Sherlock Holmes and the Eisendorf Enigma

SHERLOCK HOLMES

and the

EISENDORF ENIGMA

LARRY MILLETT

UNIVERSITY OF MINNESOTA PRESS
MINNEAPOLIS · LONDON

Map of Eisendorf, Minnesota, by Matthew Millett

Published by the University of Minnesota Press
111 Third Avenue South, Suite 290
Minneapolis, MN 55401-2520
http://www.upress.umn.edu

Library of Congress Cataloging-in-Publication Data
Millett, Larry, 1947– author. Sherlock Holmes and the Eisendorf enigma / Larry Millett.
Minneapolis : University of Minnesota Press, [2017]
Identifiers: LCCN 2016036901 (print) | ISBN 978-1-5179-0086-1 (hc) |
Subjects: LCSH: Holmes, Sherlock—Fiction. | GSAFD: Mystery fiction.
Classification: LCC PS3563.I42193 S45 2017 (print) | DDC 813/.54—dc23
LC record available at https://lccn.loc.gov/2016036901

Printed in the United States of America on acid-free paper

The University of Minnesota is an equal-opportunity educator and employer.

22 21 20 19 18 17   10 9 8 7 6 5 4 3 2 1

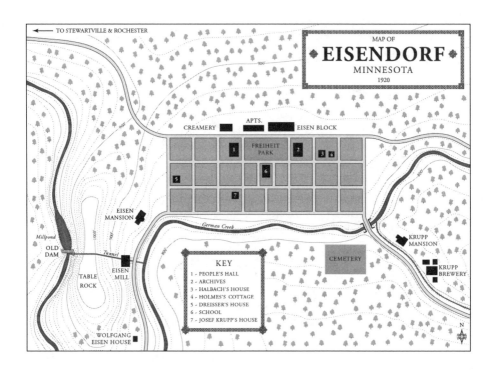

← TO STEWARTVILLE & ROCHESTER

MAP OF
◆ **EISENDORF** ◆
MINNESOTA
1920

CREAMERY   APTS.   EISEN BLOCK

FREIHEIT
PARK

1

2

3 4

5

6

7

EISEN
MANSION

German Creek

KRUPP
MANSION

Millpond

OLD
DAM   *Tunnel*

TABLE
ROCK

EISEN
MILL

KEY

1 - PEOPLE'S HALL
2 - ARCHIVES
3 - HALBACH'S HOUSE
4 - HOLMES'S COTTAGE
5 - DREISSER'S HOUSE
6 - SCHOOL
7 - JOSEF KRUPP'S HOUSE

CEMETERY

KRUPP
BREWERY

WOLFGANG
EISEN HOUSE

N

PROLOGUE

The cab, drawn by a fine black horse, stood silent on Liebergesellstrasse, a narrow street across from the park known as the English Gardens, which stretched for miles along the west bank of the Isar River. Munich, city of towers and palaces and beer halls, was quiet at three in the morning, and the cab was one of few to be found on the streets at so early an hour. Its driver, dressed in a black cape, appeared to be waiting for someone. Someone was also waiting for him.

Sherlock Holmes was on the hunt.

He'd arrived in the Bavarian capital only a few days earlier, in sweltering July heat, with no idea he would soon be pursuing a notorious murderer. Instead, it was he who was being hunted by the agents of Professor Moriarty. Ever since their master's death the year before at Reichenbach Falls, Moriarty's henchmen had been on Holmes's trail. But Holmes had managed to keep one long step ahead of them, eluding their traps like a magician disappearing from a locked box.

Holmes had made his way to Munich after staging a brilliant ruse that sent Moriarty's men careening off in the wrong direction. Before long, however, they had realized their mistake and begun retracing Holmes's steps, which meant he would have to move on very soon. Still, he'd have just enough time—or so he thought—to capture the Monster of Munich.

The Monster, a title supplied by the city's newspapers, had terrorized Munich for six months. His first three victims were so-called *Strichjungen*, young male prostitutes who plied their forbidden trade in the darkest quarters of the city. A fourth man, apparently a customer caught in the wrong place at the wrong time, had also been killed. The bodies, all horribly mutilated, had been dumped in the English Gardens like the carcasses of slaughtered animals. Meanwhile, the city's plodding police had gotten nowhere. In less than a week, Holmes had accomplished what the police had been unable to do during months of investigation. He had found the Monster, and before the night was done, he intended to bring the madman to justice.

Holmes had stationed himself on the east side of the street, in a patch of woods bordered by the stream called Schwabinger Bach. Just beyond lay Kleinhesseloher See, a pretty little lake that served as one of the English Gardens' most popular attractions. Moonlight filtered through the trees, casting faint shadows. The city was remarkably still, and Holmes could hear the stream gurgling along behind him. Too beautiful a night, he thought, for what might prove to be a deadly encounter.

The cab—an open carriage with the driver seated in the front, unlike the hansoms Holmes knew so well in London—was parked less than a hundred feet away. The driver, a broad-shouldered man, faced away from Holmes. There was no one in the back seat.

Holmes had not invited the police to his meeting with the Monster. He had suspected from the very beginning that the Monster had hidden connections to the authorities in Munich. Their investigation had been so aimless and futile, so blind to obvious clues, that Holmes saw no reason to trust them. But he did wish Watson was at his side. The good doctor, for all of the fun Holmes sometimes had at his expense, was a man absolutely to be relied upon in a tight situation, and Holmes's greatest regret during his long hiatus after the events at Reichenbach was that he had been unable to stay in contact with his one true friend.

Drawing out his Webley revolver, Holmes made his way through the trees toward the cab, which was parked in the glow of a nearby gas lamp. A light wind stirred, rustling the branches of the trees. Holmes's footsteps were as soft as the warm summer air, and the cab driver gave no evidence he heard them. Moments later, still undetected, Holmes darted from the woods and swung up into the back seat of the cab. He put his revolver to the driver's head.

"Das Monster von Munchen," he said. "Ich habe dich gefunden."

To his surprise, the reply was in heavily accented English. "Oh no, I am happy to have found you, Mr. Holmes," the driver said, making no effort to turn around. "It is a great pleasure I am sure to meet such a famous man. Shall we go for a ride?"

1

—|● ● ●|—

The message, slipped under the door of Sherlock Holmes's hotel room as he was preparing to leave Minnesota to return to England, came as a stunning surprise. Hand-printed, it read: "Do you remember the Monster of Munich? Not one of your great successes, Mr. Holmes. But you shall have a second chance. Come see me in Eisendorf."

Holmes took a deep breath. How could he forget the Monster of Munich? After twenty-eight years, the case was still a neon memory, bright and garish—the mutilated bodies found in the great gardens by the Isar, the frenzied hunt for the mad killer even as the old Bavarian capital seemed frozen with fear, the night when the Monster himself appeared, only to slip in the end from Holmes's grasp. Could the man who had terrorized one of the great cities of Europe a generation ago now be in America and close at hand?

Clutching the note, Holmes rang up the front desk. "Yes, this is Mr. Baker in room 801. Is there a place nearby called Eisendorf?"

There was a pause before the desk clerk said, "Yes, it's about twenty miles to the south."

"What can you tell me about it?"

"It's a very small town, all German, and something of a ruin, from what I've heard. Outsiders rarely go there."

"Why is that?"

The clerk paused again, as though reluctant to speak. Finally, he said, "Well, to be honest, some people think the town is dangerous."

"How so?"

"Well, because of all the troubles."

"What sort of troubles?"

"It's been in all of the papers, sir. You see, two of the town's residents have died recently under very suspicious circumstances."

● ● ●

That morning, Dr. Henry Plummer, a tall and somewhat stooped man with owl-rim glasses and no semblance of a bedside manner, had looked squarely into the sharp gray eyes of Sherlock Holmes and said, "I will be honest with you, sir. There is little to be done."

They were seated in Plummer's examination room, which reminded Holmes of a prison cell. True, there were no bars on the windows, but there was no escape either. How many others, Holmes wondered, had come to this dreary room, in this remote town at the edge of the prairies, looking for a miracle only to experience the bitter gall of dashed hope?

"Emphysema is not a death sentence," Plummer continued, in a tone so matter-of-fact he might have been talking about his prospects for lunch. "But you will certainly have to stop smoking at once."

Holmes nodded as he felt the pouch of fine Turkish shag beside the briar pipe in his coat pocket. Easier to give up life, he thought, and on the whole less trouble.

• • •

The "condition" as Holmes called it, had come on slowly in recent years. It was like a little catch at the end of each breath, as though his lungs could not quite empty themselves of air. There was a small, bothersome cough, too, and not even the fine salty air of Sussex, where he had lived since his retirement, proved to be an anodyne. He had noticed as well a slight blue tinge to his fingertips that seemed eerily unnatural. But mostly it was the shortness of breath that plagued him. His long, solitary walks along the strand near Brighton grew more labored, and even a simple flight of steps—the kind he had bounded up so readily day after day at his old Baker Street flat in London—became a test.

Holmes had never paid great attention to his health. He had always felt invulnerable, fortunate possessor of an iron constitution, and on those rare occasions when he did fall ill, his extraordinary powers of recuperation made quick work of the sickness. Even though he was well into his sixties now, he had experienced no major illnesses, no flagging of his energy, no reason to assume that he was in any way falling prey to the infirmities of old age, until the "condition" crept up on him like a footpad in the night.

Its effects had become all too evident one summer afternoon in Brighton, when a hullabaloo went up after a pickpocket lifted a man's wallet at Castle Square and tried to make his escape. The miscreant—a portly young fellow who hardly possessed the speed of a sprinter—loped right past Holmes, who instinctively turned to give chase. The pursuit did not last long. Holmes was winded within a half block, and the lumbering pickpocket got away.

And so Holmes had been forced to slow down, like an old locomotive no longer able to pull its accustomed weight. Now, every hard breath was a reminder of his age and his growing weakness. Breathing, once as unnoticed as the air itself, became a preoccupation. Holmes began to wonder if he would soon become just another old invalid, shuffling through lost days until he finally found himself at the end, fighting desperately for one last gulp of oxygen. The thought of it was almost more than he could bear. His fierce energy, as much as his great mind, had carried him to the heights of his profession. Without that energy, he wondered, would his mind begin to wither, too?

• • •

Holmes had finally decided in August 1920 to consult the famed Dr. Henry Plummer at the Mayo Clinic in Minnesota. Plummer, he knew, was considered, even among British physicians, a "top man" when it came to treating emphysema. This opinion was confirmed by no less a figure than Dr. John Watson.

Holmes had gone up to London in late August, in the midst of a boiling heat wave, to see his old friend. Watson was doing exceptionally well, with a flourishing practice on Harley Street and a comfortable townhouse on Park Square West, where he lived with his second wife. It had been months since Holmes had seen Watson, and the doctor greeted him warmly at the door. But there was also concern in his eyes when he heard Holmes's labored breathing.

"It's getting worse by the sound of it," Watson said. "Well, come in and sit down, and we'll talk things over."

Mrs. Watson—a dull and insufferable little woman in Holmes's expert opinion—was already seated in the parlor. The usual niceties were observed, after which the lady of the house did her best to monopolize the conversation, chattering on about tea caddies, lace doilies, and other tiresome topics. Only a great exercise in self-control permitted Holmes to remain civil. When he finally managed to be alone with Watson, the good doctor quickly confirmed Holmes's suspicions that emphysema, or something like it, was at the root of his problem.

"Your symptoms have been going on too long for the problem to be some temporary congestion of the lungs," Watson said. "You would be well advised to consult a specialist. Do you remember that Plummer fellow at the Mayo Clinic? I just saw one of his articles reprinted in *The Lancet.*"

Holmes, who was a regular reader of medical journals, had already absorbed the article with great interest. "Yes, it was a most fascinating piece, but it said nothing of a cure."

"I doubt there is one, Holmes. Still, you ought to go see Plummer if you can. Heaven knows he and the others did wonders for me at Mayo. Never felt better in my life after getting rid of that damned gall bladder. Perhaps they could help you as well. I would go with you, of course, but my practice—"

"I know, Watson. You are a busy man now, and I would not dream of putting you at any great inconvenience. But I will take your suggestion under advisement."

Less than a week later, Holmes was aboard the Cunard Line's *Aquitania,* sailing once again to the New World.

• • •

Rochester, Holmes found, had changed markedly in the sixteen years since he had first visited the Mayo Clinic with Watson. The town was now home to almost fifteen thousand residents but attracted four times as many patients every year, and their numbers were constantly growing. Only on a long-ago visit to Lourdes, where faith and hope served as the last drugs in the pharmacopoeia, had he seen as many supplicants. No spectral virgin ruled over Rochester, but the city was nonetheless a shrine, to the Mayo brothers and to the perceived miracles of modern medicine.

Holmes encountered crowds of other patients as soon as he checked into the Zumbro Hotel on September 4, 1920, under the name of John Baker. He was used to hotels that attracted salesmen and other business travelers, but the Zumbro's lobby resembled a hospital waiting room, full of the lame and the ill, from quivering old men and women in wheelchairs to sickly children and their desperate parents. It was not a scene calculated to cheer Holmes's flagging spirits.

The hotel itself, located next door to the clinic, was a middling sort of place, but its accommodations were of minimal interest to Holmes. What he really wanted was anonymity, and he was pleased that the Zumbro's clerks, bellboys, and other employees gave no evidence of knowing his real identity.

Holmes had long since grown weary of the fame that assaulted him like a persistent infection after Watson began publishing accounts of their exploits together. Although he was personally known to Drs. William and Charles Mayo, having met them during Watson's surgery in 1904, Holmes had asked to be registered at the clinic under a pseudonym. The Mayo brothers readily agreed to this arrangement, so that only they, and Plummer, would know the great Sherlock Holmes was in Rochester. Such, at least, had been his hope.

To make himself less recognizable, Holmes had also grown a beard. It was a shaggy affair, gray flecked with black, and it gave him the look of one of those English eccentrics of great wealth and little judgment who were a favorite subject of popular magazines. The precautions Holmes had taken made him reasonably confident no one in Rochester outside the clinic would recognize him. The note under his hotel room door soon proved him wrong.

• • •

Before arriving in Rochester, Holmes had spent the night in St. Paul with Shadwell Rafferty. Visiting with his old friend buoyed Holmes, although Rafferty, too, was feeling the cruel attacks of time. His tavern at the Ryan Hotel was gone, a victim of Prohibition, and arthritis made his every movement "a little expedition into pain," as he put it.

But they had nonetheless managed a splendid evening together, joined by Rafferty's still-vital partner, George Washington Thomas. They talked of their old adventures: the severed head in the St. Paul ice palace, the terrorists who had threatened President McKinley in Minneapolis, the rune stone affair, Elsie Cubitt in Chicago, Artemus Dodge and his locked-room mystery, and of course the remarkable Addie Strongwood, once accused of murder and now a star of Hollywood motion pictures. Only as the evening wore on, and as the Irish whiskey flowed freely in Rafferty's apartment, did Holmes bring up his own problem.

Rafferty was both sympathetic and knowing. "Ah, 'tis a nasty turn of fate, for I have always thought of you, Mr. Holmes, as man who breathes in life more intensely than anyone else I know. But do not let it throw you. You will always be Sherlock Holmes, and nothing will change that. As for those wizards at the Mayo, why I have been informed they can cure most anything. Indeed, I am hoping they will soon discover the means by which to make a fat old Irishman skinny!" Then Rafferty broke out laughing, and Holmes could not help but follow suit.

Rafferty's encouragement came at a most welcome time. Holmes's Atlantic crossing had been a gloomy business, a week of gray sky and gray water. He had hardly eaten or spoken to a soul during the entire voyage, and he had felt himself turning ever more inward, away from the world. He had always been subject to bouts of despondency, but they rarely lasted more than a few days. A new case, the more difficult and tantalizing the better, was the sovereign remedy that banished the "old dark tide," as Holmes called it.

In his retirement he had managed at first to find some measure of peace of mind without the constant stimulus of new cases. For the better part of fifteen years he had tended to his bees, conducted scientific experiments, and wrote the occasional monograph. Yet he was less a puttering retiree than a man in self-imposed exile from the world, of which he had grown weary. The Great War served only to deepen his discontent with the doings of men. Even so, he took on several demanding and dangerous assignments for the British government as a matter of patriotic duty. When the carnage finally ended, however, he wondered like so many others how any cause could be worth all the lives ground into dust on the Western Front.

The war left Holmes with a sense of disgust and a desire to forsake the world of men altogether. In Sussex, he became a shaggy hermit, rarely leaving his estate, his days consumed by idle brooding. He hardly touched his chemistry experiments. He sold his apiary, wrote nothing, and day and night seemed as one. Then "the condition" manifested itself, and Holmes fell further into a dark void. Breathing became a burden, hope faded, and contentment vanished like a glorious bird gone south, never to return. Holmes felt lost.

• • •

After a weekend spent largely in his hotel room, Holmes checked into the clinic on Monday. There, in a modern brick building Plummer himself had helped to design, Holmes underwent an extensive battery of tests. Blood was drawn, urine sampled, reflexes tested. Eyes, ears, and throat were thoroughly examined. Blood pressure was found to be normal, heart and pulse quite sound. Holmes also received a chest X-ray, the first of his life. The most important test, however, was one of the simplest. Holmes took a slow, deep breath and blew as hard as he could into a device called a spirometer. The nurse who conducted the test was coolly professional, but Holmes detected a hint of concern in her eyes as she noted the numbers registered by the apparatus.

Plummer had the all the test results in hand the next morning when he came into the examination room, where Holmes had waited for nearly a half hour with a rising sense of unease.

"Well, it is as I expected," Plummer began, offering no apology for his tardiness. "You appear to be in good enough overall health, with the exception of your lungs. The vital capacity, as it's called, should be four thousand or so milliliters for a man of your age, height, and weight. Yours is considerably less. You see—"

Holmes cut in, "By vital capacity, I presume you mean the amount of air expelled by the lungs in one breath."

"Yes. You are somewhat slow to expel your breath, and the amount of air you emit is not what it should be. However, I would classify your symptoms at this time as moderate."

It was only after much prodding from Holmes that Plummer delivered his verdict that there was "little to be done" in terms of medical treatment. Then came the equally distressing pronouncement that Holmes would "certainly have to give up smoking at once."

Plummer continued, "I know you are a smoker, Mr. Holmes, and the powerful odor of it on your person suggests you use tobacco with great regularity."

"A rather easy deduction on your part," Holmes replied. "Yes, I am quite addicted to tobacco."

"Then, as I have said, you must stop smoking. Pipe, cigar, cigarette, it makes no difference as far as I am concerned. All of them are bad for you and will make your condition worse. I have no scientific proof of it, but I am convinced smoking may well be a prime cause of emphysema. I have seen scores of patients over the years with symptoms such as yours, and in all but a few cases they have been heavy smokers. Mere association, of course, is no proof of causation, and there are doctors who might tell you my advice has no basis in fact. However, I am convinced tobacco is a scourge upon the lungs."

Holmes felt his heart sink. Tobacco had been his lifelong companion, a source of solace and relaxation as well as a profound stimulus to thought, so much so that he had come to refer to his most challenging cases, the ones that required the hardest thinking, as "three-pipe problems."

"You are asking me, Doctor, to abandon one of the great and necessary pleasures of my life because you have a theory," Holmes said. "I am not convinced."

"Then you will suffer the consequences, Mr. Holmes," Plummer said, a trace of irritation in his voice. "Ridding yourself of tobacco is the best hope you have."

• • •

Back in his room at the Zumbro, Holmes began to pack for his return trip to England. He felt restless and discomfited. He wanted desperately to enjoy a long draw of smoke from his pipe, and yet Dr. Plummer's words rang like a fire bell in his head. Holmes sighed and went over to the window. His eighth-floor room afforded a fine view of Rochester and the green wooded countryside beyond. It was a pretty enough place, but Holmes knew from experience Minnesota's fierce winter was not far off, and then there would be nothing but a long, gray chill. His own life, he sensed, was heading in the same direction, toward a winter of the spirit, and he wondered if there would ever be another spring.

He had just come back from a late lunch in the hotel dining room when he found the note. Its effect was immediate and galvanizing, and the morning's disturbing diagnosis was, for the moment, forgotten. Instead, Holmes was suddenly on the case, his mind flooding with observations and questions. In a matter of minutes, he arrived at a number of conclusions.

First, and most obvious, was the fact that someone other than the doctors at Mayo knew he was in Rochester. How had this happened? Had he been followed, perhaps all the way from England? Unlikely, but not impossible. Or had his presence first been detected in New York, or Chicago (where he'd switched trains), or St. Paul? Again, possible, but not probable. What seemed most likely was that the note writer (possibly the Monster himself) had learned of Holmes's presence in Rochester from someone at the Mayo Clinic.

Holmes had no reasons to suspect the Mayo brothers or Plummer had deliberately betrayed him. Even so, one of them might have inadvertently mentioned their famous patient to a colleague or friend. And then, somehow, word of it had reached someone lurking just twenty miles away in Eisendorf.

Holmes looked at the note and considered another question: Who had actually delivered it to his hotel room? The Monster himself? Doubtful. It was far more likely, Holmes thought, that a paid agent had done the deed. The hotel was a busy venue, and it would have been a simple manner for anyone to drop off the note while Holmes was at lunch.

But how had this agent known which room Holmes occupied? The front desk, he knew, did not as a matter of policy provide such information to strangers. Yet Holmes also knew there were a multitude of ways to obtain his room number. A clerk could have been bribed. Or someone could simply have observed Holmes's key being taken from its numbered box behind the front desk.

Yet the most intriguing questions concerned the Monster himself and what had occurred twenty-eight years earlier in Munich. Holmes had arrived there in 1892 purely as a matter of chance after a close encounter with Colonel Moran, Moriarty's most lethal assassin, at the train station in Nuremberg. By means of an elaborate deception, Holmes had managed to convince Moran he was bound for Berlin. Instead, Holmes went in the opposite direction, south to Munich, where the Monster was already engaged in his grisly work. Unable to ignore such unspeakable crimes, Holmes threw himself, at great personal risk, into the investigation.

In the short time he was able to look into the case, Holmes had concluded that the Monster was young (probably no older than thirty), powerfully built (since his victims were all strong men capable of putting up a fight), and most likely a taxi driver (which would explain his ability to dump bodies in the English Gardens without anyone taking notice).

Yet the Monster's defining quality, Holmes soon came to realize, was his towering ego. Once alerted to Holmes's presence in Munich, the Monster had gone out of his way to engineer a confrontation. He *wanted* to take on Holmes, to demonstrate that not even the world's greatest consulting detective was a match for his evil genius. Now, it appeared, he was ready to do battle again.

It still rankled Holmes that he had been forced to leave Munich not long after his encounter with the Monster in the English Gardens. Given a few more days, Holmes was certain he could have tracked down the Monster again and brought him to justice. But with Moriarty's agents closing in— Holmes had spotted one at a coffee shop not far from the gardens—he'd had no choice but to make a quick escape.

Only much later did Holmes learn the Monster had never been caught, and that his killing spree had abruptly stopped after claiming four victims.

Now, improbable as it seemed, the Monster was in Minnesota and offering Holmes a "second chance." The question was whether Holmes could afford to take it.

• • •

Despite Plummer's warning, Holmes wasn't quite ready to give up his pipe. After an hour of intense thinking, he filled up the bowl, lit it, and sat down to reexamine the note purportedly sent by the Monster. The note was clearly a formal invitation. The Monster had elaborate plans for Holmes and wanted to be absolutely certain he would come to Eisendorf. It was patently obvious to Holmes that he was being lured into a trap. The Monster—a highly intelligent man in Holmes's estimation—must have understood the situation equally well. But he had extended the invitation nevertheless, counting on Holmes's curiosity to draw him into the case.

Holmes knew his wisest course of action would be to refuse the bait. But he could not do so. If the Monster of Munich was indeed ensconced nearby in Eisendorf, then Holmes had to find him, even if it meant walking into ambush. Feeling a slight hitch in his breath, Holmes picked up the telephone and placed a call to the Cunard Line's office in New York to reschedule his return trip on the *Aquitania.* Then he went down to the front desk and asked for directions to the Rochester Public Library.

2

—⊶•••⊷—

T he library was a short distance from Holmes's hotel. He had assumed he would have to dig through copies of the local newspapers—there were two, the *Daily Bulletin* and the *Post and Record*—to find what he was looking for. But the librarians had saved him the trouble by maintaining separate clippings files of stories related to Eisendorf.

One of the thickest files was devoted to the town's troubles during the Great War. The ancestry of Eisendorf's residents, and the fact that most of them still spoke German, had cast a pall of suspicion over the community. The fact that one of the town's leading families bore the surname of Krupp— the same as that of the notorious German munitions maker—did not help matters. Holmes found a story that told of an especially unsavory incident in the spring of 1918, when a mob fueled by patriotism and alcohol ran amok through the village, setting fire to vacant houses, vandalizing buildings, and shouting "death to the Huns!"

But it was another file, labeled "Deaths—Eisendorf," that Holmes found most interesting. The news clippings revealed that within the span of just a few months in 1920, Eisendorf had been the scene of two violent deaths, both involving prominent residents and both raising the suspicion of foul play. One article said the deaths were "surprising and unprecedented in the small village, which numbers no more than forty people."

The first victim, found dead on April 9, was Hans Eisen, age sixty-two, described as "the only son of the town's founder, Dionisius Eisen." The *Daily Bulletin* reported, "Mr. Eisen, a lifelong bachelor well known for his odd ways, was found dead at ten o'clock yesterday morning of what appears to have been a self-inflicted bullet wound to the head. His body was discovered by a family member in the basement of Mr. Eisen's mansion. There was evidence he had planned his demise with great care. A revolver was found next to the body, as well as a note said to contain many expressions of despondency."

Only a few days later, however, a story in the *Post and Record* raised questions about the supposed suicide. The Olmsted County sheriff, a man saddled with the rather unlikely name of Osgood Thorkelson, was quoted as saying, "There are several inconsistencies in the evidence at the scene, and for the moment we are not closing the book on the possibility that Mr. Eisen's death may be of a suspicious nature." Holmes found, however, no additional stories regarding the sheriff's suspicions, nor did it appear any criminal charges were ever filed.

The second death occurred on July 22. This time the victim was Bernhard Krupp, age fifty-nine. He was identified as the "only son of the late Gottfried Krupp, one of the freethinking Germans who helped establish Eisendorf." A news story said Krupp had "long been head of the family business—a brewery that operated for more than fifty years before closing on the eve of Prohibition."

His death was attributed to a "tragic hunting accident" that occurred in the woods near his brewery. The *Daily Bulletin* reported Krupp had apparently tripped while carrying his shotgun, "causing the weapon to discharge. The shot struck Mr. Krupp in the upper leg, severing an artery, and he bled to death before help could arrive. Some hours after the horrible accident, a timber cruiser who happened to be in the vicinity discovered Mr. Krupp's lifeless body, which was being guarded by his faithful dog, Heinrich."

Later newspaper accounts, however, suggested Krupp's death may not have been accidental. Once again, the source of these doubts was Sheriff Thorkelson, who told a reporter, "It is a rare thing for a man to have suffered a self-inflicted wound of the type that caused Mr. Krupp's death, and so we are continuing to look into the matter." Asked whether he thought foul play was involved, the sheriff said, "It has not been ruled out." But as with the supposed suicide of Hans Eisen, Krupp's death had not resulted in any criminal charges, as far as Holmes could tell.

The names of the victims meant nothing to Holmes—yet. But if the Monster of Munich had indeed resettled in Eisendorf, then it seemed likely he'd had a hand in the two suspicious deaths. If so, why had the Monster, more than a quarter of a century after his depredations in Munich, suddenly resumed his murderous ways? Or was it possible there had been other murders in Eisendorf, years before, that Holmes knew nothing about?

That evening, in his room at the Zumbro, Holmes gave much thought to what had happened in Eisendorf. He managed, however, to limit his lucubrations to a one-pipe problem, rather than three. Plummer would not be pleased, but Holmes saw it as a step in the right direction.

• • •

"I imagine," said Sherlock Holmes, "you will find it hard to believe what I am about to tell you."

He was seated the next morning in the office of Olmsted County Sheriff Osgood Thorkelson, a man so round of body he might have been dropped, like lead shot, from a high tower and formed into a ball by the force of gravity. His face was round, his eyes were round, his belly as pendulous as a belly could be, and when he spoke, he even rounded his vowels in the manner of the florid orators of old. Yet it soon became apparent to Holmes that the sheriff, despite his resemblance to jolly St. Nick, was nobody's fool.

Holmes's first task was to convince the sheriff he was not some lunatic fresh from the asylum claiming to be the world's foremost detective. After stating his true identity, Holmes said, "Lest you dismiss me as a pretender, Sheriff Thorkelson, I would observe that your wife was born in Canada, that you have a dog—a collie, I believe—that recently delivered a litter, that you intend to visit Chicago next week, and that one of your bicuspids is causing you so much trouble that you have scheduled a visit to the dentist."

Before the startled sheriff could respond to this barrage of deductions, Holmes added, "But to save us both some time, I suggest you ring up the Mayo Clinic and ask for your friend Dr. William Mayo. He will verify I am who I say I am."

Staring at Holmes as though some exotic and wildly colorful species of butterfly had just fluttered into his office, Thorkelson said, "Well, I am impressed, sir, mightily impressed, but there is no need to call Dr. Mayo. It is well known to me, and many others here, that Sherlock Holmes has been at the clinic in recent days. Oh, and my dog isn't a collie. She's an Irish setter."

Holmes could not help smiling. "Sheriff, I must apologize for my mistake. But I feel compelled to ask how you learned of my presence in Rochester. I was assured my identity would be kept secret."

Now it was Thorkelson's turn to smile. "My wife, by the way, is indeed Canadian. How you knew that I'll never guess, unless you spotted that flag behind her in the photograph on my desk. In any event, it was she who told me you were in Rochester. She heard the news from a nurse she knows at the clinic. I expect by now half the town knows you are here."

Holmes shook his head, appalled by his own foolishness. His visit to Rochester, it seemed, was an open secret.

Thorkelson rubbed his upper lip, trying to sooth the sore tooth Holmes had noticed, and said, "I assume you're not here just to pass the time of day, Mr. Holmes. Is there something I can do for you?"

"I am here to talk about Eisendorf."

"Are you now? And why does that little town interest you?"

Holmes told Thorkelson about the Monster and the note he had received at his hotel.

"My God, that's quite a story! And you think the same fellow is in Eisendorf now? It's hard to believe."

"I can scarcely believe it myself, and yet how else would the author of the note know about what happened between us in Munich unless he is indeed the Monster?"

"You have a point, Mr. Holmes. Well, I will certainly help you all I can. But I must warn you about Eisendorf. They are a strange lot of Germans, and they want nothing to do with outsiders of any kind. You will not have an easy time of it if you go there and start digging around."

"I do not expect an easy time, Sheriff. The Monster has invited me to his lair, and I have no doubt he is spoiling for a fight. Now, what can you tell me about the two recent deaths in Eisendorf? I have read the newspaper accounts, but I have no doubt you kept certain details from the press, as is customary in police investigations."

"We did. As for the deaths, Mr. Holmes, I can tell you both are as fishy as can be. But as you well know, suspecting foul play is a far cry from proving it."

"Just how were the deaths 'fishy,' as you put it?"

"Well, let's start with Hans Eisen. The story is, he goes down to the basement of his mansion, sits in a chair, puts a nice little suicide note he'd typed out on a nearby table, picks up a pistol, and then blows his brains out. I suppose it could have happened that way. But here's what's really odd. His finger wasn't wrapped around the trigger of the revolver we found clenched in his hand. The angle of the wound to his temple was a little bit off, too, and the stippling around it suggests the gun was held a foot or so away from his head, not right up next to it, as is usually the case with suicides. There are just a lot of little things that don't add up."

"You believe, in other words, that the suicide was staged."

"It's certainly possible, but can I prove it? No. The coroner lists the cause of death as 'undetermined,' and we're leaving it at that for the time being."

"Who found the body?"

"His cousin, Peter Eisen. Both of them are—or in Hans's case, were—part of the clan the town is named after. Peter, his wife, and their daughter live in the Eisen mansion, which is the biggest house in town. Hans lived there, too, and that's where his body was found. The house is just a stone's throw from an old flour mill the family owns."

"Are there any other Eisens I should know about?"

"Just Peter's brother, Wolfgang. He's an ornery customer if there ever was one. Don't expect a warm greeting if you happen to run into him."

"I appreciate the warning, Sheriff. Now, what about the suicide note Hans Eisen supposedly left? Are you certain he wrote it?"

"Of course not. For one thing, the note was typed. Problem is, Hans was never known to use a typewriter, or so I've been told. But again, there's nothing to say he couldn't have typed the note, since we matched it to a typewriter in the house."

"What did the note say?"

"It was very simple and not very informative. It just said something like, 'I am tired of life. Good-bye.'"

"In other words, the kind of impersonal note that someone other than the dead man himself might have written."

"That's what I think."

"By the way, the newspaper stories I read suggested that Hans was an odd man. Is that so?"

Thorkelson let out a chuckle. "If you ask me, everybody in Eisendorf is odd. But, yes, Hans was considered something of a character. He never married and was known to keep to himself. He managed the family-owned mill for quite a few years. Nobody we talked to had anything bad to say about him."

"And he got along with all of his relatives?"

"So they say, Mr. Holmes."

"All right. Tell me about Bernhard Krupp and his death."

"Well, the Krupps and the Eisens are the two richest families in town. Bern, as everyone called him, was born and raised in Eisendorf and ran the brewery there for many years. Pillar of the community and all of that. The beer he brewed, by the way, was excellent. His widow, Katherine, still lives in Eisendorf. There's also a cousin named Josef Krupp, who manages what's left of the brewery.

"As to how Bernhard Krupp died, well, we have plenty of questions. The biggest one is that the wound to his leg just didn't look accidental to us. He was left-handed and so carried his shotgun in that hand, or over his left shoulder. But the wound was to the upper part of his left thigh, and it was a straight-in blast from point-blank range. If he tripped and the gun discharged, as the story goes, it's far more likely the barrel of the gun would have swung around and the shot would have hit his right thigh. There's at least one other problem."

"Which is?"

"We located several witnesses who swear they heard two shotgun blasts at about the time Mr. Krupp was shot. But there was only one expended shell in his shotgun."

"Are you thinking someone may have shot Mr. Krupp with another weapon and then fired his shotgun to make it look like as though he had accidentally wounded himself?"

"It could be. You can't link shotgun pellets to a particular weapon, so who knows? But we couldn't find any witnesses who saw Mr. Krupp in the woods that day, and the ground where the shooting occurred is so rocky there was no footprint evidence either."

Holmes said, "So you are left with strong suspicions of foul play but no definitive evidence."

"That's about it," Thorkelson admitted.

"What about motive? Is there anyone in town who might have had something to gain by the men's deaths?"

"Probably, but good luck trying to figure out who they might be."

"Why do you say that?"

Thorkelson let out a sigh and his big shoulders slumped. "In Eisendorf, Mr. Holmes, you can never be sure whether anybody is telling you the truth. They're a tight bunch and they protect their own. It's one big family—did I mention Gottfried Krupp's daughter, Maria, is married to Peter Eisen?—and they don't like talking about one another, at least not to me. We interviewed the whole damn town after the two shootings and learned next to nothing. I can't begin to tell you how frustrating it is. The town's an enigma, all turned in on itself, and you never really know what's going on beneath the surface."

"Then it sounds as though I shall have my work cut out for me," Holmes said.

• • •

Later, after the sheriff had gone through all of the evidence related to the two fatal shootings, Holmes asked for more information about Eisendorf itself. Thorkelson did his best to give Holmes an overview of the town while acknowledging how much he did not know.

"You have to understand, Mr. Holmes, that Eisendorf has always been its own little world. I don't know of another place like it. Just the way the town is laid out makes it different from anywhere else. It's also very isolated, at the bottom of a steep little valley, and the woods all around are so thick you feel like you've wandered into Sherwood Forest."

"I take it there have been no sightings of Robin Hood."

Thorkelson grinned. "Not yet, but it wouldn't surprise me. As for the town itself, it's a regular time capsule. Nothing much has changed there since the 1870s, when the mill and brewery were built."

"Was the town established at that time?"

"No, earlier than that. I believe it was in the early 1850s. Minnesota wasn't even a state then, and it was the frontier. Settlers were pouring in from all over. Yankees from the East, plus a lot of immigrants, mostly Scandinavians, but plenty of Germans, too. Among the Germans was a group of settlers from Bavaria."

"Led by Dionisius Eisen."

"Yes. He was apparently a magnetic figure, the kind of man who attracts followers. The story goes he was deeply unhappy with the state of affairs in Germany and decided to emigrate to the United States. He formed a company, preempted several thousand acres near the southern border of Olmsted County, and built the town in the valley. There are farms above, all owned by townspeople."

"Were the Krupps also among the town's founders?"

"No, I think they came along a little later, around 1870 or so. Gottfried Krupp was the head of the family."

"By the way, is Dionisius still alive?"

"Oh no, he died many years ago. As I recall, there was an accident at the mill."

"When was that?"

"I'm not exactly sure, but it must have been before the turn of the century. It seems to me there was something queer about Gottfried Krupp's death, too, but I can't remember what it was."

"Perhaps I will do some research," Holmes said. " You mentioned that Dionisius Eisen was unhappy in Germany. Do you know what prompted him to leave?"

"He was a 'freethinker,' or so he's been described to me, and I guess he just wanted a fresh start somewhere else."

"What kind of freethinker?"

"The kind who does not believe in God. To this day, Eisendorf is said to be the only town in Minnesota without a church. It's a strange place in a lot of other ways. You'll see for yourself when you get there, Mr. Holmes. You're planning a visit soon, I assume."

"Yes, tomorrow, if possible. I have been informed, however, there is no train service into the town."

"That's right. You can get to Stewartville, which is about thirteen miles south of here, by the Chicago Great Western. From there, you'll have to hire someone to drive you another ten miles or so into Eisendorf. There's a fellow in Stewartville named Tommy Boyd who runs a little taxi service. He could take care of you."

"Thank you, Sheriff. That is most helpful. I am curious, however, as to why no rail line ever reached Eisendorf."

"Well, there are two versions of the story. One is that the valley where the town lies is so deep and narrow the railroads decided they just couldn't get to it. But I've also heard that way back when, the town elders decided they didn't want a railroad because they thought it would be a bad influence by bringing in outsiders. Of course, a town without a railroad could never thrive, and that's why Eisendorf has gotten smaller and smaller."

"It now numbers only about forty residents, is that correct?"

"Might be even less than that. I think there were maybe two to three hundred people there at one time. Now, it's just wasting away. It will be a ghost town pretty soon."

"Especially if its residents continue to die in such violent fashion," Holmes noted.

"Well, maybe you can put a stop to that, Mr. Holmes. Now, as I told you, you'll be in for quite an experience in Eisendorf. The folks there just don't open up to outsiders. In fact, they can be downright hostile. Of course, I can't say as I blame them after what happened during the war."

"Ah, I read about that. A mob of so-called patriots attacked the town."

"Yes, and they probably would have burned it to the ground if I hadn't been able to get a squad of deputies down there pronto. It's a wonder no-body was killed."

"Were the ring leaders ever prosecuted?"

"Not a chance. A lot of folks around here thought the mob was just do-ing its patriotic duty. Germans weren't real popular at the time. Still aren't. That's why everybody in Eisendorf has clammed up. They see me and every other outsider as an enemy."

"Even so, there must be someone in the village who would be willing to talk with me about the recent deaths."

"There's one person who could probably help you out, Mr. Holmes. His name is Frederick Halbach. He's the official archivist in Eisendorf."

"Archivist? What exactly does that mean?"

Thorkelson explained Halbach's unusual duties.

"How remarkable," Holmes said. "Indeed, the more you tell me about Eisendorf, the more curious I become."

Thorkelson leaned forward in his chair and inspected Holmes in the manner of an officer examining his troops before a parade review. "Just re-member what happened to the cat," he said. "Curiosity could get you into trouble. You'll need to be very careful once you get to Eisendorf. Do you carry a pistol?"

"I will have it with me tomorrow."

"Good. Keep it loaded. You never know what might happen."

• • •

Back at his room at the Zumbro, Holmes lay down for a few minutes, breath-ing slowly and deeply. He glanced over at his pipe, which he'd left on the bed stand before going to see the sheriff. How pleasing a smoke would be! And yet, there was Plummer, looming in Holmes's mind like the Grim Reaper, except not with a scythe in his hand but an enormous pipe.

Holmes had made a decision, and he counted on his iron will to carry it through. There would be no more smoking. And probably not much sat-isfaction in his life either. He had become used in his retirement to a kind of imperial solitude, but with one enduring consolation—his pipe. Now, it seemed he would truly be alone in the world.

After a few more minutes of rest, Holmes called the front desk, using his real name for the first time. He was informed the Chicago Great Western offered a southbound train from Rochester at eleven every morning with a stop in Stewartville half an hour later. The desk clerk also arranged for a taxi to meet Holmes at the station in Stewartville.

Satisfied his travel arrangements were in order, Holmes turned his mind back to the case in which he was about to enmesh himself once again. Ordering the taxi had set off a cascade of memories. Cabs had been a crucial part of the Monster's murderous campaign in Munich. And it was in a cab that Holmes, for a few brief moments, had finally gotten the Monster in his grasp. Yet Holmes later realized it had actually happened the other way around. It was he who had fallen into the Monster's clutches, from which he'd managed only at the last minute to escape with his life. Sheriff Thorkelson had been right. Holmes would have to be very, very careful in Eisendorf.

Just past one, Holmes went down to dining room for a light lunch. Returning to his room an hour later, he stood outside the door for a moment. He had a premonition about what he would find inside. As before, the message had been slid under the door. It read, "I'm waiting."

3

———┤● ● ●├———

The Chicago Great Western's morning local pulled out of Rochester at eleven o'clock sharp. The coach car Holmes occupied was less than half full, and he sprawled out across two seats, with no one to disturb his thoughts. He'd taken along a light bag with two changes of clothes but wasn't sure he would need them. There was no hotel in Eisendorf—a fact he'd gleaned from Sheriff Thorkelson—so Holmes had no assurance that he could spend the night there. He would have to wait and see.

The countryside rolling by the window was what Holmes had come to expect of southern Minnesota—farm fields ambling off to the horizon, lines of distant trees dark against their green foreground, here and there a little creek meandering along in picturesque fashion. It was a handsome enough country, but not, Holmes thought, very interesting. There was no ocean to define its edge, as in Sussex, and not much visible history either—no castles or windmill towers or quaint little towns or winding country lanes banked by tall hedges. Instead, the landscape evoked a persistent sense of vacancy, too clean and open to sustain an intricate air of mystery. Eisendorf, Holmes had reason to believe, would be different.

But would he really find the Monster there? In Munich, the Monster had for many months eluded detection, moving through the night like a dark wind. He had misled the police with ease and might have gone about his lethal work indefinitely had not Holmes arrived on the scene. The little town of Eisendorf promised to be the utter opposite of Munich. Was it really possible the Monster had exiled himself to such a place? And if he had, for what reason? Holmes intended to find the answers.

● ● ●

As promised, Tommy Boyd—a freckle-faced man of forty or so with a pair of outsized front teeth lodged like shrunken tusks in his wide mouth—was at the station when Holmes arrived in Stewartville.

"Well, I just don't believe it," he announced, scooping up Holmes's bag. "Wait until I tell the wife I met Sherlock Holmes. She's one of your greatest fans. Reads all the stories. Of course, so do I. And I have to tell you, when she read about you going over that cliff in—where was it, Germany?—well, she was fit to be tied."

"Switzerland," Holmes said with some asperity, thereby bringing Boyd's spontaneous oration to a halt. "I am grateful to learn of your interest in my career, Mr. Boyd. At the moment, however, I am more interested in Eisendorf. I understand you can take me there for five dollars."

By now, they had reached Boyd's vehicle—a black Model T sedan with white lettering on the front door that read "Tommy's Taxi Service."

"Step right in, Mr. Holmes," Boyd said. "Five dollars is the price. But truth is, I'd do this job for free just to meet you."

"A man should be paid for his work," Holmes said as he slipped into the front seat next to Boyd. "How long will it take us to reach Eisendorf?"

"The roads are in good shape—not much rain of late—so a half hour or so, maybe a little more. It's a pretty drive. I'm sure you'll like it."

Once they were out of town, Holmes asked Boyd what he knew about Eisendorf. "A dangerous place, if you believe the newspapers," Boyd said. "Truth is, I've only driven through the town a few times. No reason to go there. People around here think the town is just plain weird. Kind of like a foreign country, I guess. They still speak German down there."

"But the recent deaths must have occasioned much talk," Holmes prodded.

"Sure, plenty of talk. But nobody really knows anything, and all those Germans keep to themselves. If anybody can find out what's going on, it would be you, Mr. Holmes. You know, I was just thinking if you need somebody to help you out a bit, run some errands, that sort of thing, I'd be available."

"Thank you, Mr. Boyd. I shall keep your offer in mind."

• • •

They had driven for nearly a half hour, in bright sunshine, following a series of gravel roads across open countryside, when the landscape abruptly changed. The road took a sharp turn and plunged into a dark green gash in the earth. Suddenly, a primeval forest of oaks, maples, and basswoods all but engulfed the road, forming a green canopy interspersed with yellow ribbons of sunlight draped across the high branches of the trees. Shadows flickered, the day darkened, and the air became noticeably cooler. A red-tailed hawk, sharp as a dagger, swooped past the Model T, coming so close to the windshield that Holmes was startled. He felt as if he had plunged into a lost world.

"Here we go," said Boyd, tapping his brakes. The road began descending through a long, narrow ravine. As Boyd's Model T chugged down the twisting road, Holmes noted he had not seen another vehicle, whether gasoline powered or horse drawn, in miles, and he experienced a chilling sensation of remoteness. The sunny uplands world of farm and field had vanished. Holmes was in the dark realm of the Monster now.

The road finally reached bottom, and after Boyd negotiated yet another sharp curve, Eisendorf appeared. Holmes had been in any number of small Minnesota towns, beginning in 1894 when he and Watson had traveled to the logging outpost of Hinckley at the behest of the late James J. Hill. Eisendorf looked like none of them. Set beside a fast-flowing stream between cliffs of ocher-colored limestone, the town at first glance reminded Holmes of a tiny Bavarian village hidden away in some remote corner of the Alps.

The main street struck Holmes as especially peculiar. Instead of the usual ensemble of small shops and stores, there were only three buildings, all located on the north side of the street, across from a large park. Holmes saw no indication of activity around any of them.

The first building, a low brick structure, bore the bleached-out remnants of a sign proclaiming it to be the "Eisendorf Cooperative Creamery." A smaller sign advertised the establishment as "Home of America's Best Weisslacker." But the building was obviously vacant, its windows shuttered.

Just past the creamery was a two-story wooden building of such plain design it reminded Holmes of a military barracks, with long rows of windows extending across both floors. Its red roof was pockmarked with missing shingles, the paint had all but faded away from its clapboard siding, and many of the windows were broken. The building, it was obvious, had not been used in a long time.

The last building, also two stories, was by far the largest and most impressive of the trio, its long, red brick facade culminating in a central tower flanked by a pair of ornate gables stepped up in the Germanic manner. Surprisingly elaborate, the building reminded Holmes, on a much smaller scale, of Munich's old Rathaus. The settlers of Eisendorf had clearly not forgotten the monuments of their homeland.

"I should like to look around a bit," Holmes told Boyd. "Why don't you stop in front of that building with a tower?"

Holmes got out of the taxi, grateful for the opportunity stretch his legs, and took a good look at the building. It housed a series of storefronts but only one business—identified by a sign as "Halbach's General Store"—seemed to be a going enterprise. Rusting signs advertised some of the shuttered businesses—"Muller Hardware," "People's Bank of Eisendorf," "Krupp's Drugs and Sundries."

According to a carved panel in the tower, the building was known as the "Eisen Block" and dated to 1872. Above the panel, just beneath the tower's open belfry, was a cuckoo clock outfitted with figures of a maiden and a boy in lederhosen to either side of a small bell that had once sounded the hours. But the clock's mechanism was frozen, and both of its hands, loosened from the pin that held them, had given way to gravity and drooped down to six-thirty o'clock.

Holmes turned around to look at the park, an oblong expanse the size of two city blocks. It was overgrown with weeds and devoid of amenities except for an old wooden bandstand in the center. There were no trees, no shrubs, no gardens, no benches, no walkways. An old iron sign, painted white with black letters, stood across the street in front of the park. Holmes went over for a look. The sign read "Freiheit Park, estab. 1855."

Two monumental stone buildings, both with columned white porticos in the classical manner, faced each other across the park, and their incongruous presence suggested Eisendorf had once been a town with ambitions of grandeur. The building on the east side of the park bore a carved inscription over the portico that read *Wir Sind Das Volk*, with the word *Archiv* below. There was also an inscription over the western building, but Holmes was too far away to read it. Yet another stone building, crowned by a small bell tower and looking as though it might be a school, was centered along the south side of the park. Beyond it, Holmes saw a scattering of houses and the glimmer of moving water.

What Holmes did not see yet was any obvious sign of humanity. "We are the people," said the inscription on the archives building. Despite this promise of communal solidarity, the residents of Eisendorf were nowhere in evidence. The park was deserted and so were the streets. Holmes had the distinct sensation of being in the middle of a stage set long after the play had closed. Even so, he knew he and Boyd were not alone.

As they'd driven slowly down the main street, Holmes had caught sight of a shadowy figure peering out from an upper window of the long wooden building next to the Eisen Block. It was the briefest of glimpses, and Holmes wasn't sure whether the figure was a man or a woman. Could it have been the Monster himself? Holmes didn't know, but he felt an ominous chill running down his spine. Eisendorf, his instincts told him, was going to be a world of trouble.

• • •

Holmes had gone back across the street to talk with Boyd when he finally spotted a stirring of life. A tall, broad-shouldered man emerged from the archives building and walked toward them, across the park. Once the man drew near, Holmes was able to make the usual observations and deductions. The man was sixty or so, judging by his mane of silver hair, the way his skin had begun to sag beneath his chin, and the slight elongating of his ears. He walked briskly, even though his gait betrayed a limp, very probably the result of an injury to his left knee. He wore a shabby brown suit of the kind that might have been fashionable a generation earlier. Ink stains decorated the right sleeve of his coat.

"Mr. Holmes, I presume," the man said, a marked German accent evident in his voice. "I am Frederick Halbach."

"Ah, the archivist," said Holmes. "A pleasure to meet you. But I am curious. How did you know I would be arriving?"

"We are not ill informed here in Eisendorf," Halbach replied. His manner was formal and solemn, like that of a minister presiding at a funeral. "I will simply say there has been talk of your presence in Rochester, as well as rumors that something in our little town is of particular interest to you. May I ask what that might be?"

"You are correct that I have been drawn here on a matter of great interest. Perhaps we will talk about it later."

Halbach gave a slight bow. "As you wish, Mr. Holmes. I look forward to discussing the matter with you. Now, eins nach dem anderen, or first things first, as it's said in English. Do you intend to honor us with your presence for an extended period of time, or is your visit to be regrettably brief?"

"It is difficult to say. As I understand it, there is no hotel in town."

"That is correct. However, if you do intend to stay for a while, I have a little cottage behind my house I think you would find comfortable enough. It is yours for as long as you need it."

"That is most kind of you."

"Certainly. Then let me show it to you now. Afterwards, you may be interested in seeing our archives."

"Yes, I should like to learn all I can about your town."

Holmes sent Boyd on his way with a substantial tip and an unusual instruction, then followed Halbach toward the cottage, located just behind the archives building. The cottage was nothing fancy but decent enough. Holmes unpacked, then went to see the archives.

● ● ●

Sheriff Thorkelson had already given Holmes a brief account of the archives, one of Eisendorf's most peculiar features. Now, as Holmes sat with Halbach in the tall-ceilinged room that took up most of the building, he learned a great deal more.

The room itself was curious. At first glance it resembled a small library. There were two long tables with reading lamps, shelves lined with books and what appeared to be manuscripts, a large globe, and numerous photographs on the walls depicting various groups of men, women, and children. Holmes was most fascinated, however, by a grandfather clock that stood against the back wall between two narrow windows. Its ticking was the loudest sound he had yet heard in Eisendorf. The clock had an unusual feature—a row of five brass numbers, 23231, set behind a pane of glass between the face and the pendulum. The numbers were mounted on small wheels, suggesting they changed with the movement of the clock.

Before Holmes could ask about the numbers, Halbach said, "Perhaps I should begin by telling you a little about the archives. You are seated, Mr. Holmes, in a place unique in all of Minnesota, and perhaps all of America. It is officially called the People's Archives of Eisendorf, and it was established with the town itself in 1855 by Dionisius Eisen."

"I have heard about him," Holmes said. "He led the community of like-minded souls from Germany who founded the town."

"That is correct. There were forty people in the group, all from Bavaria. Dionisius was their leader and a great visionary."

"In what way?"

"He is our prophet, I suppose you could say, although of course he had no religious beliefs. His goal was to create an ideal community, one devoted to the 'noble rule of reason,' as he called it. The community was to be free of religion, prejudice, and superstition. As part of the town's founding plan, he

established these archives, with the aim of recording everything of importance that occurred in Eisendorf."

"How extraordinary," said Holmes, who looked once again at the grandfather clock. "By the way, I must assume that the numbers below the face of
the clock have some particular significance."

"Ah, you are very observant, Mr. Holmes, very observant, as I knew you
would be. Yes, the clock was specially built to record the passing of every
day in the history of the village since its founding in 1855. Unfortunately, the
mechanism suddenly broke last New Year's Eve, and no attempt has been
made to repair it. But you may be interested to learn we are on the verge of
a milestone: Eisendorf's twenty-four thousandth day."

"Why is that a milestone?"

"A good question, Mr. Holmes. In fact, no one can really be certain. What
is known is that Dionisius was fascinated by the number twenty-four. He laid
out the town with twenty-four blocks, most of which are two hundred and
forty feet square. He also predicted in one of his many visions that an 'astonishing event,' to use his words, would occur on the twenty-four thousandth
day of the town's history."

"When will that be?"

"October 2."

"I fear I will miss it," said Holmes, who did not plan to spend more than
a few days in the town. "However, I must say Dionisius Eisen sounds like a
most interesting character, and I am grateful to him. If the archives he initiated are as complete as you represent them to be, then the two unfortunate
deaths here this year must be very well documented."

"Are those deaths what bring you to us, Mr. Holmes? I am surprised
they would be of interest to a great detective such as yourself."

"Why is that?"

"I do not think they are the source of any great mystery. But who am I
to say? If you wish to read about the deaths of Mr. Eisen and Mr. Krupp, you
may certainly do so. The Annals of Eisendorf are at your disposal."

"What exactly are these annals?"

"Let me show you."

Halbach escorted Holmes to a long table at one side of the room. A shelf
above held a long row of leather-bound volumes with gold lettering on the
spines. Halbach pulled down a hefty book labeled "Volume 1, 1–365."

"This is the beginning of the annals, Mr. Holmes," he said, opening the book. Within were pages of beautiful handwriting, in German, organized by day. "The very first entry, for Day One of Eisendorf's existence, was written by Dionisius himself. Shall I read how he began the story of our town?"

"By all means."

"Perhaps I should ask first if you understand German, Mr. Holmes."

"Passably, but a translation would be welcome."

"Very well." Halbach put on a pair of reading glasses and began to intone the founder's words as though he was delivering Holy Scripture. After a few sentences, he stopped and translated for Holmes: "'Oh glorious day! A new community in a new world has come into being. The pure, blazing light of the truth shall shine upon it and its people.'"

"Dionisius Eisen seems to have been a great optimist," Holmes remarked. "Tell me, Mr. Halbach, does the light of the truth still blaze here?"

"That is not for me to say, Mr. Holmes. Would you care to hear more?"

"Perhaps at another time. I am more interested in reading about the two recent deaths."

"Of course. They are covered in volume sixty-six." Halbach took down the volume, the last on the shelf, and marked two pages for Holmes. "You will be pleased to learn that beginning in 1900, the village decided the annals should be written in English. I will let you examine the appropriate passages. Let me know if you have any questions."

The annals, Holmes quickly discovered, were hardly a gold mine of information. Written in a stiff, formal style, they consisted largely of small-town minutiae: neighbors visiting neighbors, women gathering for a quilting bee, a fox causing trouble in someone's backyard henhouse. The two deaths were treated in the same matter-of-fact way, with only a bare recitation of the basic facts. Holmes had learned more by reading the Rochester newspapers.

Even so, he found one intriguing tidbit in the annals regarding Bernhard Krupp, who two days before he died had "paid a visit to the Honorable Walter Schmidt, in Rochester, to discuss legal matters."

When Holmes sat down again with Halbach, he asked about Krupp's visit with the lawyer.

"Naturally, I cannot say what their discussion was about," Halbach said. "You would have to ask Mr. Schmidt."

"I intend to," said Holmes. "As for the annals, I must say they were not very revealing as to the circumstances of the two deaths."

Halbach gave Holmes a chilly stare. "The annals are intended to be an unbiased and straightforward account of daily life here in Eisendorf, Mr. Holmes. Nothing more, nothing less. It is not my job to write in the sensational manner of the press."

"I see. Even so, it must give you a feeling of great power to be the one anointed to tell the town's story."

"Power, Mr. Holmes? That is an amusing thought. Of how much value is power in a place such as this?"

• • •

Holmes spent the entire afternoon with Halbach, who provided a full tour of the archives, which included a basement vault for safekeeping of the most important records. Not surprisingly, the archivist's knowledge of Eisendorf and its citizenry was encyclopedic. Yet Halbach was hardly forthcoming, and Holmes had no doubt the archivist knew much more about the two recent deaths than he was willing to reveal. During their talk, Holmes made no mention of the Monster, and he had no intention of doing so, at least for a while. Halbach was a hard man to read, and Holmes thought it unwise to share any confidences with him.

It was five o'clock by the time Holmes returned to his cottage. Before leaving Rochester, he had thrown out his pipe and tobacco. Even so, the old tobacco devil was close at hand, whispering in his ear. Holmes listened to the tempter for a time, testing his will against the lovely lure of smoke. It was almost too much to stand, and Holmes knew he had to do something—anything—to keep the devil at bay. A walk might help.

He had been assured by Halbach that all of Eisendorf encompassed little more than a square mile. Halbach had also described the layout of the streets. With that in mind, Holmes thought a quick reconnoiter would be in order. Walking at an easy pace so as not to become winded, he proceeded due south from the cottage, past two cross streets. At the south end of town, he reached a street called Mill Avenue, which ran parallel to a fast-flowing stream known as German Creek. Just past the avenue, a narrow iron bridge crossed the creek. A road on the other side disappeared around a bend into a wooded ravine where, Holmes had been informed, the old Krupp Brewery stood.

Holmes decided he would wait to have a look at the brewery. Instead, he turned west on Mill Avenue, which followed a terrace twenty feet above the creek. This terrace, according to Halbach, demonstrated how wise Dionisius Eisen had been in selecting the town site, for its elevation above the creek protected it from the floods that occurred almost every spring. Across the creek, atop another terrace, Holmes saw a graveyard wedged in front of a wooded bluff. The cemetery contained a surprising number of tombstones. Eisendorf, it appeared, had more dead than living residents.

The evening was pleasantly cool, with shafts of sunlight slanting down into the valley, and yet Holmes still saw no one. He had asked Halbach why the town seemed so deserted. The archivist explained—not very convincingly—that residents so valued their privacy they rarely ventured outside.

Holmes soon observed another peculiarity. He noted that Eisendorf's houses—all built of brick—were arranged with something close to military precision. Each block contained just four corner houses, each facing a different direction. The houses were all but identical—two-story brick cubes with wooden front porches. East–west alleys bisected the blocks, providing access to sheds, stables, garages, and other outbuildings. A passion for order, Holmes knew, could easily slide into tyranny, and he wondered what Dionisius Eisen's true dream had been in founding the town. Perhaps he had wanted not freedom for all but control of his own little kingdom, well removed from the prying eyes of the larger world.

Now, however, the town had become a museum of lost dreams, caught in a downward spiral of dissolution and decay, and most of the houses Holmes passed appeared to be vacant. He saw broken windows, peeling paint, missing roof shingles, sagging porches, yards consumed by weeds. Here and there an occupied house with a neatly kept lawn and a fresh coat of trim paint held out against the ruin. Eisendorf, Holmes concluded, was a corpse in the making. The only question was when the funeral would be.

A tap on the shoulder startled Holmes. He spun around to find a young woman in a long white smock staring at him with bright-blue eyes. A tiara made of cheap costume jewelry rested atop her lush blond hair, which fell in long waves to her shoulders. She carried a short pink wand in her right hand.

"I'm Willy," she said. "You must be Mr. Sherlock. Would you like to see a magic trick?"

4

———◖● ● ●◗———

T he girl made an immediate and unforgettable impression on Holmes. She was beautiful, her eyes sparkling and intense, and she was so small and lithe she seemed almost to float as she walked. Holmes put her age at about twenty, although her manner was childlike. He quickly learned that her real name was Wilhelmina, that she was the daughter of Peter Eisen, and that she knew "a thousand magic tricks."

She performed one for Holmes, reaching up to touch his right ear, where she discovered a penny. "It was hiding in your hair," she announced. "Did you know it was there?"

"I did not," said Holmes, who had watched her palm the coin, not very expertly. "You are indeed quite the magician. How did you manage to come up behind me so quickly that I did not see you?"

"Sometimes, I'm invisible, like the wind."

"That must be very useful."

"Yes, I see secret things. Do you want me to show you one of them?"

Holmes wasn't sure how to respond. Beyond the obvious deduction— that the girl's mind was younger than her body—he had no way to tell what she might know about the recent events in Eisendorf. But the fact she was the daughter of one of the town's leading citizens made her of more than passing interest to Holmes. He decided to play along with her for a while.

"Yes," he said, "I would like to see a secret thing."

"Come with me," she said. "It's not far."

They walked for several blocks along Mill Avenue before reaching the end of town. As the street narrowed and turned sharply to the south, fol- lowing a bend in the creek, Holmes saw a large stone house standing on a wooded hillside. It was a rambling affair, Gothic in inspiration and powerful in a grim sort of way, with a massive round tower rising above the gated front door. The house-cum-castle looked as though it had been designed to repel a peasant revolt.

"My house," the girl said. "Poppa's house."

"It's very big, isn't it?"

"Yes. Momma says it's too big. Momma doesn't like it."

"Is the secret in your house?"

"No. We have to go to the mill. The tunnel is dark. It's Wolfie's secret."

It took a moment for Holmes to realize the girl must be talking about Wolfgang Eisen. "Ah, so your uncle has a secret in the tunnel, is that it?"

The girl nodded. Up ahead, Holmes saw another stone structure, larger than the house. It had to be the town's old gristmill.

• • •

Earlier that afternoon, Halbach had told Holmes about the mill and its unusual tunnel. The archivist also revealed yet another of the town's peculiarities. Eisendorf, it seemed, had nearly vanished within two years of its founding.

"When Dionisius Eisen established the town in 1855," Halbach said, "he had no way of knowing a great disaster would soon occur—the financial panic of 1857. It hit especially hard in Minnesota. Money and credit all but disappeared, property values plunged, and men went bankrupt. The situation was so dire many of Eisendorf's settlers left. Even Dionisius abandoned the town, and the small flour mill he had built, to return to Germany. He remained there for over a decade. At one point, there were only eighteen people left in Eisendorf, all of them families who farmed the land around town. It looked as though the town was about to die."

"Obviously, that didn't happen."

"No, Mr. Holmes, salvation was at hand. Dionisius, who still dreamed of creating an ideal community here, found a man in Bavaria who possessed the wherewithal to revive Eisendorf's fortunes. His name was Gottfried Krupp. He was a wealthy brewer in Munich. But he had grown tired of Germany, and he liked the idea of making a fresh start in the New World. So he sold everything he owned, at great profit, and went into partnership with Dionisius."

"When was this?"

"In 1870. Their plan was to reestablish Eisendorf on a more secure footing. Gottfried was an excellent businessman and also quite a salesman. And, like Dionisius, he was a freethinker who hated all the trappings of religion. The two of them persuaded a new group of Bavarians to immigrate to Eisendorf. Once Gottfried arrived, he built the brewery here. He also helped build the Eisen Block and invested in the mill as well. The mill was a wonder in its day, and the only one of its kind in Minnesota."

"Because of the tunnel?"

"Yes. Old Dionisius was quite a brilliant man, and he knew his mill could be greatly improved by blasting out a tunnel to increase its fall of water and therefore its power. "

"I am not sure I understand," Holmes said. He was familiar with the wind-powered mills of Sussex and had also seen the workings of water-powered mills in his youth. But he had never heard of a mill with a tunnel.

Halbach said, "The tunnel mill here, I suppose you can say, is an accident of geography. It was built because German Creek makes a very long but narrow loop of several miles around a steep ridge called Table Rock. In the course of this oxbow, as the folks around here call it, the creek drops about thirty feet in a series of rapids. Dionisius saw the opportunity this presented, and once he had enough money, he hired a team of men to blast a tunnel six hundred feet through the limestone ridge to the mill. He also built a small dam at the tunnel's upstream entrance to assure a steady supply of water."

"Ah, I see now how it works," said Holmes. "Water enters the tunnel and races across to the mill, where it then drops thirty feet to provide power before returning to the creek. A very elegant solution."

"Yes, and very efficient as well. Eisen's Tunnel Mill, as it was called, attracted much business because of the quality of the grind it produced. It was very profitable for many years."

"Is it still operating?"

"No. It shut down five years ago. The big millers up in Minneapolis took much of the flour business, and country mills like ours found it hard to compete. It will be a ruin someday, I'm sure."

Halbach gave a regretful shake of his head. "The same fate, I fear, awaits our village. Even so, I intend to record everything that happens here, down to the last day."

"What will become of the archives once the town is gone?"

"I will make arrangements when the time comes. My hope is that Eisendorf's story will persevere even if it does not. And who knows, Mr. Holmes, perhaps you will become the last great player in the drama of this little town of ours."

"Perhaps I shall. Now, I have but one more question. What happened to Dionisius Eisen?"

"I fear that is a tragic story. There was an accident at the mill in 1893."

"A fatal accident, no doubt."

"So the authorities determined."

"And do you agree with that judgment?"

"I have no reason to doubt the official verdict."

"I wonder," Holmes said. "Eisendorf seems to be a place where accidental death is unnervingly common. Do you not find that peculiar, Mr. Halbach?"

The archivist, his blue eyes opaque panes of glass designed to mask the thoughts behind them, stared at Holmes and said, "I find many things to be peculiar, Mr. Holmes. It is the nature of the world."

• • •

As he stood before the old mill, which occupied a small clearing at the base of Table Rock, Holmes thought of Halbach's account of the tunnel dug by Dionisius Eisen. What secret might it hold? Or was Willy Eisen simply imagining a secret? Holmes couldn't see any evidence of the tunnel from his vantage point, but it had to be at the back of the mill, where Table Rock loomed. The mill, built of massive walls of yellow limestone, looked to be in good condition even though it no longer operated. Its small windows retained all of their glass, and the large double door at the base appeared to be freshly painted, in a wine-red hue close to the color of blood.

Willy Eisen wandered off to look at the mill's tailrace channel. Carved into the rocky ground, the race led down to German Creek less than a hundred feet away. Holmes went over to ask her once more about the secret in the tunnel. Then he heard doors swing open and turned around to see a burly man in overalls emerge from the mill, a shotgun cradled in his arms.

"Leave the child be," he said, "and don't you give me any trouble."

"Wolfie," the girl said, looking rather frightened, "this is Mr. Sherlock. He likes magic tricks."

"I know who he is," said the man, who wore overalls over a long-sleeved work shirt. He was in his fifties, wide through the shoulders, with a broad face, curly black hair, a barbed-wire beard of the same color, and dark-brown eyes so deep set that they looked like furtive little beasts staring out from their lairs. Holmes noted grain dust on the man's boots, dabs of grease on his callused hands, and a flashlight lodged in the pocket of his overalls.

"You must be Wolfgang Eisen," Holmes said, giving no hint of alarm at the man's sudden appearance. "I thought the mill was closed, and yet you appear to be guarding it? Why is that?"

"None of your damn business," Eisen said. "You are trespassing. Go away."

Willy said, "Don't be mad, Wolfie. Mr. Sherlock is here to see the secret in the tunnel."

"You are talking nonsense again, Willy. There is nothing to see in the tunnel."

"Why don't we have a look for ourselves?" Holmes suggested. "I would be curious to know what Willy has found."

"Curiosity can get a man killed if he isn't careful," Eisen said. "Understand this. I care nothing for the great Sherlock Holmes, nor does anyone in this town. You are sticking your big English nose where it does not belong. Don't come here again or you will regret it."

"I do not like being threatened," Holmes replied. "I have usually found that when a man makes threats, he does so because he is hiding something. What are you hiding, Mr. Eisen?"

"You're a bold one, aren't you, but you're pressing your luck. I'll give you a simple choice. Either you go, or I shoot."

Holmes looked into Eisen's cold eyes. The man just might be willing to pull the trigger.

"Very well," Holmes said, "but we shall talk again."

"I doubt it," said Eisen, who grabbed Willy by the arm. "Come along, you stupid girl. You don't want to be late for supper."

"Good-bye, Mr. Sherlock," she said. "Maybe we'll see Mr. Bones later."

"Good-bye, Willy," Holmes said, suddenly aware that the tunnel might hold a greater secret than he ever could have imagined.

• • •

Halbach was waiting by the cottage when Holmes returned just after six. "Did you have a pleasant walk?" he asked.

"Not entirely. I met Willy Eisen, who is a most charming young woman. I also met her uncle, Wolfgang. He was not as charming."

"So you must have gone to the mill. I will tell you frankly, Mr. Holmes, that the mill is a place you should avoid."

"Because of Wolfgang?"

"He is an unpredictable man with a very bad temper. I would not like to see you get hurt."

"Nor would I. But I am not a man who can be threatened, Mr. Halbach, by Wolfgang or anyone else."

"Of course. But a fearless man is not always a wise man. Let us turn to more pleasant matters. Why don't you join me for dinner at my house? It would be a great honor. Besides, Peter Eisen is there, and he would like to meet you."

Holmes, who was starving, readily agreed. They walked over to Halbach's house, which, like almost all of the others in town, was built of red brick in a simple, foursquare manner. A stone lintel over the front door bore the inscription, "Eisendorf, 1874."

Halbach said, "What you see here, Mr. Holmes, is another example of the great care with which Dionisius Eisen designed the village. The Plan of the Founders, as it is called, directed that every house should have its construction date prominently displayed over the front door. Mr. Eisen believed this would be a perpetual lesson to generations to come in the history of the community."

"How thoughtful of him," Holmes said as he stepped inside to meet another member of the Eisen family.

• • •

Like his brother, Peter Eisen was tall and stocky, with dark eyes, but there the resemblance ended. Wolfgang had struck Holmes as a bellicose, rough-cut character, the kind of man content to live in a shack in the woods with whiskey and dogs as his only companions. Peter Eisen appeared far more refined, his luxuriant salt-and-pepper hair so perfectly pomaded that it glistened like glass. Dressed in a navy-blue pinstriped suit and red waistcoat, from which a gold watch chain dangled, he had the satisfied look of a prosperous country banker. Holmes put his age at about sixty, although he could have passed for a man ten years younger.

"Mr. Sherlock Holmes," Eisen said in a hearty baritone, rising from a chair in Halbach's front parlor and coming forward to shake Holmes's hand. "Even with that beard, there is no mistaking your face. Just saw a picture of you in *Collier's*, and I must say you look even better in person. Well, it is a rare privilege to meet so renowned a man. Yes, indeed, a privilege."

"I am pleased to meet you as well," Holmes said, struck by how much more loquacious Peter Eisen was than his sullen brother. "Mr. Halbach tells me you are the head man in this little community."

"Oh, now, don't believe everything Freddy tells you. Eisendorf belongs to its people, not to me. Besides, if anybody rules this town, it's Freddy. We couldn't do without him. Has he shown you the archives?"

"He has. The annals are quite intriguing."

"Aren't they? My uncle Dionisius was a genius in his own way. He truly wanted to create a new kind of community here. What a dreamer he was!"

"And yet he does not seem to have been especially successful. Mr. Halbach tells me that Eisendorf is shrinking away."

"Perhaps, but the future may hold a surprise or two for our little town. Don't you agree, Freddy?"

Halbach stared at Eisen for a moment, as though trying to fathom some great mystery, then said, "The future is always a surprise, Peter. Now, why don't we go into the dining room? I am sure Mr. Holmes would enjoy a glass of beer."

Once they were seated at the dining-room table, where three steins of beer awaited them, an elderly woman came in from the kitchen bearing a plate of cheese, pickles, and relish.

"Ah, Mrs. Dreisser, this is Sherlock Holmes," Halbach said. "He has come all the way here from London."

"Guten abend," the woman said, without much warmth. "The rest will be served shortly, I am sure."

Halbach sliced off a wedge of cheese and handed it to Holmes. He took another wedge for himself and said, "Weisslacker, or beer cheese as we call it. It used to be a specialty of our creamery, but now we have to get it from Wisconsin. The taste, I assure you, is much better than the smell."

Holmes tried a bite of the pungent cheese and agreed. Feeling parched, he also took a stein of beer. "I see that Prohibition does not hold sway here," he noted. "Yet the brewery is closed, is it not?"

"It is," Eisen said. "Krupp's Cave-Aged Lager is officially a thing of the past. The brewery shut down some years ago. Poor Bern didn't have the heart to sell off any of the equipment, but his cousin, Josef, is trying to do that now. It really is a pity! I may be biased, Mr. Holmes, but if there was a better beer brewed in Minnesota, I do not know of it. Yes, a very fine beer indeed. Fortunately, it is still possible to find a spare bottle or two, if you know where to look."

"As Mr. Halbach obviously does," Holmes said, raising his stein. "And now let me propose a toast to Eisendorf. I am finding it to be a most remarkable place. Mr. Halbach has already told me something of the town's history, but I should like to know more. In fact, as we were coming in, Mr. Halbach, you mentioned the Plan of the Founders. What exactly is this document?"

Eisen provided the answer. "It is our Bible, I suppose you could say, only God plays no part in it. The Plan of the Founders, which Uncle Dionisius wrote in his own hand, is the law of Eisendorf. Not, mind you, the law insofar as the state of Minnesota is concerned—we are subject to that when it comes to criminal and civil matters—but the law that governs the structure of the community, which includes the farms on the uplands."

Eisen paused to take a long draft of beer before continuing. "Dionisius's plan described precisely how Eisendorf would be laid out, how land and resources would be controlled, and how its finances would be administered, among many other things. You may not be aware of it, Mr. Holmes, but all of Eisendorf—the village, the farms, the carefully managed forest here in the valley—is owned by the people. Eisendorf is a cooperative, to use the legal term."

"I take it that is a novel arrangement?"

"For a village, yes. There are many cooperatives in Minnesota, mostly formed by farmers to run businesses like creameries, but Eisendorf is the only cooperative community."

"And who governs this cooperative?"

"Freddy does," Eisen said. "He's the administrator. Has been for twenty-five years."

Halbach shook his head. "Peter is being facetious. The people themselves govern Eisendorf. I merely do their bidding. We have an annual meeting every December at the People's Hall, which you may have noticed, Mr. Holmes, on the other side of the park. Numerous issues affecting the community are discussed and voted on. The meetings can last for quite a while."

Eisen chuckled. "Freddy is given to understatement, Mr. Holmes. The annual meetings are hell on earth, as far as I'm concerned. The good people of Eisendorf like to talk about every damn thing you can think of. Why, didn't last year's meeting go on for twelve hours, Freddy?"

"Seemed like twelve days," Halbach said.

"Democracy is not a pretty thing," Eisen said, "but it is the way of Eisendorf."

"Unfortunately, violent death also appears to be the way of your town," Holmes said, yanking the conversation in a new direction. "There have been two suspicious deaths in the span of a few months in a community of just forty people. It must be cause for great concern, Mr. Eisen, especially since one of the victims was a relative of yours."

Eisen's bluff geniality suddenly gave way to a more confrontational tone. "And you have come to investigate these two unfortunate incidents, is that it, Mr. Holmes? I must admit I am surprised. I know Freddy is, too. We welcome you to our little town, and we are truly honored by your presence, but it is a mystery to us why you would find such matters of interest."

"My reasons are my own, Mr. Eisen, but I will tell you I have cause to believe the recent deaths here are connected to events that occurred long ago in Munich."

"Is that so? Well, I am sure Freddy and I would like to hear more. What are these old events of which you speak?"

"I cannot say at present."

"Then you have us in a difficult place, Mr. Holmes. You leave us groping in the dark. How can we be of help to you if we do not know why you are here?"

"You will know soon enough, Mr. Eisen. But for the moment, you and Mr. Halbach can be of help by answering a few questions regarding the two recent deaths."

Eisen let out a long sigh. "All right, but I do not see the point of your inquiries. Bern Krupp's death was a terrible accident, pure and simple. As for poor Hans, you appear to believe his suicide was something far more sinister. I assure you, it was not. My dear cousin was a deeply troubled man. His death was a tragedy, but it was not unforeseeable. He had entertained thoughts of self-destruction for many years."

"And yet the sheriff of this county believes his death may not have been a suicide."

A flash of irritation crossed Eisen's face. "Thorkelson is a good enough man, but he often lets his suspicions get the better of him. He appears to believe some great evil is lurking in Eisendorf. It is not. Accidents happen, Mr. Holmes, and so do suicides. Our town is not immune to the troubles of the world."

"On the contrary, I would say it has experienced more than its share of troubles. As for your cousin's death, I am sure Sheriff Thorkelson has pointed out to you all of the inconsistencies he found at the scene."

"Yes, yes, yes," Eisen said impatiently, "and none of them proves a thing. Besides, anyone in town could tell you all about Hans's troubles. The truth is he made a mess of everything he tried. Take the mill, for example. It was failing when I got here. Dionisius was growing feeble, but poor Hans wasn't really up to the job of running the mill, so Wolfgang had to take over."

"When was that?"

"In 1892, the year we arrived in Eisendorf."

Holmes found this news fascinating. "So you weren't born here, Mr. Eisen?"

"Oh no, I came over from Munich, just like the others that year."

"The others?"

"We call it the 'third immigration,'" Halbach explained. "Peter and Wolfgang and about twenty others arrived from Munich in 1892. They were the last Germans to come over here from the old country."

"What brought you here?" Holmes asked Eisen.

"It was Dionisius's doing. He went to Munich to recruit new settlers. I had a decent enough job there but not one with any great future, and I liked the idea of making a fresh start. So did Wolfgang."

"I encountered Wolfgang and your daughter, Willy, when I walked over to mill," Holmes said. "I cannot say your brother was very welcoming."

"Oh dear. I hope he didn't threaten you."

"He had a shotgun and seemed prepared to use it."

Peter Eisen looked mortified. "Let me apologize to you, Mr. Holmes. My brother has a rather gruff manner, I'm afraid, and he's very possessive when it comes to the mill. We've had some vandalism there, and he's been standing guard. But he at least should have been polite. I should probably apologize about Willy, too. She's always trying to convince people she knows 'secret things,' as she calls them. The fact is, they're all in her head. I love her dearly, but she can be a trial."

"There is no need to apologize for Willy," Holmes said. "I found her to be quite delightful and informative. She even offered to show me one of her secrets in the old mill tunnel."

"Oh Lord, my little girl must be in heaven with you here, Mr. Holmes. She knows you're a famous detective but not much else, and she'll want to let you in on all of her imaginary secrets. I remember once she found an old brass lamp—God only knows where—and swore she saw Aladdin coming out of it."

"Let us hope the genie granted her three wishes," Holmes remarked.

"I wouldn't be surprised if he did," Eisen said with a smile.

Mrs. Dreisser entered to announce that dinner would be served shortly. Eisen smiled at her and asked, "How are you and Georg doing?"

"Well enough," she said.

"Ach, das ist gut," Eisen said, turning to Holmes. "Mrs. Dreisser's son, Georg, also came over in 1892. He's done very well for himself. So has our host. Isn't that right, Freddy?"

Holmes was caught by surprise. "So you, too, were part of the 1892 immigration, Mr. Halbach?"

"Yes, but I am not so sure I have found any great success here, as Peter seems to suggest."

Before Holmes could ask another question, Eisen rose from his chair. "I am sorry to say I cannot stay for dinner. I have another engagement tonight. But I am sure we will talk again, Mr. Holmes."

After Eisen had left, Halbach asked, "What did you think of Peter?"

"He's certainly more pleasant than his brother."

"I would not dispute the point," Halbach said. "Would you care for more beer?"

• • •

Halbach's house overlooked the town's main street, and from his chair Holmes could look out a window toward the Eisen Block. It was almost seven, darkness closing in, and the street was deserted. But not for long. Holmes saw the headlights of an automobile, coming in from the west. The car drove slowly past the Eisen Block, as though the driver were looking for someone. Then it disappeared down the street, only to reappear moments later, heading back in the direction from which it had come.

The car, Holmes knew, was Tommy Boyd's taxi. He'd asked Boyd to swing by Eisendorf every night at seven o'clock, just in case. Eisendorf was isolated, with no telegraph service and uncertain phone lines, and Holmes wanted to be sure he had a means of sending and receiving messages. Boyd would also be available to whisk Holmes out of the town if he found himself in grave danger.

The sight of Boyd's taxi, with its headlamps penetrating the coal-black night, touched off an unsettling memory. In Munich, the Monster's horse-drawn cab had also featured two lamps, and Holmes suddenly saw them in his mind, sending out shafts of light into the silent, shadowy murk of the English Gardens. Holmes had nearly met his death in that cab. Now, once again, he could feel the Monster close at hand, waiting for him in the darkness.

5

————⊣● ● ●⊢————

The dinner—a Teutonic repast of plump sausages, sauerkraut, and potato salad, all washed down with copious quantities of excellent lager beer— went on for two hours. Halbach, who grew more expansive with each stein of beer, did most of the talking. Holmes did not object. Listening—not just to the meaning of words but also to how they were spoken, how they were arranged, how they suggested what might lie hidden beneath—was a detective's most vital skill.

In his younger days, flush with the bright bloom of his own genius, Holmes had not always been a good listener, his mind often racing ahead of the speaker's words in a tumult of ideas and deductions. Once, in fact, he had ruefully admitted to Watson, "I sometimes see everything but hear nothing." But Holmes was older now and in less of a hurry, so he carefully absorbed everything Halbach had to say.

The archivist's wide-ranging disquisition included one item Holmes found of particular interest. It concerned the "third immigration" of 1892. If the Monster was in fact in Eisendorf, he must have arrived with that late company of settlers. Holmes needed to know the name of every man in the group. So far, he knew of four—Peter and Wolfgang Eisen, Georg Dreisser, and Halbach himself. How many more were there? He put the question to Halbach, who remained cagey despite his ample consumption of beer.

"Why would you want to know such a thing?" he asked. "Come now, you must have a reason."

"I am simply trying to get a clearer picture of the town's history," Holmes lied.

"Ah, I think you are fibbing, Mr. Holmes. You know something, don't you, and that is why you are here."

"Perhaps, Mr. Halbach, but I do not know why the 'third immigration,' as you call it, should be shrouded in secrecy."

"It is not, Mr. Holmes, I assure you. But do you really expect me to remember all the names? I will have to look it up in the annals. Come see me tomorrow, and I will give you what help I can."

"I shall," Holmes promised.

As they moved on to dessert—a rich chocolate torte bursting with whipped cream—Holmes returned to the subject of his encounter with Wolfgang Eisen. "Mr. Eisen was quite threatening. Do you know why?"

"It is as Peter told you," Halbach said, attacking the torte with gusto. "Wolfgang is a difficult man. I am also sure the break-ins at the mill over the past few months have made him quite anxious. Young troublemakers from some of the neighboring towns are undoubtedly the culprits. In any case, Wolfgang is a man best avoided. That is all I can say."

"And what about his niece, Willy? Do you agree with her father that she is not to be trusted?"

"Dear little Willy is the sweetest girl you could ever imagine, but the poor thing is a bit touched, as they say, and she has a very vivid imagination. She is always talking about secrets and magic and who knows what else. I would not pay too much attention to it."

"So I take it you have no reason to believe there is a secret hidden in the tunnel? No old skeletons, perhaps?" Willy's parting reference to "Mr. Bones" had left Holmes wondering whether the girl might have found human remains of some kind in the tunnel. But if she had discovered old bones, whose might they be?

Halbach delivered a glassy-eyed stare, then said, "There are secrets everywhere, are there not? However, I know of nothing hidden in the tunnel. There are rumors, of course, but I am sure they have no basis in fact."

"What sort of rumors?"

"Oh no, I will not fall into that trap, Mr. Holmes. I have no interest in rumor mongering. We already have enough of that here in town."

"In my experience, rumor is sometimes the first dim light of the truth," Holmes noted.

"Well, I do not share that sentiment," Halbach said, making it clear he wasn't about to share any gossip with Holmes.

"Very well," said Holmes, "let us forget about secrets and rumors for the time being. However, I should like to know more about the tunnel itself. It must be quite a remarkable feat of engineering. How did Dionisius Eisen manage to excavate it?"

"Well now," Halbach said, suddenly warming, "that is indeed quite a story. He hired six local men do the work. They started on either end of Table Rock, and they used black powder—keg after keg of it—to blast their way through. Took them eighteen months until they finally met in the middle."

"How extraordinary. Now, I believe you told me earlier he also built a dam on the creek at the far end of the tunnel."

"Yes, to maintain a reliable flow of water to the mill."

"So the opening at that end of the tunnel must be under water."

"It used to be, at least for much of the year. But the dam was washed away some years ago, so you can see the tunnel entrance now. Wolfgang tried to board it up, but I hear that some young people still get in there and go exploring. I'm sure I don't know why. As I told you, there's nothing to see. It's just an old tunnel."

"Ah, Mr. Halbach, are not all young people detectives at heart?" Holmes observed. Then he pushed back his chair and rose to his feet. "Please thank Mrs. Dreisser for the excellent dinner. It is time I retire."

"Well, I wish you a good night's sleep," Halbach said.

"Oh, I am sure I shall rest most peacefully," said Holmes, who in fact had no intention of doing any such thing.

• • •

When Holmes returned to his cottage, he found the front door ajar and light glowing from within. He had locked the door when he left for dinner after dousing the kerosene lantern in the parlor. Holmes took out his revolver and pushed in the door. He found Willy Eisen sitting in the parlor, a manila folder in her lap. A tiara glittering with costume jewelry once again crowned her head. She wore a flowered pink dress beneath her long coat.

"Don't shoot me, Mr. Sherlock," she said, cringing when she saw the gun.

Holmes slipped his revolver back into his jacket pocket. "My dear Willy, I most certainly am not going to shoot you. But how did you get in? The door was locked."

She shook her head. "It was open."

"Really? I find that most interesting. Now, is there something you want to show me? I see you have a folder with you. Is it another secret?"

She gave no answer. Instead, she stood up, the folder falling to the floor, and rushed over to Holmes. She wrapped her thin arms around Holmes's waist and said, "I'm afraid, Mr. Sherlock. Wolfie is very mad at me."

As Holmes hugged Willy, he felt her trembling. She really was terribly frightened. He tried to reassure her. "Come over to the couch, and sit next to me. It will be all right. There is no need to be afraid. Why is your uncle so mad? Does it have something to do with what's in the folder?"

She nodded before retrieving the folder and handing it to Holmes. He opened it to reveal a collection of yellowed newspaper clippings, all in German. They were held together by a heavy staple.

"Ah, and what are these?" Holmes asked.

"Wolfie says I stole them."

"Did you?"

"No, I found them."

Some of the clippings included a masthead, and Holmes recognized the newspaper at once. It was the *Münchner Neueste Nachrichten*. He had read it every day during his brief stay in Munich in 1892. The newspaper prided itself on getting scoops, and one of them had nearly cost Holmes his life. Yet the paper had also provided the most thorough coverage of the Monster's murder spree. Holmes scanned the clippings. All of them appeared to be from 1892 and dealt with the Monster's crimes.

Holmes felt a surge of excitement. "Where did you get these, Willy?"

"It's a secret."

Holmes knew he had to be patient with the girl. A "secret" one minute might not be the next. The trick was not to push her too hard. "I see. But I have to tell you something, Willy. I am a great detective, as you know, and I find out things. So I know you found these clippings at your house."

"Did not," she said. "Fooled you!"

"Yes, you did. You are a sly one, aren't you? Well, let me see now. Where could they have come from?"

When Holmes took a closer look at the clippings, he detected a faint odor. Holmes's nose was legendary—Watson had once called him "a perfectly good bloodhound disguised as a man"—and what he now smelled was malty, with a bitter tinge of hops, along with a certain mustiness.

"I stand corrected," Holmes said. "You found these at the brewery, didn't you, Willy?"

The girl was wide-eyed. "How do you know, Mr. Sherlock?"

"I told you. I am a great detective. There are caves at the brewery, are there not? Is that where you found the box?"

"Maybe," she said.

"Do you ever see Wolfie at the brewery?"

"He works there for Big Joey."

Holmes assumed Big Joey was Josef Krupp, whose family owned the brewery. Sheriff Thorkelson had brought up his name earlier.

"I see. Now, Willy, I want you to listen very carefully. When did you find these clippings?"

"I don't remember."

Holmes suspected the girl had only a vague sense of time, and he didn't press the point. But he very much wanted to know why the clippings had caused Wolfgang Eisen to become so upset.

"How did your uncle learn you had these clippings?"

"Wolfie finds out everything. He's mean. He came to my room, and his face got red, and he yelled at me and said I was a thief and I'd better give them back."

"What did you do?"

"I ran away and came to see you, Mr. Sherlock. I don't want Wolfie to strangle me."

Willy, Holmes began to think, could be a vital ally. She was like a nosy little mouse who knew every hiding place and every secret in Eisendorf. But if knowledge was power, it could also be a peril. Her uncle's threats had to be taken seriously.

"I will not let Wolfie hurt you," Holmes told her. "I will talk to him. May I keep these clippings for now?"

"Yes, I don't want the ghost to take them."

"The ghost?"

"He lives in the big house. It's empty but I hear him sometimes."

"The big house? Where is that, Willy?"

"You know, the wood building with the red roof."

During his dinner with Halbach, Holmes had asked about the wooden building next to the Eisen Block. He had learned it had been built as temporary apartments for the immigrants of 1892, since no other housing was available at that time in town. Known as the Wohngebäude, the building had been vacant for years.

"Have you ever seen this ghost?" Holmes asked.

"Ghosts are invisible, Mr. Sherlock. Don't you know that?"

"Of course they are. But why do you think there's a ghost in the big house?"

"He talks."

"What does he say?"

"I don't know. I can barely hear him. Ghosts are very quiet."

Holmes tried to question the girl further about what she had heard in the Wohngebäude, but her answers grew increasingly vague. In the end, he wasn't sure what Willy had actually seen in the old apartments, but he thought the "ghost" might be real. Someone had been watching from the apartments when he arrived in town. Now, Holmes wondered whether the building had at least one part-time occupant and perhaps two, if Willy was also a frequent visitor.

"Are you thinking, Mr. Sherlock?" she suddenly asked.

"Yes. It's a habit of mine."

"I like to think, too, but it's hard," she said, reaching into her coat pocket for a piece of hard candy. When she pulled out the candy, she had something else in her hand—a photograph.

"Look at this, Mr. Sherlock. I found it."

The photograph was a tintype of the kind popular in the nineteenth century. It showed five men in suits standing in front of a large stone building with the name "Treuer" incised above the doorway. It was a name Holmes recognized. Curiously, the face of one of the men in the photograph had been rubbed out. Holmes wondered why.

"Where did you find this, Willy?"

"In the box."

"The same box with the clippings?"

She nodded.

"Willy," said Holmes, "I do not know what I would do without you. Now, I want to ask you about one more secret. It concerns Mr. Bones."

"No, I can't go there anymore," she said, shaking her head. "Wolfie will catch me."

"You mean, in the tunnel?"

The girl looked at Holmes. There was wonder in her blue eyes but no guile. "I can't talk about it. I must go, Mr. Sherlock. Maybe I'll see you again."

Then she was out the door, like a wisp of smoke gone in the night.

• • •

After Willy left, Holmes retreated to his small bedroom at the rear of the cottage. There, he made a disturbing discovery. Atop the vanity next to his bed he found a pack of Lucky Strike cigarettes. A hand-printed note beneath the pack said, "How about a smoke, old man? Breathe easy now. I'll see you soon."

Clearly, the Monster or someone working with him had broken into the cottage while Holmes was having dinner with Halbach. It explained why Willy had found the door open. Holmes made a thorough search of the cottage but found nothing else out of the ordinary.

The cigarettes, he had to admit, were a terrible temptation. The easy draw of smoke, the pleasure of exhaling it in a slow blue curl, the aroma more inviting than any perfume. Holmes stared at the green-and-red pack, an oasis in a desert of denial, but finally turned away as desire gave way to deduction. The cigarettes were a revelation. The Monster obviously knew about the diagnosis Holmes had received at the Mayo Clinic. But how had he acquired this knowledge, since medical records were supposedly private? Holmes intended to find out.

• • •

The cottage lacked electricity and indoor plumbing, but Holmes hardly noticed the inconvenience as he settled in for the night. His conversation with Halbach had been a rich larder stocked with savory morsels, and Holmes wanted to digest them all. Lying on the lumpy, saggy old bed in the cramped bedroom, a kerosene lamp providing all the light he needed, Holmes let his mind range through a sequence of possibilities, based on what he had learned of Eisendorf's unique history. But it was the "third immigration" that drew Holmes in like a whirlpool, his mind circling and circling.

The more he stared into the swirl, the more he saw a likely connection to Munich. His memories of Munich in the summer of 1892 remained vivid. A hunted man, he had arrived in the old city by the Isar in late July. He'd gravitated at once to the coffeehouses and cafés of the Schwabing neighborhood, Munich's bohemian quarter, where he had found a small apartment on a quiet little street. His aim was to lie low for a time before possibly returning, in secret, to England.

Holmes had been in Munich for only a few days when the newspapers trumpeted the Monster's latest outrage. This time he had murdered and mutilated two men, a twenty-one-year-old male prostitute and a young businessman the police assumed had been his customer. The businessman's name was Martin Treuer. Both bodies had been dumped in the English

Gardens, their naked, grossly violated remains left for all to see in the first light of dawn.

The park was a short walk from Holmes's flat, and when he went to see where the body had been found, near the little round temple known as the Monopteros, he was struck at once by the Monster's daring. The temple occupied a highly visible hilltop lovers were known to frequent even in the early morning hours. Yet instead of looking for a secluded spot to dispose of his latest prey, the Monster had deposited the bodies in a spot where he could easily have been seen. Was the Monster simply brazen, Holmes wondered, or had he found a way to hide his activities in plain sight?

Given his situation, Holmes knew it would be risky to pursue the Monster. If the press got word Holmes was on the case and revealed his presence in Munich, Moriarty's agents would be at his doorstep in no time. But investigating crimes—the more strange and grotesque the better—was an addiction Holmes found all but irresistible. The Monster of Munich was calling to him, and he had to answer.

• • •

Early the next morning, Holmes went to the archives to see Halbach. The archivist, a green visor shading his eyes, was hard at work writing the latest chapter in the Annals of Eisendorf. He did not look especially pleased to see Holmes.

"I suppose you want that list of men who arrived with the third immigration," he said. "I am very busy now, as you can see, but if you go to the annals for 1892, you will find what you are looking for. As I recall, they arrived in September."

"Thank you," Holmes said and walked over to the long table with the annals arrayed on a shelf above. He found the volume for 1892 and, after a brief search, located an entry dated September 6, 1892. The writing, in German, was difficult to read, but Holmes finally found the list of names he was looking for. Eisendorf being the carefully planned place it was, the names were in alphabetical order. Holmes got out a pad and pencil and jotted down all of the men's names. There were twelve, beginning with a certain Theodore Abel and ending with Oskar Wohl. In between he found Georg Dreisser, the two Eisens, and Halbach. He also came across one other name he recognized—Josef Krupp.

An age was listed with each name, providing Holmes with a handy way to eliminate suspects. The Monster he had tried to corner in the English Gardens was young and very strong. In their brief, violent encounter he had seen strands of the Monster's black hair. It had no gray streaks. The Monster, Holmes thought, could not have been much over thirty years old at the time.

Holmes studied the list. Dreisser was twenty-eight when he reached Eisendorf. Peter Eisen was thirty; Wolfgang Eisen, twenty-seven. Halbach was twenty-nine. Holmes ran down the remaining names. All the rest except one were either too old or too young to have been the Monster. The exception was Josef Krupp, age twenty-six at the time of his arrival in town.

Holmes was well aware that simply because five men of the right age had arrived in Eisendorf from Munich in 1892, logic did not dictate that one of them must be the Monster. The Monster could have arrived later. Indeed, he could have lived elsewhere for years before moving to Eisendorf. It was even possible whoever had invited Holmes to Eisendorf was not in fact that Monster but someone else—an associate, a relative, or merely a troublemaker with knowledge of the case.

Still, Holmes thought it more likely than not that the Monster was in Eisendorf and that he had arrived as part of the 1892 immigration. And that meant Holmes had five suspects. What he didn't have was any reason, for the moment, to favor one over any of the others. He put the list in his jacket pocket and went over to talk with Halbach again.

"Did any newcomers from Germany or anywhere else arrive here after 1892, to your knowledge?"

Halbach glanced up from his work and said, "Mr. Holmes, I have work to do. I am not a walking, talking encyclopedia."

"When it comes to this town, that is exactly what you are," Holmes said. "Please answer my question, and I will be happy to leave you alone."

Halbach rubbed his forehead, as though trying to massage away a persistent headache. "A lot of people have left Eisendorf since the 1890s, but I can think of only a few—prodigal sons, I guess you could call them—who have returned."

"Who might these prodigals be?"

"Well, there's Georg Dreisser, who lived in Rochester for many years. He just came back in March, I think it was, to help take care of his mother. And of course, there are the Eisens."

"Which Eisens?"

"Peter and his family. They were up in St. Paul for a long time but returned here last year. Oh, and there's Josef, too."

"Josef Krupp?"

"Yes. I don't know where he was, but he came back to help out Bernhard with the brewery."

"How strange all of these men would return to live in a town that even you admit is dying. What brought them back?"

"Must be the exciting nightlife," Halbach said, "Now, if you don't mind—"

"I appreciate your help," Holmes said. "I will not keep you from your work any longer."

"Thank God for that," Halbach muttered as Holmes went out the door.

• • •

A walk appealed to Holmes, so he set off once more toward the mill. He wanted to have a better look at it. When he reached the massive stone structure, he stood outside the main doors for a few minutes, making a bit of noise, just to see if Wolfgang was lurking inside with his shotgun. But there was no response, so Holmes examined the padlock and bar securing the doors. The padlock, he soon determined, was of a type he could easily pick. But when he pushed against the doors, he felt something heavy against them. Wolfgang, he suspected, had erected a barricade of some kind inside. Gaining covert access to the mill and its tunnel, it now seemed, would be a difficult proposition.

Holmes circled around toward the rear, to look for the tunnel entrance there. It was an uphill walk over rocky ground, and he went slowly. A new appreciation for the force of gravity had arrived along with Holmes's emphysema, but he resented his condition nonetheless. Why should what had once been so effortless now be so difficult?

At the rear of the mill, he paused to take a breath and survey the situation. The mill's back wall, a good twenty feet high, stood next to the steep hillside forming one side of the long ridge known as Table Rock. An unruly growth of small trees and shrubs crowded into the narrow space between. Holmes soon spotted what he was looking for—an elongated wooden box, suitable for sheltering a flume, that extended from the mill directly into the hillside. Here, he was sure, was the tunnel that Willy Eisen said contained a secret.

In his younger days, Holmes might have tried to scramble through the trees and break into the flume. But such athletic maneuvers would be far more challenging now. Besides, the flume's plank walls and slightly pitched roof looked very sturdy. It would take a heavy crowbar at the least to pry open the walls, and with Wolfgang Eisen always hovering around, there was a strong chance he might discover Holmes in the act of breaking and entering.

There was, however, one other possibility, which was to enter the tunnel from its west portal, on the far side of the ridge. But how accessible was that opening? Holmes wasn't sure, but one way or another, he wanted to see the tunnel for himself.

Of course he could not be sure the tunnel really held a secret in the form of "Mr. Bones," as Willy claimed. The girl had a tenuous grasp of reality, and her secret discovery could be nothing more than the scattered bones of a rat or some other animal. Or "Mr. Bones" could simply be a figment of her imagination. And yet, Holmes was inclined to think Willy was in her own strange way a truth teller, that rarest species of humanity. She just might be the one person in Eisendorf he could trust.

6

————|● ● ●|————

After returning from the mill, Holmes lay down on the spongy, old couch in the cottage's parlor and tried to collect his thoughts. But his mind, always the sharpest of instruments, especially when stropped by a few pipefuls of good tobacco, seemed to lack its old powers of concentration. Had Eisendorf, with its enervating stillness, begun to envelop him in a kind of mental fog? Or was he in a state of nicotine withdrawal? He remembered what it had been like to give up cocaine, his mind so absorbed by the loss of the drug he could barely think. Was his abrupt decision to stop smoking having the same effect? Whatever the cause of his malaise, Holmes knew he had to snap out of it, and quickly. The Monster, on his home ground, promised to be even more dangerous than he'd been in Munich. Now more than ever, Holmes needed to be at the top of his game.

Feeling restless and in need of company, Holmes went out for a breath of fresh air. Gazing across the park, he noticed that Halbach's General Store, Eisendorf's only going business, appeared to be open. Holmes went over for a look. The store occupied the east end of the Eisen Block. A sign over the door, its block letters faded almost to illegibility, announced that the store had been established in 1893. Below, a smaller sign read, "U.S. Post Office, Eisendorf."

The store, Holmes discovered when he stepped inside, was like so much else in Eisendorf, a place where time seemed to have stopped dead, encased not in amber but in a thick coat of dust. A bewildering miscellany of items—ceramic jugs, china, tinware, coffee grinders, bushel baskets, lanterns, boxes of ammunition—packed the shelves. Rakes, pitchforks, and other farm utensils hung from hooks on the walls. Overhead, big spools of twine, rope, and wire dangled from the ceiling. Halbach, dressed in a white apron, stood behind a glass display case that held pocket watches, jewelry, and other valuables, including a revolver with a small, white price tag attached to its trigger guard. Jars of candy and an old brass cash register occupied the counter above the case.

Halbach was behind the counter when Holmes walked in. He was the store's only customer. "It would seem, Mr. Halbach, you are running a museum here," he said.

"Yes, it does look that way, doesn't it?" Halbach admitted. "I started the store right after I got here, but I don't think I ever turned a profit."

"How do you manage to stay in business?"

"'I suppose you could say this place is my hobby," Halbach replied, a touch of rue in his voice. "I keep it open a few hours a day just because I want to. Oh, I sell some staples"—Holmes had noted bags of flour and sugar arrayed behind the front counter—"but not much else. There are bigger, better stores in Stewartville and Rochester with all the latest things, or people just order what they want from Sears and Roebuck."

A bell over the front door rang, announcing the arrival of another customer. Holmes turned around to see Wolfgang Eisen.

"Ah, Mr. Eisen, how nice to meet you again," Holmes said, "especially without your shotgun."

Eisen glared at Holmes and said to Halbach, "I'll come back later. It stinks in here."

"I would not leave just yet," Holmes said, walking over to Eisen and blocking his path to the door. "I had a fascinating talk with Willy yesterday. She says you threatened her, apparently because she found something you have been hiding."

"She's always making things up," Eisen said. "I don't know what you're talking about."

"So those Munich newspapers from 1892 and that old photograph from Martin Treuer's business are merely products of her imagination, is that what you are saying?"

Holmes hoped the mention of Treuer's name would spark a reaction, but Eisen gave no hint of surprise or concern.

"Get out of my way," Eisen said, his saturnine eyes boring in on Holmes, "or I will knock you over."

Holmes didn't move. Staring back at Eisen, he said, "I am thinking you must have worked for Mr. Treuer. Is that you in the photograph, with your face scratched away? Why would you do that? What are you hiding?"

Eisen uttered an expletive and pushed Holmes aside.

"I should be very unhappy if you even think of hurting Willy," Holmes said.

"I'm quaking," Eisen said. "I'm quaking in my goddamn boots."

He left without another word, slamming the door behind him.

"I must say Mr. Eisen is not growing on me," Holmes told Halbach.

"Wolf isn't much for socializing, I'm afraid. But he's really quite harmless, once you get to know him."

"I look forward to that day. I am sure he and I will have many fruitful discussions."

• • •

Willy Eisen came into the store a few minutes later. She was wearing a light-blue dress with small white wings attached to the shoulders. As always, a tiara balanced atop her head. Her ballet slippers were also white, as was the marching baton she spun slowly in her right hand. Her left hand was balled into a fist.

"Hello, Mr. Sherlock," she said. "Wolfie didn't see me. I know where to hide."

"Of course you do," Holmes said, his mood instantly brightening. Willy was the one person in Eisendorf he had taken an immediate liking to. Most of the town's residents, as far as Holmes could tell, had turned in on themselves, hunching down like hunted animals in their remote little valley. But Willy was different. She had managed to blossom in her own odd way, a bright flower in a dark garden, and Holmes felt himself curiously free and relaxed in her presence. She represented something he had lost long ago and had only in his old age come to miss. Holmes wasn't sure what to call this lost thing, but it was there in Willy, a sharp, mysterious spark, and he knew it would be good to have it back, if only he could.

"Are you here to buy candy?" she asked Holmes.

"No, but I suspect you are."

She nodded, then paused to adjust her tiara. "I would like some things," she told Halbach. Examining the candy jars with great care, she pointed to her selections one by one: "Two of those, three of those, one of those, none of those—I don't like them at all—and five of those. How much?"

Halbach bagged the candy and added up the bill. "Looks like ten cents, Willy. Can you handle it?"

She opened up her left hand and dropped a pile of pennies, seven in all, on the counter. "There," she said. "Good-bye, Mr. Halbach. Good-bye, Mr. Sherlock."

Holmes said, "Could I walk a bit with you, Willy, on your way home? I like candy, too"—he took two sticks of licorice from one of the jars and left a nickel on the counter—"and we could talk."

"I don't like licorice," she said. "But you can come along, Mr. Sherlock. I think you're nice."

"Thank you, Willy. I think you're nice, too."

• • •

They left the store and walked south toward German Creek. The day was cool and pleasant, a few thin clouds roaming far above the bluff tops. Holmes was again struck by how quiet the town was, its streets deserted, its residents invisible behind the drawn curtains of their houses. Even the birds had stopped singing, as though bound by some secret code of silence. Holmes had never been in a place that felt so empty and yet somehow so menacing.

"I'll show you something," the girl suddenly announced.

"I'd like that. Is it another secret?"

"Maybe," she said, adding as though it were an afterthought, "They're sleeping in white sheets."

Holmes had no idea what Willy meant. "Who's sleeping?"

"The men in the picture."

"A picture of men sleeping?"

"Yes."

"Where did you see this picture?"

"It's a secret."

"But you said you'd show it to me, didn't you? Is it another secret you found in the brewery cave?"

"Maybe."

"Was it with those newspaper stories and that other picture you found?"

"Maybe."

"How many men were sleeping in the picture?"

"Two."

"And why do you think they were sleeping?"

"Their eyes were closed."

Holmes began to have the glimmer of an idea. Could Willy have seen a photograph of two dead men covered with sheets, perhaps in a morgue? If so, why would Wolfgang have kept such a picture? Holmes had another thought. Could the photograph be a grisly souvenir from a long-ago crime?

"Do you have the picture, Willy? I would like to see it."

She ignored Holmes's question. "Do you like lemon drops, Mr. Sherlock?" she asked, reaching into her bag of candy.

"Sometimes."

"I like them all the time," she said, taking two drops from the bag and handing one to Holmes. "Wolfie never eats candy. I hope he dies."

"That is not a very nice thing to say, Willy. Is Wolfie still mad at you? Does he want his things back?"

"Wolfie is always mad. Poppa has to tell him to be nice."

"Good for your Poppa. Everybody should be nice. And you know, Willy, you could be really nice to me by showing me that picture of the sleeping men."

"No, it's a secret," she said, skipping away from Holmes as she twirled her baton. The iron bridge spanning German Creek lay just ahead. She went halfway across before pausing to gaze over the railing. "Mr. Frog lives down there," she told Holmes when he came up to join her. "He's very big. He likes me."

"I'm sure he does. It's too bad Wolfie doesn't like you just as much. Did he get angry at you when you showed him Mr. Bones?"

"I didn't show him. Mr. Bones is my secret."

"I would really like to see Mr. Bones," Holmes said. "He must be an interesting fellow."

"Yes, I like him. Do you know how many secrets I have, Mr. Sherlock?"

"I'm sure you have quite a few."

"Seventeen," Willy said without hesitation. "Let's go to the other side."

She ran to the far end of the bridge, then stopped so Holmes could catch up to her. She unwrapped another piece of candy and popped it in her mouth. Holmes received the discarded wrapping.

"Put it in your pocket, Mr. Sherlock. Momma says it is a bad thing to make a mess."

"Your Momma is right," Holmes said, looking into Willy's eyes. They were so blue and bright and free from the taint of the world that he felt a sudden urge to sweep her up and shield her from all the rot and deception around her. But it was not only her sweet spirit that was at risk. Holmes sensed that dark events were about to unfold, and he feared she would be in their midst.

"I liked Cousin Hansy," Willy suddenly announced. "He was happy."

Holmes was intrigued by this spontaneous observation. He knew little about Hans Eisen, Dionisius's only son, other than that he had supposedly committed suicide following a long bout of despondency. "I thought he shot himself because he was sad," Holmes said.

"It was Wolfie's gun. I saw it."

"The gun that your cousin Hans used?"

Willy nodded. "Wolfie kept it in his jacket, but I saw it. I can see secret things."

"I know you can, Willy. Did Wolfie give the gun to Hans?"

"Oh, no, Hansy didn't like guns. He told me never to touch them or I would die. Hansy was nice. I miss him. Who do you miss, Mr. Sherlock?"

"I miss many people. But I would really like to hear more about Wolfie's gun."

"I'm tired. You didn't answer me, Mr. Sherlock. Who do you miss most?"

"Well, I have one dear friend whom I miss very much."

"Where is he?"

"In London."

"Does he live in a palace with the king?"

"Not quite," Holmes said, "although I am sure he would like to."

They were walking now up a winding gravel road that led into a wooded ravine. A tiny stream coursed beside them. Holmes had many more questions for Willy but realized he would have to tread lightly. The girl was fragile and airy, like the angel's wings attached to her shoulders, and Holmes knew she would become flustered or simply go silent if he tried to push her too hard. Better to go slowly. He wanted Willy to be comfortable and spontaneous. He hoped she would reveal her secrets—all seventeen of them—in due time.

Holmes changed the subject. "I am still thinking about that ghost you heard, Willy. You know, the one in the big house. It must have been very scary for you."

"I don't go there anymore," she said before halting by a road that branched off to the west, toward the cemetery Holmes had seen on his earlier walk through town. She put a finger to her lips and whispered, "Shhh, we have to be quiet, Mr. Sherlock. The people are resting. Sometimes I see them at night."

"What do they look like?"

"They're invisible, except to me."

"Can they see you?"

"Yes, but they're nice."

"Unlike the ghost?"

Ignoring Holmes's question, Willy picked up the pace again. "The beer house isn't far," she announced. "Big Joey will be there but not Auntie Kate."

The road started to steepen, and Holmes slowed his pace. Willy noticed his labored breathing. "Are you sick, Mr. Sherlock?"

"Just old, Willy. Tell me about Big Joey. Is that Mr. Krupp, who runs the brewery?"

"Yes. Auntie thinks he's smarter than he looks. She told me."

"Why does she think he's smart?"

"I don't know. She just does."

"Do you like your auntie?"

"Yes. Auntie Kate is nice."

Holmes had not yet met Katherine Krupp, although he intended to talk with her. He hoped she could shed additional light on the supposedly accidental death of her husband, Bernhard.

Holmes said, "I would really like to know more about the secret in the cave. Is it a really big secret?"

"Yes. Maybe I'll tell you when we get there."

"That would be lovely. Now, where exactly is this cave?"

"You'll see," she said and took Holmes by the hand, as if she were guiding a small child to safety. She spun the baton in her other hand, the leader of a marching band of which Holmes was the only member.

A hundred yards or so up the ravine, a driveway entered from the east, and Holmes looked up to see the town's other mansion—the Krupp family estate—looming above the trees in a Germanic festival of arches, towers, and gables.

"Auntie's house," Willy said. She moved a few steps ahead of Holmes now, dancing to her own imaginary music.

Holmes nodded and did his best to keep up. Before long, they reached the brewery, a substantial cluster of stone and brick buildings occupying a clearing in the woods. The largest building, constructed of blocks of limestone, bore a carved sign with the word "*Sudhaus*" over its main entrance. Clearly, the Krupp Brewery had once been a substantial operation, but it was shuttered now, and no one appeared to be around.

Holmes had learned from Halbach that the brewery had closed in 1915, a few months after a German U-boat sank the *Lusitania,* claiming nearly

1,200 lives. The attack on the ocean liner touched off a storm of anti-German sentiment that caused the brewery to suffer a disastrous drop in business. But with Prohibition looming, the brewery wouldn't have survived much longer in any event.

Behind the brewery a sheer cliff rose to a height of one hundred feet. There was a large cave at the base of the cliff, its opening in the form of a parabolic arch. Willy led Holmes into the cave, where they encountered two iron doors just inside the entrance.

"This way," Willy said, pushing open one of the doors.

As they started to go deeper into the cave, Holmes heard heavy footsteps coming up behind them, and then a man's voice boomed out, "What are you doing here?"

• • •

The speaker was yet another of Eisendorf's broad-shouldered men, with a substantial belly, muscular arms, and a big, balding head mounted on a neck fit for a bull. A small forest of a beard, more white than black, spread its foliage well beneath his chin. His dark, probing eyes suggested shrewd intelligence. He wore overalls, a checkered shirt, and heavy boots caked with mud, and he carried himself with easy confidence.

"You must be Josef Krupp," Holmes said, extending his hand. "I am Sherlock Holmes. My apologies if we were trespassing. Willy is hard to resist when she wants to show me something."

"I know all about Willy," Krupp said, shaking Holmes's hand with an iron grip. "She noses around here all the time, even though she knows better. Now, is there something the two of you want?"

Holmes said, "As you must be aware, Mr. Krupp, I am investigating the recent deaths that have occurred in Eisendorf."

"So I've heard. But I just can't figure out why the illustrious Sherlock Holmes would take an interest in our small problems. Don't you have enough to do in London?"

"I don't live there anymore," Holmes said. "Actually, one of the most interesting cases I ever encountered was in Munich, years ago. Wasn't that your birthplace, Mr. Krupp?"

"Is there some point to all of this?" Krupp asked in a tone that was not friendly. "I'm not much for idle chatter."

"The point is murder, Mr. Krupp. It is a crime that interests me no matter where it occurs, and I should like to put a few questions to you. I understand Wolfgang Eisen sometimes works here."

"Not anymore. I know a snake when I see one."

"I imagine you do. What did Mr. Eisen do to make him a reptile in your eyes?"

"That's my business."

"Perhaps, but it may soon become mine as well. Before he was dismissed from your employ, did Mr. Eisen's work here take him into this cave on occasion?"

Krupp glared at Holmes, suspicion lurking in his eyes. "Why do you ask?"

"Because it could be important. Have you ever run across any old German newspapers in the cave? Or perhaps some old photographs?"

Krupp gave a telltale blink, and his head dropped slightly. "No," he said, "and why would it matter anyway?"

Holmes, who during his long career had been lied to in every conceivable way by miscreants of every conceivable kind, was sure he was being lied to now.

"Then you would have no objection, I presume, if I took a look in the cave for myself."

Krupp took a step forward, his big belly almost touching Holmes, and said, "So you think because you're the almighty Sherlock Holmes you can do anything you want, is that it? Well, think again. Did you see the sign when you came in that says, 'No Trespassing'? You're trespassing now, and you're not welcome here. Either leave or I'll throw the both of you out."

"You are the second person who has threatened me today," Holmes said, standing his ground, "and I'm growing tired of it."

"Too bad. Maybe you should take the hint. Nobody wants you here. Nobody needs you here. You should leave."

"I find it peculiar, Mr. Krupp, that you are so uncooperative. I should think you would be interested in getting to the bottom of your cousin Bernhard's suspicious death."

"I know better than you ever will what happened to my cousin," Krupp said, glaring at Holmes, "and justice will be served soon enough. I will see to that. But it's none of your damn business. Now, this is the last time I will say it. Get out!"

"Very well," Holmes said coolly, "but I am sure we will speak again soon."

"Not a chance," Krupp said, adding, "and don't ever come back here. That goes for you, too, Willy. I don't want to catch you sneaking around anymore, or there will be big trouble."

"I don't think Big Joey likes you," Willy said as she and Holmes headed back to town.

"So it would seem," Holmes said. "I think you, my dear Willy, are the only true friend I have here."

• • •

Willy soon flitted away, saying she had to go home. By the time Holmes returned to his cottage, he was feeling weary, even though it was only a little past noon. Why did he feel so bereft of energy? Was it the emphysema? Or was it the simple fact he had gone two days without the stimulus of tobacco?

Holmes sat down on the couch, took off his shoes, rubbed his feet. A fine pipeful of tobacco, or a nice long draw on a good cigarette or cigar, was what he really needed. He still had the pack of Lucky Strikes provided by the Monster. The pack looked to be fresh and tightly sealed. Even so, the Monster might have found some elaborate means to poison the cigarettes. Holmes wasn't quite desperate enough to take that chance. Besides, he knew it would be entirely illogical—and if Dr. Plummer was to be believed, suicidal—to give in to tobacco's siren call. Ah, but how he wanted a smoke!

In hopes of staving off his tobacco urges, Holmes let his thoughts once again drift back to Munich in 1892. There, in that strange city where beauty and terror danced together in the moonlight, he had quickly discovered the Monster was a most formidable foe.

Holmes had begun his investigation at one of Munich's libraries, where he spent a long afternoon reading everything he could find about the murders. He learned that all four victims had been left in open areas of the English Gardens, near a well-traveled road or pathway. Evidence clearly showed the men had been killed and eviscerated elsewhere. No one had seen the bodies being dumped. Nor had the police been able to discover where any of the murders had actually occurred.

Munich's police had focused their investigation on the city's underground community of male prostitutes and the Monster's presumed connection to it. The police believed the Monster must be "a customer of such perverts," as one newspaper put it, killing them in grisly fashion only after satisfying his "forbidden lust." Holmes thought this could indeed be true, but what really puzzled him was how the Monster had managed to dispose of four bodies in the English Gardens without arousing the least bit of suspicion.

The more Holmes thought about the case, the more convinced he became that the police were on the wrong track. If the murderer was a frenzied sex criminal, how could he at the same time be so clever and calculating? The Monster was surely a vicious murderer. But did he really kill out of some uncontrollable passion, or did he just want it to look that way? The answer to that question would not be long in coming.

1

—⊰ • • • ⊱—

ater that afternoon, Holmes heard a knock at the cottage door. He glanced
out the window. His caller was a heavyset man, whose fancy attire—dark
wool suit, red bow tie, starched white shirt, and black homburg hat—
was decidedly out of the ordinary for Eisendorf.

"I am Georg Dreisser," the man announced when Holmes opened the
door. "I thought I would stop by to introduce myself."

"Of course. Please, come in."

"Not quite Baker Street, is it?" Dreisser said, inspecting the cottage's thin-
ly furnished parlor.

"I gave up Baker Street long ago, Mr. Dreisser. I am a country gentleman
these days."

"And supposedly retired, from what I have read. And yet here you are in
Eisendorf, on the hunt."

"True enough, Mr. Dreisser. Have a seat."

Dreisser nodded and parked himself in one of the parlor's two side
chairs. He removed his hat and let it rest on his lap. He said, "I am not one for
casual pleasantries, Mr. Holmes, so I will get to the point. My dear mother,
who in addition to being Mr. Halbach's cook is Eisendorf's busiest gossip, informs me my name came up in one of your recent conversations. Naturally,
I am curious as to why."

Holmes studied his visitor. Dreisser was stocky, with the broad, florid
face and dark, suspicious eyes Holmes had come to associate with Eisendorf's male population. Beyond certain obvious deductions—Dreisser
owned a white cat, played billiards, spoke French, and carried a pistol in his
jacket pocket—Holmes couldn't tell much about the man.

Holmes said, "You are of interest, Mr. Dreisser, because you arrived
here in 1892. Is that correct?"

"Yes. But why is that of any importance?"

"That will become clear in due time."

Dreisser slowly shook his head. "Come now, Mr. Holmes, there is no
need to be coy. You are the world's most famous detective. You have worked

on behalf of kings and lords and great titans of business, and yet here you are in this stupid little town in the middle of nowhere, trying to chase down a murderer. A most strange circumstance, if you ask me. When I learned of your arrival here, I naturally had to ask myself why you would bother. After a while, I began to think that it must because of what happened in Munich in 1892. Am I right?"

Holmes deflected Dreisser's question with one of his own. "And just what do you believe happened in Munich that might have led me to come here?"

Dreisser toyed with his hat and said, "The Monster, Mr. Holmes. What else could it be? As I'm sure you already know, I was in Munich at the time of the murders there. I read all of the papers, of course, and followed the case very closely, as did everyone else. In any event, I now find you are asking me about how I and others happened to leave Munich in 1892 and resettle here. From this I have made a deduction. Do you wish to hear it?"

"Deductions are always fascinating, Mr. Dreisser. Please, go on."

"Very well. Putting two and two together, as it were, I have concluded you are on the trail of the Monster right here in Eisendorf. You think he arrived in 1892, Germany perhaps having become too hot for him, and that he is now continuing his murderous ways before our very eyes."

"That is quite a deductive leap."

"Yes, and you are entirely free to deny the truth of it. Yet somehow I doubt you will. Oh, and by the way, I am not the Monster, if that is your next question, nor do I know who is."

Holmes scrutinized Dreisser's face, looking for telltale signs of deceit—averted eyes, rapid blinking, an involuntary tic. He saw nothing out of the ordinary but took no comfort as a result. The Monster, he knew, would be nothing if not a consummate liar.

"Your theory is most interesting," Holmes said, "and perhaps we will talk of it another time. For the moment, however, I should like to return to the matter of your emigration from Germany. How did it come about that you and about twenty other people decided to leave Munich and relocate to Eisendorf?"

Dreisser's shrewd eyes honed in on Holmes. "So you will not confirm my deduction, I see. Sly of you, Mr. Holmes, very sly. But a refusal to deny a thing is, as often as not, a tacit affirmation. Or so I believe I read somewhere. No matter. I am happy to answer your question as to why we all came here. The answer requires but one word: 'desperation.'"

"And why was that?"

"Come now, you must have seen the problem firsthand when you were in Munich. The early 1890s were a terrible time in Germany. There was a deep depression, and like so many other young people, I found myself out of work and with no prospects. My mother, with whom I lived, was also in a poor way. That's when I saw the posters Dionisius Eisen had put up in the beer halls, offering to pay full steamer fare to come to the United States and settle in Eisendorf."

"And you found the idea attractive, I take it."

"Yes. Dionisius did quite a sales job by painting a very pretty picture of Eisendorf. Green hills, fine farmland, thriving businesses, nice houses. Oh, and did I mention the climate? It was cold, yes, but dry. Why, a person would hardly notice when the mercury sank to the bottom of the thermometer. Naturally, I should have known it was a fantasy, but I was young and therefore foolish, and I had nothing to lose. So I took the chance and came over with my mother and the rest of the group from Munich."

"And yet, if I am correct, you are not from that city, Mr. Dreisser. Your accent suggests you hail from Lorraine, where much French is spoken."

"Très bien," Dreisser said. "Yes, I moved to Munich in 1891 to look for work but did not have much success."

"What sort of work did you find?"

"Odd jobs here and there. Why do you ask?"

"Mere curiosity. Did you ever drive a taxi?"

Dreisser cocked his head to one side and gave Holmes a sidelong glance. "No, that is one job I never had."

"I see. Now, when did first you see the posters advertising Eisendorf?"

"It must have been in the summer of 1892, around the time the Monster was going about his disgusting business. But it wasn't until late August that everything was arranged and we set sail for America."

"Did you know Peter and Wolfgang Eisen in Munich?"

"Only vaguely. There was a big meeting with everyone in the group before we left, and I met them there."

"Did you strike up a friendship?"

"Well, I got to know Peter pretty well. A nice enough fellow, at first. As for Wolfgang, let's just say he's not known for making friends."

"So I have discovered," Holmes said.

"Ah, I see you've already met him," Dreisser said with a smile. "Wolfgang doesn't exactly ooze charm, does he? However, you should know he wasn't always the miserable hermit he is today. He's actually quite capable. He ran the mill here for years and did a good job by all accounts."

Holmes said, "I believe Frederick Halbach also came over with your group, as did Josef Krupp. Did you know either of them beforehand?"

"No, I first saw them at the same meeting where I met the Eisens. I got to know them better during our crossing, which was very stormy. I remember all of us got sick. Perhaps it was an omen."

"It must have been a rough crossing indeed. I assume you eventually came to know everyone in the group. Can you name any other of the men who are still living in Eisendorf?"

"No, it's just the five of us now. The others are gone."

"Do you mean they are dead?"

"Well, they could be for all I know. When I say they're gone, I mean they left town."

"Recently?"

"No, they left long ago."

"Why?"

Dreisser let out a bitter laugh. "Well, Mr. Holmes, Eisendorf didn't exactly turn out to be the Eden we were promised. Far from it, in fact. We all got here not long before the big depression of 1893 hit, and there were hard times all around. And that first winter! Mon Dieu, I had never been so cold, for so long, in my life. Mother and I lived in that damn barracks they called the Wohngebäude for two years because no houses were available in town and there was no money to build new ones. Most of the men who came over had families, and they couldn't find decent work, so they left. I think some of them even went back to Germany."

"I see. And yet you stayed, Mr. Dreisser."

"Yes, but not for all that long. I had a little training in Germany as a chemist, and I managed to get a good job in Rochester. I lived there, in fact, until this spring, when I moved back here to help my mother. She has become rather forgetful and simply can't keep up her house anymore."

"And where do you work in Rochester, Mr. Dreisser?"

"At the Mayo Clinic."

"How interesting," Holmes said. "How very interesting."

• • •

Over the next hour, Dreisser had much more to say about Eisendorf. He depicted the town and its citizens in the worst possible light, referring repeatedly to what he called "a foul odor of corruption."

"This whole place smells to high heaven," he said. "Eisendorf is the rotting carcass of an ideal, Mr. Holmes, and nothing stinks worse than a dream gone bad."

Holmes recalled something Halbach had said about Dreisser, calling him "*the* village atheist in a town full of atheists." Yet Holmes had long ago come to understand that a man who believes in nothing is a man who will believe in anything. Dreisser's cold cynicism, Holmes suspected, might well disguise some dark purpose.

"Those are harsh words, Mr. Dreisser."

"But they are also the truth. Idealism is just another source of human misery in my estimation. Old Dionisius was an honest enough dreamer, I suppose, but he was foolish to think he could remake human nature. The ideals drained out of this place a long time ago, and now all that's left is the sludge. You will be pleased to know, Mr. Holmes, that the good people of Eisendorf are today just as foolish and grasping as everybody else."

"And what are they grasping for, if I may ask?"

"Money, what else? It's what makes the world go round, as they say. Incidentally, do you have any idea how much Eisendorf is actually worth?"

"I cannot say the town strikes me as having any great value," Holmes observed. "Indeed, it looks as though it will be utterly abandoned before long."

"Bah! Forget about the town, although you are right enough—its days are numbered. Come back in twenty or thirty years and there'll be nothing here but a wide spot in the road choked with weeds. No, I'm talking about the whole cooperative, Mr. Holmes. Four thousand acres of some of the best farmland in Minnesota, plus another thousand acres of virgin hardwood forest. That's where the value is."

"But the farms and forest belong to the cooperative, do they not?"

"For the time being. But who knows what the future may bring?"

"What are you saying?"

Dreisser raised his hands, palms up, in a gesture of uncertainty. "I am merely saying there may be some big changes in the wind. Naturally, it's all a secret at this point. As you perhaps have already discovered, if there's one thing the rulers of this benighted little village love, it's a good secret."

"Those rulers being the Eisens, I presume."

"Yes, they are the almighty lords of this town, especially now that Bernhard Krupp is gone. It was most convenient for them he died when he did, if you ask me."

"Why do you say that?"

"Well, there is a story—I don't know if it's true, mind you—that when old Gottfried Krupp arrived in town in 1870 with a bulging bagful of money, he insisted on certain changes to the cooperative agreement Dionisius Eisen had drawn up when he founded the community. The changes were designed to benefit the Krupp family at the expense of the Eisens, or so I've heard."

"So I take it you think Bernard Krupp's death was no accident?"

"Perhaps, but I really don't know one way or the other. What does the sheriff think?"

"He has his suspicions."

"And what about you, Mr. Holmes?"

"I am reserving judgment," said Holmes, who was growing tired of Dreisser's insinuating manner. "Let us talk about what you know, Mr. Dreisser, as opposed to what you merely suspect. Take that cooperative agreement you claim was amended to benefit Gottfried Krupp. Do you know its actual contents?"

"No, but neither does anyone else in town outside the charmed circle."

"The charmed circle being Peter and Wolfgang Eisen?"

"Yes. Of course, Bernhard Krupp would also have been aware of the document, but the dead can't speak, can they? As for Peter and Wolfgang, I doubt either one would be willing to tell you a thing about it, Mr. Holmes. They're canny fellows, the both of them."

"And no one else in town would know about the amended agreement?"

Dreisser thought for a minute. "Oh, how silly of me. Good old Freddy must be in on the secret."

"You mean, Mr. Halbach?"

"Yes, and I will offer you some free advice, Mr. Holmes. Be very wary of Freddy. Very wary. He is the prince of liars and always has been. No one in town trusts him."

"Why is that?"

"He's a maneuverer, Mr. Holmes, the snake in our bloody little garden of intrigue. Not that it really matters what happens here, I suppose."

"It matters if there is a cold-blooded murderer loose in Eisendorf. Is that why you're carrying a pistol, Mr. Dreisser? Who is it you're afraid of?"

"Why, no one in particular, I assure you. But it never hurts to take pre-cautions, does it? Besides, I note you, too, have a pistol in your coat pocket," Dreisser said, rising from his chair and donning his homburg. "Well, it is time to go. It has been an honor to meet you, and I wish you well. Still, it is a worrisome time, is it not? Who can say what might happen next? It behooves us all to be vigilant, but especially you, Mr. Holmes. I would not be surprised if the man you are looking for has you in his sights."

"I shall take that as a friendly warning," Holmes said as he escorted Dreisser out the door.

• • •

Holmes did not treat Dreisser's warning lightly. In Munich, the Monster had shown himself to be extremely treacherous once Holmes had picked up his trail. He had also proved to be very clever, and Holmes's breakthrough didn't come until he began to take a closer look at the Monster's victims.

One peculiarity stood out. The Monster's first and second victims had both been *Strichjungen.* Then the Monster had committed a double murder that did not fit the pattern. True, one of the victims was a male prostitute. The other, however, was the young businessman Martin Treuer, who owned a flour mill in a small community just outside of Munich—the same mill visible in the background of the photograph Willy Eisen had discovered.

The Munich police theorized Treuer was a victim of circumstance, killed during an assignation with the prostitute who was the Monster's real target. But that scenario struck Holmes as most unlikely. Killing and muti-lating two men at once would have been far more difficult than dealing with a single victim. Besides, wouldn't a murderer hunting down male prostitutes select his victims in the easiest way possible, by hiring them first, then kill-ing them once they had been lured to his lair?

Treuer's murder, Holmes believed, might just be the key to the case. It didn't make sense unless Treuer had been carefully targeted, for some rea-son, by the murderer. But why had the businessman been marked for death? It was only after Holmes talked to Treuer's grieving widow that he began to see a possible answer.

• • •

Before going off to dinner with Halbach, Holmes decided to take a closer look at the Wohngebäude. It was there Willy Eisen had supposedly heard a ghost.

It was there, too, that Holmes had seen a shadow moving behind one of the second-floor windows. Had Willy been the shadow, or was it someone else?

Holmes couldn't be certain, but he thought it likely Willy maintained a hideout in the abandoned building. In her meanderings around town, she picked up all manner of things, souvenirs of her secret adventures, and she needed a place to store them—a private archives, as it were. What better spot for her secret collection than in her own room in the Wohngebäude? There, she could be free of her parents and her prying uncle Wolfgang.

Perhaps it was while in her hideout that Willy had heard the "ghost." Holmes suspected this spectral figure was real, someone else who had established a hideaway in the abandoned building, someone who might have been watching Holmes as he arrived in town. Perhaps it was the Monster himself.

With the sun poised just above Table Rock and long shadows spreading like dark fingers all across the town, Holmes strolled over to the apartments. Unlike almost every other structure in Eisendorf, the Wohngebäude was built of wood rather than masonry, and it had not aged gracefully. Its clapboard siding, once painted a deep red to match the roof, was warped and peeling, and many of the windows, arranged in long rows, were broken or boarded up. The building was a ruin in a town destined for the same fate. Holmes could see why Georg Dreisser had not liked living there.

The eastern end of the building was close to the Eisen Block. A dilapidated wooden fence ran between the two buildings, sheltering what must once have been a side yard for residents of the apartments. After taking a quick look around, Holmes slipped through an open gate into the yard. One of the apartment building's two doors was just past the gate. It was a heavy wooden door, with no windows, and it looked too substantial to be easily kicked in. Holmes tried the door and discovered it was open.

Inside, Holmes encountered a long central hall decorated with spiderwebs and dimly illuminated by pale shafts of light coming from open doors on both sides. A staircase by the door led up to the second floor. Holmes climbed up to another long hallway, narrower than the one downstairs. It presented a musty, vaguely nauseating odor, along with a substantial collection of rodent droppings. Holmes went down the hall, past a series of half-open doors with apartment numbers still affixed to them. He stopped at apartment 210. Its door, unlike the others, was shut and locked. Was someone living inside? Holmes decided it would be best to knock.

He did so and immediately heard footsteps beyond. He slipped his hand into his coat pocket and felt the reassuring heft of his revolver. "This is Sherlock Holmes," he announced. "I need to speak with you."

A lock turned, and the door suddenly swung open. Wolfgang Eisen, wearing a black raincoat and a scowl to match, stared at Holmes. "What in blazes do you want?" he asked. A cockroach, his expression suggested, would have been a more welcome visitor.

"Why, Mr. Eisen, what a surprise," Holmes said. He looked past Eisen's hulking figure into the room. He saw a tattered couch, a rocking chair, and a small desk littered with what appeared to be old newspapers. A threadbare rug covered part of the floor. "I didn't realize you lived here."

"I don't," he said. "Now go away."

Holmes ignored the command. "So this must be your office. I see you are doing some research. Old newspapers by the look of it. Tell me, why are you so fascinated by the Monster of Munich?"

Eisen responded with a low growl and tried to slam the door shut. Holmes had faced just such a situation many times before, and he planted one foot inside the door before Eisen could close it.

"Why don't we sit down and have a nice talk about the old days in Munich?" Holmes said. "You can tell me about the Treuer Mill—you worked there, didn't you?—and your days as a cab driver."

"Move that foot or I will move it for you," Eisen said. There was genuine menace in his voice.

Holmes leaned his shoulder into the door and said, "You can talk to me now or to the sheriff later."

What happened next left Holmes stunned. Without a word, Eisen yanked open the door, stepped forward to wrap his massive arms around Holmes in a crushing bear hug, lifted him off the floor, and then carried him down the hall as though he were an old piece of furniture. Holmes, his arms pinned, was powerless to resist. When they reached the stairs, Eisen relaxed his grip. Holmes felt as though he had just been pincered in the claws of a giant lobster.

"Go on, get out," Eisen said, shoving Holmes in the chest to emphasize the point. "And don't come back. This is private property now."

Holmes backed away and pulled out his revolver. He would not let Eisen attack him again.

Eisen was not impressed by Holmes's show of force. "Are you going to shoot me, Mr. Holmes? I doubt it. You have no power here. You are nothing to me."

Then he turned around and walked back to his apartment.

Holmes collapsed on the steps, fighting for breath. He suddenly felt old and feeble. His body, once so lithe and strong, had betrayed him, and he wondered if he could possibly be a match for the Monster when the time came.

• • •

Holmes made no mention of his bruising encounter in the Wohngebäude when he had his usual dinner with Halbach. But he fully intended to take up the matter with Sheriff Thorkelson at the first opportunity. Holmes's confidence in his own powers had begun to sag, and he was by no means sure anymore he could take on the Monster alone. He would need the sheriff's help at some point.

After dinner, Holmes returned to his cottage, if only because there was nothing else to do. The town, which as far as Holmes could tell, had only two street lamps—both in the park—was all but pitch black at night. There was nowhere to go and nothing to see. Holmes didn't mind the solitude, but he also realized, not for the first time, how much he missed Dr. Watson.

In the old days, they would have talked for hours about the case. Or at least Holmes would have talked, and Watson, with his usual forbearance, would have listened, breaking in now and then to ask the kind of question that might cause Holmes to start thinking along new lines. They would have smoked, too, the glorious aroma of tobacco a spur to inspiration. Now, Holmes thought glumly, he had neither Watson nor his pipe, and he felt poorer for the loss of both.

It was nearly two in the morning by the time Holmes finally managed to fall asleep. He had fitful dreams. Then, after what seemed only a few moments of rest, he was awakened by loud voices from somewhere outside the cottage.

Holmes put on his robe and stepped out into the night. At first he couldn't make out the words being shouted. Then he heard a chilling cry: "Kommen Sie! Kommen Sie! Es ist Mord!"

8

—|•••|—

H olmes checked his pocket watch. It was just after six, and the first thin
coat of morning light had begun to paint the town. He went back inside,
threw on some clothes, grabbed his Webley, then headed out to Freiheit
Park. There had been rain during the night, and a soft mist hung in the air.
Holmes spotted a light in Halbach's house but did not see the archivist. The
village, usually so empty, had suddenly come to life. Small groups of men,
some carrying weapons, were walking toward the park. They looked like
ghosts in the subdued light.

Holmes crossed the park, past the old bandstand at the center, moving
as quickly as he could. At the park's far west end, in front of the People's Hall,
he found about a dozen men gathered around a motionless body someone
had covered with a blanket. Only the victim's lower legs and feet—a man's
feet—were visible.

"Does anyone know who this is?" Holmes asked, looking into the circle
of faces staring down at the blanketed corpse. He didn't recognize any of
the men.

"We know," one of the onlookers said. "Just you leave him be."

Holmes was exasperated. Apparently the corpse's identity was to be another of the town's closely held secrets. Ignoring the advice to leave the body
alone, he bent down to uncover the dead man's face.

One of the men in the crowd tried to shove Holmes away. "What did we
tell you?" he said. "This is not your business."

"Now, now, what's going on?" asked a familiar voice. Holmes looked up
to see Halbach, who had joined the crowd. "Come, let us not be unreason-
able. There is no need to be suspicious of Mr. Holmes. He is here to help us,
I am sure. I heard cries of 'murder.' Who has been killed?"

"It is Josef Krupp," one of the bystanders said. "Someone shot him."

•••

Krupp's body, Holmes discovered when he looked under the blanket, had
been left naked in the park. He lay on his back, his legs spread. A bullet had

penetrated his heart. Stippling around the chest wound indicated Krupp had been shot at very close range, but Holmes would need a better look, preferably with a magnifying glass, to be sure. There was no evidence of blood in the weedy grass around the body, suggesting Krupp had been shot elsewhere and then left in the park. The townsmen who rushed to the scene after the shouts of "murder" had trampled the ground, making it impossible for Holmes to detect any footprints the murderer might have left behind.

"Who found the body?" Holmes asked.

An elderly man in a gray raincoat, with a feisty dachshund on a leash, reluctantly stepped forward. The dog growled at Holmes. Even the canines of Eisendorf, it seemed, did not care for outsiders. Holmes discovered that the man, named Fritz Jungbauer, spoke poor English, so Halbach came forward to help translate.

Jungbauer's account proved to be of limited use. He walked his dog early every morning. It was dark when he set out, but the sun was rising by the time he and the dog headed back home. They took a shortcut through the park, where Jungbauer spotted Krupp's body in the emerging light. Jungbauer said he had seen no one else on his walk. It was all perfectly routine, except for the naked body with a hole in it.

The old man's story matched the facts, as far as Holmes could tell. Krupp's body showed signs of early rigor mortis and lividity, which meant he likely had been dead for six hours or more. Whoever dumped the body in the park would have been long gone before Jungbauer stumbled on it.

Holmes wanted to turn the body over to look for additional clues but decided against it. The sheriff or the county coroner would be the best person to undertake that task. Although there was little evidence at the scene, Holmes had no doubt who had killed Josef Krupp. The Monster was back at work in Eisendorf, as deadly and brazen as ever.

• • •

Holmes had just finished talking with Jungbauer when a tall, middle-aged woman made her way through the cluster of men still gawking at the body. She wore a gray dress cinched at the waist and a bright red shawl. A thick head of hair, black mixed with gray, drifted down in curls to her shoulders. Sharp blue eyes set off by high cheekbones commanded her face.

"What is going on?" she asked Halbach.

"It is very bad news, Mrs. Krupp. I'm afraid Josef has been murdered."

"Murdered?" she repeated. Her next words took Holmes by surprise. "So it's not over, I see. First Bernhard, now Josef. I wonder who will be next."

"I do not think you need worry about that," Halbach said. "As you have no doubt heard, we are fortunate to have Sherlock Holmes among us. I am sure he will help us get to the bottom of this. Mr. Holmes, this is Katherine Krupp, Bernhard's widow."

Holmes bowed slightly and said, "I am very sorry, Mrs. Krupp, that we must meet under such tragic circumstances. Were you close to Josef?"

"No one was," she said matter-of-factly, "except perhaps for Maria."

"Maria Eisen, Peter's wife," Halbach reminded Holmes. "She's Bernhard's sister."

"I am aware of that," Holmes said, irritated that Halbach had felt the need to provide a prompt. Holmes's legendary memory needed no such assistance. "Now, Mrs. Krupp, do you know of anyone who might have wanted to murder Josef?"

"Probably the same person who murdered my husband," she said.

Holmes studied Mrs. Krupp's face. Her lips, he noted, were quite sensuous and seemed at odds with her flinty eyes. Everything about her decisive manner suggested she was a woman of both strong passions and high intelligence. Had he finally found someone willing to speak honestly and openly about what was happening in Eisendorf?

"Why are you so certain your husband was murdered?" Holmes asked.

Mrs. Krupp glanced at the circle of men surrounding them. "This is not the place to speak of such things," she said. "Come by my house later and we will talk. But I will tell you this, Mr. Holmes. Something is terribly wrong here, and it cannot go on."

As Mrs. Krupp turned to go, Peter Eisen arrived with Willy in tow. Mrs. Krupp greeted the girl warmly but said nothing to her father. Holmes noticed the slight. The Eisens and the Krupps, it appeared, were by no means on friendly terms.

• • •

"I just heard the news," Peter Eisen said, planting himself in front of Holmes. "This is very distressing. How did it happen?"

"That is what I intend to find out. It would seem Eisendorf has become a very violent place of late. Why do you think that is?"

"I wish I knew. I really do. But I can't imagine why anyone would want to kill Josef. He caused no trouble."

"And yet now he has died a violent death, just like your cousin, Hans, and Bernhard Krupp."

"True, but Hans took his own life, and with Bernhard, it was an accident. Are you suggesting their deaths and Josef's murder are somehow connected?"

"Anything is possible. May I ask when you last saw Mr. Krupp?"

"Goodness, I think it's been a week or more. I was over at the brewery, and we were chatting about some of the equipment he's been selling off."

"And you were on good terms with him?"

"Let us just say we were always civil. But I know he and my brother, Wolf, didn't get along. They had some big falling out. Not sure why. I try to stay out of other people's business."

"A wise policy, no doubt. By the way, I am surprised your wife did not come along with you. I am told she and Josef were close."

"Really? Well, I'm not so sure about that, but you can ask her if you want. She is up at the house. She doesn't get out much these days."

"Is she ill?"

"You might say that."

An odd answer, Holmes thought, but he did not pursue the matter. Instead, he asked about Wolfgang. "I'm a bit surprised your brother isn't here. It's not every day a man is found naked and murdered in the town square. I should think Wolfgang would be curious to see what happened."

"He probably doesn't know about it yet," Eisen said. "He's something of a recluse."

"I see. By the way, I understand he and Willy had quite a row recently over some German newspapers and old photographs she had found. Apparently, he believes she stole the items from him."

Eisen's shoulders slumped, and he slowly shook his head. "Willy is just like a little bee buzzing in your ear, isn't she? But as I'm sure you can tell, Mr. Holmes, she can't always be trusted. Willy is a wonderful child, but she's not quite right, if you know what I mean."

"I have found she is actually quite right about many things," Holmes replied. "Indeed, I should like to speak with her right now."

But when Holmes turned around to look for the girl, she had vanished into the mist.

"Sorry," Eisen said. "She never stays in one place for long. Shall I see if I can find her?"

"No, she will turn up. She always does. Now, tell me more about the disagreement she had with your brother."

"There's not much to tell," Eisen said. "Wolf claimed she'd taken some things of his, and naturally he was upset. It's silly when you think about it because all he ever collects is worthless junk. Still, I'm puzzled why you're asking about all of this. What does it have to do with Josef's murder?"

"Humor me, Mr. Eisen. As I understand it, Willy took some old newspaper clippings about a series of murders that occurred in Munich in 1892, just before you and your brother left for America. Do you know why Wolfgang might have found those murders so interesting?"

"Good Lord, Mr. Holmes, I don't have a clue. You'll have to ask Wolf. It was all so long ago."

"Did your brother ever show you an old photograph of a group of men standing in front of a flour mill in Germany?"

"Truly, Mr. Holmes, I am at a loss here. Why would Wolf have such a picture?"

"Do you know if he ever worked in a flour mill in Germany?"

"Not that I am aware of. But again, what is this all about? It sounds as though you suspect Wolf of something."

"At this point, Mr. Eisen, everyone in town is a suspect. But I would like to speak with Wolfgang. Do you suppose he will be coming along shortly?"

Eisen shrugged. "Who can say? Wolf keeps his own counsel and his own time. Always has. I rarely see him except at supper, which he usually has at our house."

"As it so happens, I saw him yesterday in the old apartment building."

"At the Wohngebäude? What was he doing there?"

"I thought you might know. He appears to have an office of sorts on the second floor."

"I know nothing about that," Eisen said. "How utterly strange! You say he has an office?"

"Yes. It appears that's where he keeps his collections of newspapers and other documents. I was treated quite roughly when I tried to question him about it."

"I don't know what to tell you, Mr. Holmes. This is all a mystery to me.

But my brother is by nature a secretive man. He keeps to himself. He has a house out in the woods, and he seems happy enough there."

"When did you last see him?"

"Yesterday, at supper. As I said, he often comes over to eat with us."

"What time did he leave your house last night?"

"I'm not sure. He was still there when I left just before seven. Maria could tell you when he went, if she's so inclined. But I doubt he stayed for long."

"And you haven't seen him since?"

"No, but I'm sure he'll be around today. You could always talk to him out at his place. It's just a half mile or so past the mill."

"Very well. Now, may I ask where you were last night?"

"You weren't joking, were you, Mr. Holmes? Everybody is a suspect. Well, as I told you, I left my house about seven. I drove to Stewartville to meet a fellow there who's interested in buying some equipment from our mill. John Thompson's his name. I got back home about ten and went to bed."

"And you heard no disturbances during the night?"

"No, I slept like a log," Eisen said. "I always do."

• • •

"The sheriff should be here pretty quick," Halbach said after Eisen left. "I called him as soon as I could. I guess we'll just have to wait now until he arrives."

"On the contrary, there is much to do. For one thing, I should like to take a much closer look at the body. I am wondering if you have a large magnifying glass of any kind in your possession."

"Oh, I don't think so . . . Wait, I believe there is one at the store. Been there for years. Do you want me to look for it?"

"Yes, and I might as well join you," Holmes said. "Mr. Krupp certainly is not going anywhere."

They walked over to the store, where Halbach began a one-man expedition to locate the magnifying glass. "I know it's here somewhere," he muttered before disappearing into one of the back aisles.

Holmes, who took a spot by the front counter, was about to volunteer his considerable skills as a searcher when he made a curious discovery. It concerned the revolver he had seen the day before in the display case. Then, a small white tag had been attached to the trigger guard. Now, the gun bore a much larger, red tag. And instead of a price, the tag contained a message: "Look at me."

Holmes went around to the back of the case, opened it, and gingerly lifted out the weapon. It was a six-shot, .44 caliber Smith and Wesson with a four-inch barrel. The gun was old but appeared to be in excellent condition. Holmes broke open the cylinder, which contained a single spent round. A sniff of the barrel told him the gun had been freshly fired. Holmes found something even more telling on the reverse side of the red tag.

Halbach returned from the back of the store with a triumphant look animating his usually stoic features. "Found it," he said, handing Holmes a four-inch magnifying glass. "Compliments of the house. Ah, I see you're looking at that old revolver. God knows how long I've had it." Then Halbach noticed the red tag. "Well, that is very strange. I don't—"

Holmes cut in. "Yes, it is very strange. You see, it is perfectly obvious this gun was fired quite recently. Perhaps as recently as a few hours ago, when I suspect it was used to murder Josef Krupp. How do you suppose that happened, Mr. Halbach?"

Halbach's face betrayed no alarm. "I have no idea. If it was fired, then somebody must have stolen it. I always kept it unloaded, and I certainly have never fired it."

Holmes slipped the gun into his jacket pocket, then stared at Halbach for a moment, trying to read past the mask of his face. Nothing registered. The archivist's thoughts and emotions remained hidden. "For the moment, I shall have to take you at your word, Mr. Halbach. Still, it is a most suggestive state of affairs, don't you agree?"

• • •

Osgood Thorkelson was duly surprised when Holmes handed him the gun. They were standing next to Josef Krupp's shrouded corpse, waiting for the coroner to arrive from Rochester. The sheriff and two deputies had reached Eisendorf at eight o'clock. One deputy was already making a canvas of every house around the park. The other was searching Josef Krupp's residence, located just a block away.

"I believe this is the weapon used to murder Mr. Krupp," Holmes said before explaining how he had come upon the revolver.

"What makes you so certain?"

Holmes said, "Whoever used it to kill Mr. Eisen left a little message on the back of the price tag. I will save you the work of reading it, Sheriff. It says, 'Good work, Mr. Holmes.'"

Thorkelson glanced down at Krupp's body and said, "Well, this is a mighty strange business, isn't it?"

"So it would seem," Holmes agreed. "I have already looked for fingerprints on the gun, and you are free to do the same, but I believe the killer wiped it clean."

"And then returned it to Halbach's store. Very cheeky, I would say, unless Halbach did it himself."

"That is certainly possible. Unfortunately, until we find the bullet that killed Mr. Krupp, we will not be able to make a ballistics match."

"Any idea where the bullet might be?"

"Perhaps. I suggest you have one of your men look around Mr. Krupp's brewery, paying particular attention to the cave."

"Do you think Krupp was murdered there?"

"Either there or at his house."

"Well, I guess we'll find out one way or the other. Do you have anything else for me, Mr. Holmes?"

Holmes related his conversations with Katherine Krupp and Peter Eisen. He also told the sheriff about Willy Eisen and "Mr. Bones."

"That's peculiar," Thorkelson said, "but even if the girl did find a skeleton in the tunnel, how does that tie in with anything happening here now?"

"I cannot be sure," Holmes admitted. "I hope to learn more from Willy in the next day or two. I also have information of more immediate interest concerning our murder victim."

After describing his harsh encounter with Josef Krupp the day before, Holmes said, "He made one especially revealing statement. He said he knew what had happened to his cousin and that, to use his exact words, 'justice would be served soon enough.' I took that to mean Mr. Krupp not only believed his cousin had been murdered but that he knew, or at least thought he knew, who did it."

"Well now, that would be a good motive for someone to murder him. Who was his suspect?"

"Wolfgang Eisen. Mr. Krupp referred to him as a snake and did not disguise his deep dislike of the man. But he offered no proof."

Holmes went on to tell Thorkelson about the German newspaper clippings and the old photographs Willy Eisen had found. He also narrated the tale of his violent confrontation the night before with Wolfgang in the Wohngebäude.

"I'd be happy to bring him up on assault charges," Thorkelson said.

"No, that would not be useful. But I would like to have a look at Wolfgang's little collection of memorabilia."

"Sounds like a good idea to me. When do you want to go over there?"

"Soon, but first I have something else to tell you." Holmes then shared his suspicions regarding the five men, Krupp among them, who had arrived in Eisendorf as part of the "third immigration" in 1892.

Thorkelson was intrigued. "I take it you believe one of the remaining four murdered Krupp."

"I think it very likely. But bear in mind I have no hard evidence against any of them, not even Wolfgang. Nor, for that matter, can I be absolutely certain one of them is indeed the Monster."

"Ah, here comes the coroner now," Thorkelson said, looking across the park at a black sedan that had just pulled up. "Do you want to talk to him?"

"Not right away. Let him examine the body first. In the meantime, I suggest we have a look at Wolfgang Eisen's hideaway."

• • •

The side door into the Wohngebäude was still unlocked when Holmes and the sheriff arrived. They climbed up to the second floor and walked down the dim hallway to Wolfgang Eisen's secret office. Holmes tried the door, expecting it would be locked, but instead it swung open with a turn of the knob.

"Curious," he said. "I should think Wolfgang would keep it locked at all times."

"Maybe he doesn't see the use of it now that you've found him out," Thorkelson said. "From what I hear, you're a very handy man with a lock pick."

The office appeared to be just as Holmes had seen it the night before, except for one crucial difference. The stack of old newspapers was gone.

"I see Wolfgang has cleaned up," Holmes said as he began rummaging through the old desk on which the newspapers had once been piled. "Let us hope he is not an entirely tidy fellow."

"I'm thinking we might need a search warrant for what you're doing," Thorkelson noted.

"You might need one, Sheriff, but I am merely a private citizen. Stop me if you see fit."

"I'm not even here," Thorkelson said, "so I couldn't stop you even if I wanted to."

In the bottom drawer of the desk, Holmes came across a repository of lewd magazines. He began paging through them.

Thorkelson looked on with amusement. "Enjoying yourself, Mr. Holmes?"

"I assure you, Sheriff, my interests are not prurient. I am merely . . . ah, what have we here?"

Holmes removed a sheet of paper that had served as a place marker in one of the magazines to indicate where a photograph of an especially voluptuous woman could be found. The paper contained a letterhead for the "Martin Treuer Getreidemuhle, Puchheim, Bavaria."

Thorkelson came over for a look. "Does this mean something to you, Mr. Holmes?"

"It means a great deal. Martin Treuer was one of the Monster's victims in Germany."

• • •

Holmes had gone to see Hilda Treuer two days after the murder of her husband and a male prostitute. She had already been questioned at length by the police.

"They were awful," she told Holmes. "They made it sound like Martin was a pervert. He was not. It is ridiculous to think he was interested in men in that way. And now they have ruined his reputation and my life."

Holmes believed her, for the simple reason that the murder of Martin Treuer did not fit the pattern of the Monster's crimes. Cornering young prostitutes and killing them in the thrall of some demented sexual fury was one thing. It was quite another to kill two men at once, one of them a powerfully built businessman in the prime of his life, as the thirty-year-old Treuer had been. And so Holmes had come to suspect Treuer's murder had nothing to do with sex.

Just two year earlier, in 1890, Holmes had investigated the bizarre case of the Red-Headed League, in which cunning criminals used a cover story to lure a pawnbroker out of his shop so they could rob a bank vault beneath it. The murders and mutilations of the prostitutes in Munich, Holmes thought, might be a similar, albeit far more terrible kind of ruse, designed to disguise the fact Treuer was the killer's real target.

With that idea in mind, Holmes decided to ask Mrs. Treuer, who not only was intelligent and pretty but also spoke excellent English, about her husband's business activities. If sex was not the motive behind Treuer's murder, Holmes reasoned, then it might well be money. What Holmes learned from the widow soon convinced him he was on the right track.

"Martin, as you know, owned a flour mill just outside Munich, and he was having some serious trouble there," she told Holmes. "He believed a great deal of money was missing and must have been stolen."

"How much money?"

"At least ten thousand marks."

"A very substantial sum indeed. Did your husband have a suspect in the theft?"

"Yes. He believed it was his accountant, a man named Paul Geist. Martin was having the books audited. Once that was done, he told me he intended to press charges against Mr. Geist with the police."

"And when did you have this conversation with your husband?"

"It was only about two weeks ago, as I remember."

"Did you ever talk to Mr. Geist about this matter?"

"No, I never even met him."

"Then I imagine you do not know where he lives."

"Actually, I might. Martin kept a book with the address and telephone numbers of all of his key employees. I could look if you wish."

"Please do."

Mrs. Treuer quickly returned with the book and began thumbing through it. "Yes, here it is," she said. "Mr. Geist lives on Herzogstrasse in Schwabing, near the English Gardens."

"How convenient," Holmes said, deciding he would pay a visit to the mysterious Mr. Geist as soon as possible.

9

——|● ● ●|——

Holmes and Thorkelson returned to the park to speak briefly with the coroner, Dr. Michael Speck, who was also a pathologist at the Mayo Clinic. After a cursory examination of the body, Speck agreed with Holmes's conclusion as to the manner and time of Krupp's death.

"Strange he was left naked," Speck remarked. "Why go to the trouble of taking off his clothes?"

"I think it was done for my benefit," Holmes said, then gave Speck a brief account of what had happened in Munich in 1892.

Speck let out a low whistle. "That's quite a story. And you think this fellow is now in Eisendorf?"

"I do," Holmes said.

"Whoever could have imagined such a thing? Well, I'm not sure how much Mr. Krupp's body will tell us, but I promise we'll do the most thorough autopsy possible."

"Excellent," said Holmes. "The sheriff will keep me posted as to your findings."

"That I will," Thorkelson said. "So what's next, Mr. Holmes? Do you want to have a look at Krupp's residence?"

"Later. I think I'd like to speak first with Maria Eisen." Holmes wanted to talk with her to see what she could tell him about the late Josef Krupp. He also hoped she might have some useful information about her brother-in-law, Wolfgang.

"We can do that," Thorkelson said, "but I must warn you we'll be in for quite a time of it."

"How so?"

Thorkelson rubbed his chin and said, "Maria Eisen is—how should I put it?—a very peculiar woman. I've had some dealings with her over the years, and I can tell you she's not exactly overflowing with the milk of human kindness. In any event, let's drive over there. It will be much quicker than walking."

Thorkelson led the way to his big sedan, which was parked in front of the People's Hall. As Holmes got into the front seat, he noticed that Dr. Speck, with the help of two men, was preparing to turn over Krupp's body. What he would find beneath it, as Holmes would soon learn, was deeply disturbing.

• • •

Perched part way up Table Rock, the Eisen mansion resembled a feudal castle lording over the town. Its crenellated front tower, tall hooded windows, and ponderous walls conveyed a sense of stony gloom. Attached to these sober Gothic aspirations was a wooden front porch pulsing with gaudy gingerbread ornament. It was a house that seemed to be at war with itself.

Thorkelson maneuvered his sedan up the mansion's steep, twisting driveway and parked in front of the porch, where Willy Eisen was rocking in a swing seat.

"Mr. Sherlock, Big Joey is dead," she said when Holmes came up to greet her.

"We know. Are you sad?"

"No. Big Joey was mean, just like Wolfie."

"Is your mother inside?" Thorkelson asked.

"Momma and Poppa are both here. Would you like to see a trick, Mr. Sherlock?"

"Perhaps later, Willy. Could you come in with us for a while? We want to talk to the whole family."

"No," she said. "You go."

"Now, see here, Miss Eisen—" the sheriff began, but Holmes cut him off.

"That is fine, Willy. We will talk later."

• • •

Peter Eisen answered the doorbell. "Well, you're not wasting any time, are you, Mr. Holmes? Come in. I suppose you're here to see Maria."

"It will be a pleasure to meet her," Holmes said. Thorkelson made no attempt to second the motion. Instead, he delivered a crooked grin.

The mansion's front parlor was a testament to the dark, stuffy opulence of the Victorian era. Holmes surveyed the scene with a certain grim appreciation. The room was furnished with dark mahogany chairs and tables, chocolate-brown drapes designed to resist the intrusion of light, red patterned wallpaper of a particularly hideous sort, and bric-a-brac everywhere, piles of it infesting shelves, étagères, and any other piece of furniture that could be commandeered. Holmes nearly sighed. He had grown up in just such a house in England, and it had made him a lifelong victim of clutter, as Watson had proclaimed, with considerable asperity, more than once.

The funereal room instantly came alive with the appearance of Maria Eisen, who swept in like a tidal wave, filling the room with her perfumed presence. The perfume, Holmes determined with a single sniff, was undoubtedly from Paris—Jicky, perhaps—and by no means inexpensive. She wore a flowing pink dress with puffed white sleeves and a lacy, low-cut bodice, as though she was preparing for a night at the ballroom. In her right hand was a lighted cigarette in a long silver holder.

Tall and full-figured, she was younger than Holmes had expected— late forties, perhaps—and quite striking. Not exactly a beautiful woman, Holmes decided, but a strong and interesting one. She had wide-set black eyes, short-cut black hair untouched by gray, and thin, rather cruel lips.

"You are here to discover what happened to Josef," she said in a smoke-singed contralto, "but you will have no answers in this house, I am afraid, for I do not know. He was murdered by some foul beast who prowls this ruin of a town, and I would leave if I could but I cannot. It is all quite awful! I only hope my dear Peter isn't next."

"How kind of you to say so, my love," her husband said with a mock bow.

She walked up to Holmes and said, "And now the greatest detective in the world is here to make things right. The immortal Sherlock Holmes himself! Ha! There are things that can never be made right and secrets that can never be known. This you will learn, you vain and foolish man, and then you will leave and wonder why you came here in the first place. As for my friend the fat sheriff, I gave up on him long ago. He sees nothing, he knows nothing. Now, would the two of you like some tea?"

"Well, Mrs. Eisen, greetings to you as well," said Thorkelson, who appeared to take no offense at her insults. "Tea would be nice."

"Get them some tea," she ordered, gesturing toward Peter. "And do try to be quick about it. The sooner they have their tea, the sooner we can be rid of them and enjoy all the wonders of our existence in this rotten, stinking hellhole. I will never know why my beloved Peter dragged me back here."

"Maybe he was just trying to torment you," Thorkelson said, getting into the spirit of the moment.

"Ha! He could do that in St. Paul as well as here. It's that dreadful mill that drew him back. 'Why, I've got grist in my blood,' he told me. Isn't that what you said, Peter?"

"No, but it makes for a good story, my sweet."

Holmes couldn't tell whether to be amused or appalled by Mrs. Eisen. But he now understood why Thorkelson had warned him about her. "I am struck by your mention of a 'foul beast' at loose in Eisendorf. Do you think this person has murdered others here as well? Perhaps even your brother, Bernhard?"

Her voice suddenly softened. "My darling Bern was a good and kind man, and such men are rare in this idiotic world to which we are all condemned. I am sure it was an accident. It must have been. Besides, you are the one who is supposed to know everything, Mr. Holmes. You are the masterful solver of riddles. What do I know? I am merely a poor woman, trying her best to get by, and it is not easy."

As she talked, the smoke from her cigarette drifted like ambrosia into Holmes's eager nostrils. How he missed his tobacco!

She noticed his longing. "You like to smoke, don't you, Mr. Holmes? I read that somewhere. The 'three-pipe problem' or some such nonsense. I can tell you've got the devil's itch in your throat. Yes, it's a terrible habit. But then is not life itself a bad habit? At least it is if you are living here amid dullards, fool, and criminals. So I smoke myself to death. Why not? Who cares? What does it matter?"

Holmes noticed that she grew short of breath after delivering her speech. A brief coughing fit followed.

"Your optimism is most inspiring," Holmes said. "But perhaps we can return to the matter at hand, although I must say, Mrs. Eisen, you do not seem prostrate with grief over Josef's death. I have been told the two of you were close."

She shrugged and said, "You will no doubt be told many things while you are here, Mr. Holmes, but there is little chance any of them will prove true. However, I will say I did not detest Josef. He was dull-witted, of course, but then how can one not be in a place such as this? But if you are expecting me to grieve his passing, you will be disappointed. There are things I do not like, Mr. Holmes, and what I do not like I do not allow to disturb my life. I do not like grief. It serves no purpose, for the dead are dead and the living are living, and that is all there is to it. I do not like music, which irritates my sinuses, so I do not listen to it. I do not like cheese, which gives me

88

indigestion, so I do not eat it. I do not like dogs, which are filthy beasts, so I do not have any. It is that simple. Now, why don't the two of you have a seat?"

"Yes, why don't we," Thorkelson said, giving Holmes a conspiratorial wink as they sat down on a long, immensely overstuffed sofa, into which they sank like a pair of merchant ships torpedoed on the high seas. Moments later, Peter returned with two cups of very potent black tea, then sat on a rocking chair across from his wife.

Struggling to keep from disappearing entirely into the depths of the sofa, Holmes asked, "When did you last see Josef, Mrs. Eisen?"

"Who can keep track of things such as that? Josef came here now and then to talk of one thing or another. I may have seen him last week. Or perhaps I didn't."

"Can you be more specific as to what you and Josef talked about? For example, did he seem worried in any way or mention a problem with someone in town?"

"I suppose if he had said something interesting, I would remember it. But he didn't, so I don't. How is your tea?"

"Strong," said Holmes, who found Mrs. Eisen's casual evasions to be quite interesting. He suspected she was more concerned about Josef's murder than she was letting on. "What about your brother-in-law, Wolfgang? Did Josef ever mention any particular problems with him?"

"Wolfgang, I dare say, is the very definition of a problem. Why my divine Peter tolerates his presence in our home I cannot fathom. I suppose it has to do with brotherly love or some such foolishness."

"Wolfgang was here for dinner last night, was he not?"

"He is here every night. He believes my only purpose in the world is to cook him dinner. So he honored us with his gracious presence, ate as always like a filthy, rooting pig, and then went back to that awful shack where he communes with the dirty creatures of the forest and no doubt spends his useless days whittling."

Holmes glanced at Peter Eisen, but he seemed unmoved by his wife's verbal assault on his brother. "Did Wolfgang say anything about Josef last night?"

"Oh, you may be sure, Mr. Holmes, that Wolfgang was a veritable fountain of scintillating conversation. Isn't that right, Peter dear?"

"My wife is being sarcastic," Peter said.

"No kidding," said Thorkelson.

Mrs. Eisen said, "Wolfgang is not up to the challenge of eating and talking at the same time. It would overtax his stunted intellect. Therefore, the answer to your question is that he had nothing to say about anything. Does that satisfy you?"

"No," said Holmes, "it does not. Did he talk, for instance, about the items he believed your daughter had stolen from him?"

Mrs. Eisen let out a long sigh, then fixed her chisel-sharp eyes on Holmes. "Why do you bring up such trivialities? My dear daughter has the mind of a four-year-old, which puts her on Wolfgang's level. I do not concern myself with their petty arguments. Isn't that right, Peter dearest?"

Eisen, who had sat through his wife's dramatic performance like a bored stagehand at a play he'd seen far too many times, finally spoke up. "Whatever you say, my darling. But I think Mr. Holmes wants to know about some old German newspapers and photographs Willy might have gotten her hands on. He thinks they could be clues."

"Clues to what?"

"Murder," Holmes said.

"Well, I know nothing of it, so why bother me with your impertinent questions? Ask Willy. Perhaps she will favor you with one of her many outlandish fairy tales."

"I am inclined to find your daughter more enlightening than you are, Mrs. Eisen, and considerably more honest as well," Holmes said. "Now, please tell me what time your brother-in-law left last night."

Mrs. Eisen gave Holmes a long, cold look. It was like being pelted with sleet. "You are becoming quiet tiresome, Mr. Holmes."

"The same might be said of you, madam."

"Ha! So now you are resorting to petty insults. Very well, I will answer your inane questions in the hope you will go away and leave me in peace. As for Wolfgang, he left last night not long after Peter did. What time was that, my dear?"

"I left just before seven. So Wolfgang must have left about then, too."

"Did he say where he was going?" Holmes asked.

"Really, why should you care?" Mrs. Eisen said. "How suspicious you are! It must be a common defect in a mind of your type."

"I think of it as a virtue. Now, please do me the favor of answering my question."

"Oh, very well, let me think. Yes, I recall he managed a few words to the effect that he was going to see Freddy."

Peter Eisen chimed in, "That could well be. Wolf likes to hang around the archives. He and Freddy are friends. But I don't know if he went over there or not."

"What did you do after Wolfgang left, Mrs. Eisen?"

"I went to bed early, for what else is there to do in Eisendorf but sleep and dream of better things? My lovely Peter returned about ten and made sufficient noise to wake me up. He is very dependable in that way. Then I went back to sleep. Now, I trust you will go away, Mr. Holmes. You are giving me neuralgia."

Sensing Holmes might soon become inclined to homicidal violence, Thorkelson stepped in with a question. "Was Josef particularly close to anyone here in town?"

It was Mrs. Eisen who answered. "You might ask my dear sister-in-law, Mrs. Krupp. They have been thick as thieves, or so I am led to understand. If a man is skulking about in the depths of the night, there is usually a woman involved, is there not? You would be surprised how many loose and suspicious females inhabit this wretched village. It is a veritable nest of vipers."

"And you believe Mrs. Krupp is among them?" Holmes asked.

"You may decide that for yourself," Mrs. Eisen said, waving her hand in a dismissive gesture as she rose from her chair. "I am feeling very weary. My spirit is much afflicted, and I need rest. Peter will show you out."

After lighting another cigarette, she walked out of the room.

"Well, it looks like our audience with the queen is over," Thorkelson said.

"I'm sorry my wife could not be of more help," Eisen said. "But Maria is Maria. Do you have a wife, Mr. Holmes?"

"No."

"Ah, then take my advice. Never acquire one."

• • •

Holmes hoped to find Willy on the porch, but she had disappeared once again.

"We could take a quick look around town," Thorkelson suggested.

"No, it would be a waste of time," Holmes said. "She has too many hiding places. Why don't we see if Wolfgang Eisen is home?"

"That's easy enough," Thorkelson said. "His place is just down the road."

Thorkelson edged his big sedan down the mansion's driveway, then headed out toward the mill on a gravel road. Past the mill, the road turned to dirt, and Eisendorf's forest—an untrammeled Eden of elm, basswood, red oak, and sugar maple—enveloped them. The rugged heights of Table Rock loomed to the west.

"Quite the forest, isn't it?" Thorkelson said. "Dark as night when you get back in there. A man could disappear in these woods and who knows if you'd ever be able to find him."

"Let us hope Wolfgang has not already done so," Holmes said.

Maria Eisen's description of Wolfgang's dwelling as a "shack" turned out to be accurate. Unmolested by maintenance, the ramshackle cottage offered a sagging front porch, warped shingle siding, and a weed-choked yard decorated with a miscellany of discarded items that included an impressive colony of empty whiskey bottles.

"Don't think Wolfgang is much for housekeeping," Thorkelson said once they had pulled up into the yard.

They quickly discovered that the shack's occupant was at home. Wolfgang Eisen stepped out on the porch, cradling his double-barreled shotgun.

"How are you today, Mr. Eisen?" Thorkelson said as he and Holmes got out of the car.

"I'm all right. What do you want?"

"Just a little talk, that's all. Could I ask you to put that shotgun down? Don't want to have any accidents."

Eisen grunted and set the shotgun on one of the porch chairs.

"Thank you. Could we talk inside?"

Eisen looked at the sheriff, then Holmes. "We can talk here. What's this about?"

Holmes said, "It's about the murder of Josef Krupp. Have you heard the news?"

"I've heard."

"I see. Who told you about Mr. Krupp's death?"

"Word travels," Eisen said. "You still haven't told me what you want."

"The truth would be handy," Thorkelson said.

"I don't know anything about what happened to Josef, if that is what you are after. You are wasting your time."

Holmes and the sheriff went at Eisen for the next fifteen minutes, peppering him with questions. The answers were invariably short. Among other things, Eisen told them he had indeed argued with Krupp over his work at the brewery. The cause? "Josef was too bossy," Eisen said, "so I quit." But he claimed there were "no hard feelings" as a result.

And where had he been at the time of Josef's murder? "Sleeping." After dinner with his brother, he'd paid Halbach a brief visit, just as his sister-in-law had said, and then gone straight home, to be by himself. Nothing had disturbed his slumbers.

Eisen became animated only when Holmes again brought up the matter of the old newspapers and photographs Willy had unearthed.

"I have told you before and I will tell you again the girl is an idiot. Why do you waste my time with this foolishness?"

"If it is such foolishness, Mr. Eisen, why did you remove all of the memorabilia from your secret office last night? Unfortunately, you overlooked something. You left behind a little souvenir from Martin Treuer's flour mill. How long did you work there?"

Eisen's eyes narrowed, and he glanced at his shotgun. "Who said you could go there? You have no right!"

Holmes slipped his hand into his coat pocket, feeling for his revolver. Then Thorkelson stepped forward. "Let us be calm here. Mr. Holmes is simply playing the devil's advocate. You are accused of nothing, Wolfgang. We just want to find out all we can about Josef's murder."

"Well, I know nothing, as I have told you. We are done, unless you wish to arrest me, in which case I will call a lawyer." He picked up his shotgun and went back into the house.

"I guess that's it for now," Thorkelson said. "I could have predicted how this would go. Wolfgang is a hardhead, and you'll never get much out of him."

"Perhaps. Which is why I should very much like to see the inside of his house."

Thorkelson gave Holmes a stern look. "I know what you're thinking, Mr. Holmes, and I would not try it if I were you. He'd shoot you in a second if he caught you burgling his place. Besides, I wouldn't be surprised if he has the house booby-trapped. He's just that kind of extremely suspicious man. As for me, I'd need a search warrant to get in there, but there's no probable cause I can see."

"So it would seem we are stymied," Holmes said.

"For the moment," Thorkelson said, "but things can always change. Now, would you like to take look around Mr. Krupp's house? No warrant needed there."

"Lead the way," said Holmes.

• • •

Josef Krupp's house was one of Eisendorf's standard red-brick foursquares, distinguished only by the purple paint covering its wooden trim.

"Mr. Krupp did not have a future as a home decorator," Holmes, whose eye for color was precise and discriminating, remarked to the sheriff when they arrived at the house. A uniformed deputy was stationed outside the door.

"Nichols, this is your lucky day," Thorkelson said to the deputy. "Say hello to Mr. Sherlock Holmes."

"An honor to meet you, sir," the deputy said. He was young and thin and looked nervous.

"Find anything in there?" Thorkelson asked.

"No, sir. Deputy Carter and me, we went through the place as best we could but couldn't find much. We looked real close for any signs of blood, just like you told us, but we didn't see even a drop of it."

"All right. Mr. Holmes and I will have a look for ourselves."

The house was surprising tidy. "The perils of prolonged bachelorhood when it comes to matters of housekeeping are well known," Holmes said. "Dr. Watson could testify to that. And yet Mr. Krupp, who was not married, seems to have been remarkably neat."

"He was a German," Thorkelson said. "That's just the way they are. Now, is there something in particular you're looking for here, besides blood?"

"Clothes and paper," Holmes said. "I do not think Mr. Krupp was naked when he was shot. If he was killed in this house, the clothes he was wearing could still be here. As for paper, I would be curious to see whether Mr. Krupp maintained files of any sort."

"What kinds of files?"

"I will know when I find them."

Their search yielded no clothing that looked to have been hurriedly discarded. And, like the deputies, they found no blood.

"It is safe to say Mr. Krupp was not murdered here," Holmes told the sheriff. "The brewery may be a better place to look."

I've got another deputy nosing around there now," Thorkelson said. "Maybe he'll find something."

The hunt for paper turned out to be more successful. In a small metal file in a study on the second floor, Holmes found a thick folder that contained police reports, newspaper clippings, autopsy findings, and other documents relating to the supposedly accidental death of Bernhard Krupp.

"It is as I thought," Holmes said after he had gone through the documents. "Mr. Krupp was investigating his cousin's death. However, it does not appear as though he found any incriminating evidence. Still, it makes me wonder about the argument he had with Wolfgang. Perhaps Mr. Krupp came to suspect Wolfgang knew something about Bernard's death, or was directly involved in it."

"Do you think Mr. Krupp was murdered because of his suspicions?"

"It is entirely possible," Holmes said. "All we lack is proof."

As they were leaving the house, Dr. Speck came up to greet them.

"I was hoping I would find you two," he said. "I discovered something very interesting under Mr. Krupp's body. I thought you'd want to see it right away."

The coroner handed Holmes a note, hand printed on a three-by-five-inch index card. It read, "Zu spät, zu spät."

Thorkelson took a look and said, "What does *zu spät* mean?"

"Too late," Holmes said. "These words were written by the Monster. He left the message because he wishes to show me how clever he is, just as he did in Munich."

• • •

The identical message had been delivered to Holmes at his apartment in Munich after the double murder of the young prostitute and Martin Treuer. It had come as a surprise, not because of its taunting content but because of its timing. Holmes received the message only hours after his presence in Munich had been revealed in the press. How, he wondered, had the Monster known where he was staying? It was a question Holmes had never been able to answer to his satisfaction.

A similar question nagged at him now. How had the Monster managed to learn, almost immediately, that Holmes was in Rochester and being treated for emphysema? Holmes wasn't sure, but he thought Dr. Henry Plummer might have the answer.

10

—|● ● ●|—

"I guess we've done all we can here today," Thorkelson said from behind the wheel of his sedan, which was parked near Holmes's cottage. Holmes, one foot resting on the running board, leaned in to talk with the sheriff. It was five o'clock, and Thorkelson looked eager to leave Eisendorf in his rearview mirror.

His deputies had already returned to Rochester after an unproductive day of canvassing. No one in town claimed to have seen or heard anything suspicious on the night of Josef Krupp's murder. Thorkelson's men had made one important discovery. Deep in the recesses of the lagering cave at Krupp's brewery, a deputy had found bloodstains, blood splatter, and a pile of clothes. Clearly, Josef Krupp had met his end there.

"Did you find anything else?" Holmes asked.

"If you mean old German newspaper or photographs, the answer is no. Maybe Willy found all there was."

"Or the Monster took whatever was left after murdering Mr. Krupp. What of the fatal bullet? Was it found in the cave?"

"No, and it doesn't make much sense. We know the slug went right through Mr. Krupp, but we couldn't find it anywhere in the cave."

Holmes said, "It is quite possible the Monster picked it up. There was ample time to do so. I imagine he's keeping it as a souvenir."

"Or maybe he just doesn't want us to do a ballistic comparison on that gun from Mr. Halbach's store."

"I doubt he cares," Holmes said. "In any event, we have made some progress today. We know where Mr. Krupp was killed, and we are fairly certain we have the weapon used to kill him. But there are still a great many questions to be answered."

"Such as why he was killed. Do you still believe it was because he'd figured out who might be responsible for his cousin's death?"

"It's as decent a theory as any at the moment, but as I said before, we have no proof. And yet, I am of a mind there must be some larger purpose behind the murder."

"What do you mean?"

"I mean that the Monster is the kind of man who plays a long game. He did so in Munich, committing a series of murders tied to strategic goal. He may be doing the same here."

"And what might his goal be?"

"Ah, that is a very good question, Sheriff. I will let you know when I have an equally good answer."

"Well, as you said, many questions remain. I'd like to know, for instance, how Mr. Krupp's body was transported to the park. Any ideas?"

"I do not see how it could have been done by one man unless he used a vehicle of some kind, most likely an automobile."

"That seems logical enough," Thorkelson agreed. "But the killer went to an awful lot of trouble to make his point. He had to drag the body out of the cave—the blood we found was a good two hundred feet from the entrance—and then lug it to the park and dump it there without being seen by a single soul. It was a risky business all the way around, and pretty damn bold, if you ask me."

"True enough, but you must remember the Monster thrives on his own audaciousness. He also has a great deal of experience when it comes to dumping bodies. It was all worth it for him, just to rub what he had done into my face. We are dealing with a strange, twisted man who is both perfectly rational and perfectly mad, and that is why he is so dangerous. By the way, when will the autopsy be performed on Mr. Krupp?"

"Tonight. I'll get Dr. Speck's report to you as soon as I can. But I don't expect any big surprises. Time of death was probably around midnight, just as you figured."

"Yes, and that is not a time conducive to ironclad alibis."

"You're right. The Eisen brothers were asleep at that hour, or so they told us, and there's nobody to contradict them. Same with your other suspects, Halbach and that Dreisser fellow. Sleeping like babies, or so they told my deputies. But there's nobody to back them up—Halbach lives alone, and Dreisser's mother was in Rochester—so it's just their word."

Thorkelson started his car. "Well, I guess you'll have plenty to occupy that big brain of yours tonight, Mr. Holmes, but I have to tell you I'm worried, so I'm going to suggest something. You probably won't like it, but here it is anyway. You should leave Eisendorf right now. Pack up and come back to Rochester. I can't protect you here, and whoever this Monster is, he has you in his sights. The fact is, you could be next."

"Yes," said Holmes, "which is why I must remain. Indeed, I would like you to make arrangements to have my suitcases sent down to me. They're being stored at the Zumbro Hotel. I am going to need more clothes."

Before the sheriff pulled away, Holmes handed him an envelope. "I had occasion late this afternoon to write a rather detailed letter to Dr. Plummer. Please deliver it to him as soon as possible. I would call the good doctor, but Mr. Halbach informs me all of the telephones here are party lines and listening in on the conversations of others is a regular pastime. I do not wish my inquiries of Dr. Plummer to become public knowledge. If he can answer my questions, we may learn something very useful."

Thorkelson nodded. "He'll get your letter tonight, and I'll have your luggage sent down. In the meantime, remember what I said before. You must be very careful."

• • •

Holmes lay uneasily in bed that night, his revolver close at hand. Questions assailed him in the darkness, and time danced in his head. Holmes had read of Einstein's new theories, and while cosmology as a whole held little interest for him, he was fascinated by the problem of time. He knew it was a trickster and that calendars were merely a convenient fiction. Time was fluid and unpredictable, like water sloshing in a pail, and it was rushing through his brain now, a flood of possibilities and connections. The events in Munich and Eisendorf were years and continents apart but also closely bound. Once Holmes could see them together, fully joined at last, he would have the truth.

A thunderstorm swept through just after dawn. Holmes woke up with a start, the lightning flashes like a sharp stimulant. Munich was still on his mind, but he knew he had to concentrate on the present. He had never seen the Monster's face in Munich, but he was sure he had seen it now, in Eisendorf.

The problem was that he didn't know whose face it was. The Monster's powerful physique should have made him stand out, even after a span of nearly thirty years. But big, broad-shouldered men were so common in Eisendorf it all but amounted to a communal trait. Peter and Wolfgang Eisen certainly fell into that category, as did Georg Dreisser and Frederick Halbach. The few other men of the right age he'd seen in town were built along the same lines.

It was all very frustrating. The Monster was right in front of Holmes, in a town of perhaps no more than twenty-five men, and yet he still remained elusive. As a young man, Holmes had read all of Edgar Allan Poe's detective stories. His favorite was "The Purloined Letter," which told of a much-coveted document hidden in plain view. So it was now with the Monster. Finding him would require, among other things, one of Holmes's most carefully cultivated skills—an ability to see the obvious.

• • •

Sunday morning was church time in most communities, but not in Eisendorf, where atheism supposedly flourished. Even so, when Holmes awoke and went outside to stretch his legs, he saw a pair of old Model T sedans, both fully occupied, heading out of town toward Stewartville. He suspected the drivers and their passengers were on their way to church, having rejected the "freethinking" principles of Dionisius Eisen. Holmes was not much of a churchgoer himself—he viewed ritual as a pernicious form of tedium—but he would not have minded an opportunity to leave town for a while. Eisendorf's lonely silence was wearing more on him with each passing day.

The morning was dreary, fog lingering over the wooded bluffs, and Holmes once again felt his spirits lagging. Until recent months, loneliness had never really affected him. In Sussex he had found a kind of solitary peace for more than a decade. But then his illness had struck, quite literally taking the air out of his sails, and the windswept downs, with their bleak immensity, began to seem cold and inhospitable.

The shadow haunting every life had also begun to make its presence felt more strongly than ever before. Holmes had never been certain what to make of the prospect of his inevitable demise. It was perfectly logical on one hand and perfectly ridiculous on the other, but for most of his life he had simply been too absorbed in his work to give it much thought. Now, however, it seemed to be in the very air, like a special form of gravity, pulling him toward the grave.

But what nagged at him even more fiercely was the hole that had been bored into his life since his consultation with Dr. Plummer. God, how he wanted a smoke. Without tobacco and the silken pleasure it brought, Holmes felt incomplete, as though some vital part of his being had been ripped away. Yet Plummer's warnings could hardly be ignored. Holmes's choice was to breathe or to smoke, and logic told him the answer should be obvious. But reason did not appreciate the taste, the aroma, the deep sense of ease that came with a pipeful of good shag.

A knock at the door of his cottage interrupted Holmes's tobacco dreams. He found Halbach standing outside. "May I come in, Mr. Holmes?"

"Of course. I was intending to call on you shortly as it was."

Halbach took a seat in the parlor. He said, "I imagine you wanted to ask me if I had a visit from Wolfgang the night of the murder."

"You have talked with the Eisens, I see."

"Just with Peter. He came by this morning and said you and the sheriff had quite an interview with Maria yesterday. I am happy to see you survived."

"She is indeed a redoubtable, if strange, woman," Holmes said.

"Perhaps even stranger than you think," Halbach said. "But it doesn't matter, does it? Now, I am here to tell you Wolfgang did indeed stop by my house Friday night."

"What time was that?"

"Half past seven or thereabouts. He didn't stay for long."

"Was there some particular reason he wished to see you?"

"A very particular reason, Mr. Holmes. I intended to mention it to you yesterday, but with all the excitement, I never had the chance. Here is what I can tell you. Wolfgang came by my house to show me something he had found. Would you like to see it?"

"By all means."

Halbach removed a photograph from his coat pocket and gave it to Holmes. It was another tintype, but smaller than the one Holmes had received from Willy Eisen. The picture showed a cab driver, in a top hat and cowled coat, buggy whip in hand. Several other cabs were visible to the rear, along a broad street lined with ornate stone buildings of the kind Holmes had often seen in Munich. The driver's face looked familiar. Holmes studied it for a moment and soon realized he was looking at a young Georg Dreisser, perhaps about age thirty.

Just two day earlier, Dreisser had told Holmes he'd never been a cab driver in Germany. Now, it was obvious he had lied.

"This is most interesting," Holmes said. "Did Mr. Eisen say where he obtained this photograph?"

"He did not. Naturally, I was curious about it, so I pressed him a bit. But he was a sphinx. He refused to say anything about the source of the photograph. I must say, Mr. Holmes, it was a very peculiar conversation. It was as though Wolfgang was trying to tantalize me."

"Why did he bring it to you?"

Halbach, suddenly looking pensive, folded his hands, let out a small sigh, and said, "Well, I suppose you could say I am Wolfgang's only real friend in town. He does not get on well with his family, especially his sister-in-law. But despite his rough appearance and manner, he is Eisendorf's best amateur historian. He spends more time at the archives than anyone else in town, except for me, of course."

"Did he say what he expected you to do with the photograph?"

"As a matter of fact, he did. He said I must show it to you. He told me you had been 'badgering' him—that was his word—about certain events in Germany long ago. He said you apparently thought he had been a cab driver there at one time. He said he hadn't but Georg had. The photograph is proof. That is why he wanted you to see it."

"Why didn't he show it to me himself?"

"You will have to put that question to him. All I can tell you is that Wolfgang is a bit odd, as you have noticed."

"Does Mr. Dreisser know about the photograph?"

"Yes, I showed it to him last night, and he was very surprised. He said he had donated the photograph, along with other family memorabilia, to our archives just a few months ago. He had no idea how it had come into Wolfgang's possession."

"Did he in fact make such a donation?"

"Yes, Georg brought in several boxes of things, but I have not yet had a chance to sort and catalog them. The photograph may well have been in one of the boxes, but I can't say I ever saw it."

"Is it possible Wolfgang took the photograph from the archives?"

"I would not like to think so, Mr. Holmes, but I suppose he could have slipped out with it. I can't imagine why. Of course there is another possibility."

"That Mr. Dreisser is lying for some reason?"

"The thought has crossed my mind," Halbach admitted. "What do you think, Mr. Holmes?"

Holmes wasn't immediately sure what to think. He said, "As you have suggested, Mr. Halbach, it all depends on where and how Wolfgang obtained the photograph. It could be an attempt on his part to shift attention from himself and implicate Mr. Dreisser in wrongdoing."

Halbach scratched his head." I don't understand. How could an old picture of Georg sitting in a cab implicate him in something?"

Was Halbach genuinely confused, or was he simply trying to extract more information from Holmes about his investigation? The archivist's bland, distant eyes gave no clue. Holmes decided the time had come to talk about something else.

"For now, I have told you all I can about the matter," he said. "But you can answer more questions. You mentioned Wolfgang's interest in history. Has his research ever led him to old newspapers from Munich? I am thinking in particular of editions dating to 1892."

"That is an odd question, Mr. Holmes, but the answer is no. We have no such newspapers in the archives."

"I see. What about other photographs or documents relating to the Treuer Mill in Puchheim, Germany? Do the archives contain anything like that?"

"No. I have never heard of the Treuer Mill."

"Are you aware of the office of sorts Wolfgang maintains, or perhaps I should say, used to maintain in the Wohngebäude?"

"That is news to me, Mr. Holmes. I've seen him going into the building a few times, but I didn't make much of it. Wolfgang doesn't like being interrogated, so I never asked what he was doing there."

"Your discretion is most commendable, Mr. Halbach. Ask no questions and you shall stay happily in the dark, is that it?"

"It is safer there sometimes, Mr. Holmes. Don't you agree?"

"Perhaps for the moment, but in the long run it is always more dangerous. Now, since you have come to me with this photograph, it would a good time to tell me more about Georg Dreisser. Is he well respected here in Eisendorf?"

Halbach rubbed at his chin and said, "It is not my place to say. I prefer to speak well of people, not ill."

"Very noble on your part, Mr. Halbach, but if you adhere to that principle, you shall endure a lifetime of uninteresting conversation."

A hint of a smile creased Halbach's lips. "Well put, Mr. Holmes. All right, I will tell you Georg Dreisser is not well liked in town. It goes back to the war. He was still living in Rochester then, but he stayed here almost every weekend with his mother. As you may be aware, the entire town came under great suspicion during the war. Beer was German, and Germans were Huns, and Huns were sinking American ships and killing American boys, and well, you get the idea. We were just those nice quiet folks down in Eisendorf for all those years, and then we suddenly became enemies of the nation, never mind that some of our farm boys were already serving overseas with Pershing. In any case civic leaders in the county demanded we all sign loyalty oaths and otherwise declare our patriotism."

"There was even a mob that ransacked the town in 1918, was there not?"

"Yes. The newspapers called it a 'patriotic gathering,' if you can imagine that. It was a dark day in the history of Eisendorf, and it didn't have to happen. You see, most of us were willing to sign the oath. But Georg had other ideas, and he started talking to the Rochester newspapers. He said America had no business fighting in Europe against Germany or any other nation. He also dismissed the oath as 'stupid nonsense,' to use his words."

"I imagine that did not endear him to many people."

"No, and it did great damage to all of us here. Before long there were headlines suggesting the whole town was disloyal. The governor even cited of our supposed lack of patriotism in a speech at the state capitol. Not long after that, the mob arrived. I thought the whole town might burn, but the sheriff stepped in just in time. Naturally, when the dust settled, people here were very upset with Georg for bringing on so much trouble."

"And as a result, I take it, he became something of a pariah."

"Yes, especially after Hans Eisen and Bernard Krupp, among others, spoke out very forcefully again him. It was a very bitter and divisive time in our little town."

"And you think Mr. Dreisser carries a grudge because of what happened?"

"Oh, I know he does. I do not wish to make accusations, Mr. Holmes, but I believe Georg is the sort of man who might readily resort to violence if he grew angry enough."

"Are you suggesting he was behind the deaths of Hans Eisen, Bernard Krupp, and now Josef Krupp?"

"No, no, dear no, Mr. Holmes. I am merely offering some information you may find useful. I am in no position to accuse Georg Dreisser of anything. Believe me when I say I have nothing personal against him."

Holmes was amused by Halbach's protestations. The archivist had a sly way of impugning other people even as he proclaimed himself free of any malign intent.

"Let us return for a moment to Wolfgang's visit Friday night. When he left, did he say where he was going?"

"No, but I did see him walking straight south, instead of cutting through the park like he usually does when he's going home."

"So he was walking toward the brewery?"

"That's what it looked like," Halbach said.

"Very well," said Holmes. "If you do not mind, I shall keep the photograph of Mr. Dreisser."

"Do what is necessary, Mr. Holmes. Please trust me when I say my only concern at this point is that you find the killer who is ravaging our little village."

"I intend to," said Holmes.

• • •

Early in the evening, Thorkelson stopped by the cottage to give Holmes an update. He'd brought along Holmes's two suitcases, and he set them on the floor before depositing his big, round body on the parlor's well-aged sofa.

"I have bad news," he began. "The press is nosing about. The Rochester papers are interested in the murder, as you would expect, and others are sure to follow. I'll try to keep the press boys at bay as long as I can, but they'll be here pretty soon. So you might want to lay low, if you can."

"That was good of you to deflect them," Holmes said. "Reporters are a troublesome lot, although I have found they can be quite useful on occasion. What else can you tell me?"

"Well, to begin with, I delivered your letter to Dr. Plummer. He promised to get back to you as soon as possible."

"Excellent. I am guessing you also have some news regarding Josef Krupp's autopsy."

"I do, Mr. Holmes, but it's not exactly a revelation."

"I'm listening."

"All right, here's the gist. He died of a bullet through the heart, which is hardly news. Looks to be a large caliber round, maybe a .44, and it could easily have been from that gun at Halbach's store. But since we don't have the slug, there's no way to be one hundred percent sure. That's about it. I'm hoping you'll have something better to report."

"Perhaps I do. As it so happens, I have come across yet another old photograph that may bear upon the case." Holmes then showed Thorkelson the photograph of Georg Dreisser and described how he had obtained it. He also noted that Dreisser had denied ever working as a cab driver.

The sheriff listened intently, then said, "That's quite a tale, but what are we to make of it? Is Mr. Dreisser now our chief suspect because he lied about being a cab driver? Or do you believe it's all a setup of some kind on Wolfgang's part?"

"There is no way to be certain," Holmes admitted. "We will need to talk to Wolfgang again, and also Mr. Dreisser. But I'd prefer to wait awhile before we do so. Let us see how the situation develops."

"OK, but I would like to know why Halbach didn't tell us about the photograph yesterday?"

"He claims he did not have the chance to do so, but who really knows? Mr. Halbach can be quite devious. It seems to be a trait in Eisendorf. The truth, I am beginning to think, is a fugitive that fled the town long ago."

"Shall I put out a warrant?" Thorkelson asked with a grin. "Maybe I can locate the fellow. What does he look like?"

"Alas, no two people in the history of the world have agreed on that point," Holmes replied with a smile of his own.

As Thorkelson was preparing to leave, Holmes put one more question to him.

"Have you ever been inside the tunnel that brings water to the Eisen Mill?"

"Funny you should ask, Mr. Holmes. I think about that tunnel every time I come here. I was in it twice as a kid, when I was ten years old or so. I grew up in Stewartville, and I had a buddy there named Jake Bailey who knew a kid in Eisendorf. Can't remember his name. We're talking way back now, around 1880, not long after the tunnel was bored. There were families in Eisendorf then with young kids. All gone now, of course. Anyway, the three of us snuck into the tunnel a couple of times just because, well, we were ten years old and it seemed like a great adventure."

"I imagine it was," Holmes said. "How did you get in?"

"We used the far entrance, on the other side of side of Table Rock, by the old mill dam. The Eisens had an iron gate across the entrance there to try to keep people out, but we managed to squeeze around it."

"And that entrance is still there today?"

"Far as I know. The dam washed away some years ago, but that really didn't affect the tunnel other than to leave it high and dry."

"Is the tunnel entrance still gated?"

"No, I think the gate is gone. But the Eisens may have boarded up the entrance. I'm sure kids still try to sneak in there now and then." The sheriff gave Holmes a knowing look and said, "Am I right in thinking you're planning a little expedition of some kind to look for Mr. Bones?"

"Perhaps, but since anything of the sort would involve trespassing, I naturally can't speak of the matter to law enforcement."

"Naturally. Fact is, I don't care to know a thing about any plans you may have."

"Sheriff, you are a man of great discretion and judgment. I salute you. Now, tell me this: What did you and your friends find inside the tunnel?"

"Nothing, really. There's a channel in the floor where the water ran, and we followed it all the way through the tunnel to the mill itself. Then we went back out the same way we came in."

"Are there any chambers off the main tunnel?"

Thorkelson closed his eyes to think. Finally he said, "As a matter of fact, there was a small side chamber near the middle of the tunnel. It was mostly filled with loose rock. I imagine it's still there."

"Yes," said Holmes, "I imagine it is."

11

———•◦•———

A
s had become his custom, Holmes ate supper with Halbach. The talk turned at once to Josef Krupp's murder and the attention it was beginning to attract in the press.

"It would appear that Eisendorf is about to gain some notoriety," Holmes said, "albeit not of the flattering kind."

Halbach took a deep breath and exhaled with a sigh. "Oh dear, that is not a good thing. The newspapers can never be trusted to tell the truth. You know, Mr. Holmes, Dionisius Eisen foresaw just such a problem when he established the archives. He wished to ensure the story of the town would be told in the proper way and not subject to the sensationalism of the popular press."

"How prescient of him. And yet I wonder whether there might not be another explanation, which is that he simply wanted to control the story for himself. In my experience, Mr. Halbach, the official version of events is often more instructive for what it leaves out than for what it includes. I imagine, for example, that in your role as the town's archivist there are many stories you have chosen not to tell."

Halbach smiled in his familiar, irritating way. It was the self-satisfied smile of a man who believes he alone speaks the truth. "Not all stories deserve to be told, Mr. Holmes. Be that as it may, there will certainly be a story of interest for you tomorrow. Services for Josef Krupp will be held at four o'clock in the People's Hall. Most of the town should be there."

"Then I shall attend as well," Holmes said. "I should like to meet more of the good citizens of Eisendorf. Thus far I have far seen mostly shadows behind curtains."

Halbach's dinner table, as always, was well stocked with beer, and the archivist grew more loquacious as the alcohol flowed. Eventually, the conversation drifted toward the topic of Eisendorf's cooperative form of governance.

"How did such a novel arrangement come about?" Holmes asked.

"It's quite a story. The official name is the Eisendorf Cooperative

Community. Dionisius established it as part of the Plan of the Founders, and it's the only one of its kind in Minnesota. Everything here is controlled by the cooperative. Between the town and the surrounding farms and forests, as I think I told you earlier, it comes to about five thousand acres in all."

"Am I correct in assuming that because of the cooperative, there is no individually owned property in Eisendorf?"

Halbach shook his head vigorously. He was growing tipsy, and his normal reserve had eroded. "No, sir, you would be wrong. Very wrong. The fact is, four properties are specifically exempted from the cooperative. They are the mill, the brewery, and of course the two mansions."

"You mean the houses belonging to the Eisen and Krupp families?"

The archivist nodded, then hoisted his stein of beer in a mock salute. "To the almighty Eisens and Krupps! They run this town and always have, so they can make their own rules."

"So the town's two leading families decided cooperation was good for everyone except themselves, is that it?"

"You have hit the nail square on the head, Mr. Holmes, and I hear it penetrating the soft wood that passes for intellect in Eisendorf. Whup! Whup! Ah, what a fine, mighty noise it is. Yes, sir, you have struck the truth." The archivist leaned over toward Holmes and added in a conspiratorial whisper, "Oh, and don't think there isn't some resentment about such a cozy arrangement here in town."

"And what about you, Mr. Halbach? Do you resent the special treatment afforded to the Eisens and Krupps? I assume, for example, that unlike them, you don't own your house."

"I am not a resentful man, Mr. Holmes. But you are right. I do not own this fine domicile. I simply inhabit it with the cooperative's permission, as it were. All hail the Eisendorf Cooperative! When I die, it will be theirs. Of course, that assumes the cooperative will outlive me."

"Is there a reason to think it will not?"

"A very good reason," said Halbach, who had begun to slur his words. "Oh yes, there is a reason so good it is downright juicy. But don't you see, I can't tell you. No, I cannot utter a word about it." The archivist put one finger to his lips. "Shhhh. It's a secret. But what does it matter? All will be ruin here soon enough, and Eisendorf will be no more. We are all ghosts here, Mr. Holmes, living lost lives, but we don't know it yet."

"Well, then, let us drink to the ghosts of Eisendorf!" Holmes exclaimed. "I am enjoying our little talk so much that I think we should have another stein of beer."

"An excellent idea. Mrs. Dreisser, more beer!" Halbach commanded. "More beer for the men of the house!"

After the elderly cook had delivered two more quarts of Krupp's Cave-Aged Lager, Halbach's tongue continued to loosen, and Holmes was eventually able to tease out a bit more about the "secret."

"Mark my words," Halbach said, "there will soon be a day of reckoning in Eisendorf. It will be the end of Dionisius Eisen's dream."

What followed was a rather garbled account of events going back half a century. The gist of it, arrived at only after several lengthy detours, was that Dionisius Eisen and Gottfried Krupp in 1870 had made a key decision about the future of Eisendorf. Holmes recalled what Georg Dreisser had told him about a secret change made to the cooperative agreement in 1870. It seemed likely Halbach was referring to the same thing.

"What exactly will this 'day of reckoning' entail?" Holmes asked.

"Ah, a very good question," Halbach said. "Let us just say Dionisius and Gottfried, in their infinite wisdom, decided that after a span of fifty years, there would be an opportunity to reconsider the cooperative. Now, do the math, Mr. Holmes, do the math! Eighteen seventy to nineteen twenty. How long a time is that?"

Holmes wanted to keep Halbach talking, so he gave the appearance of performing a complicated mental calculation before arriving at the answer. "Why, Mr. Halbach, I believe that is fifty years."

"Exactly! Exactly! So now you see what I am talking about."

Holmes in fact was not at all sure what Halbach meant, other than that some unspecified change to the cooperative agreement might be in the works. Yet even after a half-dozen steins of beer and much muttering in German, the archivist remained tight-lipped, refusing to provide additional details. "I do not spill the beans," Halbach said, his words sliding into a soft slur, "but thersh to be a great shock. Yesh indeed."

"How so?" Holmes asked.

It was too late. Halbach's head slumped to the table, and he fell fast asleep.

• • •

When Mrs. Dreisser came in to tend to her drunken employer, Holmes stood up and said, "I shall wait a bit in the parlor to make sure Mr. Halbach has suffered no ill effects from his unfortunate overindulgence."

The old woman responded with a suspicious stare. Holmes ignored her doubting eyes and went into the parlor, where he had seen Halbach's telephone atop an end table. A man as organized as the archivist, Holmes assumed, would keep a directory of local numbers on hand. Holmes soon located it in the table's top drawer. He found Bernhard Krupp's number and placed a call.

"Ah, Mrs. Krupp," he said when her heard her voice, "this is Sherlock Holmes. I have been terribly remiss in not getting back to you. I am wondering if I could stop by this evening for a talk."

There was a pause before Mrs. Krupp said, "Yes, I do not see why not. I have a friend over right now, but I could see you around nine. Would that be too late?"

"Not at all."

"Good. Are you still staying at that cottage behind Mr. Halbach's house?"

"Yes."

"Then I'll pick you up there just before nine."

"I would be happy to walk up to your home."

"No, I will come and get you. I look forward to talking with you."

• • •

Back at the cottage, Holmes lay down on the creaky old bed that had yielded him few nights of restful sleep, rested his hands behind his head, and began to think again about Munich.

There, after his interview with Hilda Treuer, he had made inquiries with the police regarding Paul Geist, the accountant at Martin Treuer's mill suspected of embezzlement. Although the Munich police were, like many Germans, fanatical record keepers, they could tell Holmes nothing about Geist, who had no criminal record. Even so, Holmes decided it would be worth his time to pay a visit to the accountant at his apartment near the English Gardens.

It was a warm, cloudy evening, and Holmes stopped for coffee at a small café, where he bought the latest edition of the *Münchner Neueste Nachrichten*. What he saw when he opened the paper came as a shock. On the front page was a story announcing "the renowned English detective Sherlock

Holmes has now joined forces with the Munich police to find the Monster responsible for the horrible series of murders in the English Gardens." Citing "very reliable sources in the police department," the newspaper went on to report "Mr. Holmes has vowed to find the killer who has terrorized the city if it is the last thing he ever does."

The rest of the story was a farrago of fact and fiction leavened with plenty of wild speculation, but it hardly mattered. Holmes had suddenly become a marked man, and it would not take long for Professor Moriarty's agents to be at his heels. He would have to escape Munich in short order. But before he left, he still wanted to talk with Geist. An interview with the accountant, Holmes believed, might be his last, best chance to identify the Monster.

Holmes went back to his rented apartment to begin laying plans to leave Munich. Norway, he thought, might be a good place to hide out for a time. Once he had sent his bags to the train station and made other necessary arrangements, he walked over to Geist's apartment, located in a small building with just two units. Holmes rang the doorbell but received no answer.

There was a little café across the street with sidewalk tables. Holmes sat down, ordered coffee, and waited. It was already almost ten o'clock. He watched the apartment for several hours in hopes he would spot a stocky young man fitting Geist's description. But there was no sign of life at the apartment.

Then, just before midnight, a cab—its license number obscured—came racing up Herzogstrasse and stopped in front of Geist's apartment. What happened next was utterly unexpected. The cab driver stepped down from his seat, secured his horse, and quickly walked off down the street. Moments later, a man wearing a black cape and hat emerged from the apartment. He untethered the horse and climbed up into the seat of the cab.

It was too dark for Holmes to make out the man's face, which in any event was obscured by a scarf pulled up over his chin. But the man was well built, with broad shoulders and a barrel chest. Holmes could tell by the way he walked that he was young.

Could it be Paul Geist? Holmes thought so. But why had the accountant suddenly become a cab driver? Perhaps, Holmes thought, because that is how he did his murderous work. A cab driver in the English Gardens after dark would have attracted little notice. It would have been the easiest way to dispose of the bodies of his victims.

The man in the cape flicked the reins and slowly began moving down

Herzogstrasse toward the gardens, just a few blocks away. Another cab appeared, coming in the opposite direction, and Holmes hailed it. "Turn around," he ordered the driver, "and follow the cab that just went by. But don't get too close."

Five minutes later, they entered the English Gardens, realm of the Monster.

• • •

At precisely nine o'clock, by Holmes's watch, a long, red touring car, its top down, pulled up in front of the cottage. Mrs. Krupp, wearing a sporty black hat and a pink scarf, was at the wheel. Holmes came out to greet her.

"Hop in," she said. "It's much easier to drive up to my house than to walk."

The engine of her automobile—a 1919 Packard, she told Holmes proudly—produced a pleasing, throaty roar as she sped up the hill toward her mansion. Around them, the dense forest that ringed Eisendorf like a heavy fur wrap was a pitch-black mystery.

"Do you drive, Mr. Holmes?" she asked. "I find it quite exhilarating."

"No, I have never felt the need," Holmes said. In truth, he didn't care for the idea at all. Driving required attention to the road, and Holmes much preferred the comfort of a railroad carriage, where he was free to think without the constant worry of crashing into something. Dr. Watson, on the other hand, had embraced the automobile with great enthusiasm and would natter on about horsepower, engine displacement, and other tiresome topics if given half a chance.

"Well, here we are," Mrs. Krupp said as they pulled up in front of the mansion. "Castle Krupp, or so it used to be called."

Two bright yard lights illuminated the home, a cream-colored confection of towers, tourelles, gables, and round-arched windows that had the look of a jolly old Bavarian castle. The Eisen mansion on the other side of town, Holmes thought, was sepulchral by comparison.

"I know," Mrs. Krupp said, anticipating Holmes's reaction. "It's all rather crazy, isn't it? Bern's father, Gottfried, loved the Hohenschwangau Castle in Bavaria, and he tried to build his own small version of it here. I'm not sure he was all that successful, but I've grown fond of it."

Mrs. Krupp ushered Holmes through the front door. A German shepherd came bounding up to greet them.

"Oh, how are you, my dear one," Mrs. Krupp said, bending down to rub the big dog's chest. "This is Heinrich. My husband loved him very much, as do I."

"He is a beautiful specimen," Holmes said, letting the dog nuzzle his hand. " I recall reading he was with your husband when he died."

"Yes, and if only he could speak, we might know the truth at last. But come, have a seat, Mr. Holmes. I will make us some tea."

Holmes followed Mrs. Krupp down a barrel-vaulted hall into a surprisingly cheery living room filled with plants. A massive stone fireplace dominated one wall. Holmes noticed a photograph of a striking young couple, posed in front of a studio background.

Mrs. Krupp caught Holmes's eye. "My husband and I just after our wedding," she said. "We honeymooned at Niagara Falls."

"You made a lovely couple," Holmes said. "How long were you married?"

"Thirty-six years. Bern, as everyone called my husband, was a wonderful man. We were very happy together. I still find it hard to believe he's gone. His absence has become the biggest presence in my life. But I have to go on living. What other choice is there?"

"And do you have children?"

Holmes saw at once by Mrs. Krupp's expression that he had touched a wound. "No, we were unable to," she said. "It is my greatest regret. Now, let me get that tea for you."

When Mrs. Krupp returned with the tea, Holmes said, "As you have no doubt surmised, I am investigating Josef Krupp's death. I talked yesterday with your sister-in-law, and she said you and he were quite close."

Anger flashed in Mrs. Krupp's eyes. "Did Maria really say that? She is such a liar. I do not doubt she even suggested we were sleeping together. She is a venomous woman, Mr. Holmes, full of anger and hate. There is not an ounce of love in her heart."

"Peter Eisen must have thought differently when he married her," Holmes observed.

"Perhaps, but he's learned his lesson by now. If I were he, I would have left her long ago. I just feel bad for little Willy. I think of her as the town angel. It is sad she was brought into this world by such a cruel mother."

"You are right about Willy," Holmes said. "However, I have found she is an angel who is very much of this world. Indeed, she seems in her own strange way to know more about this town than anyone else."

Mrs. Krupp smiled. "You have been talking to her, I see. Has she told you any of her 'secrets'?"

"She has. There is one in particular that interests me. Did Willy ever tell you about certain items she had discovered in the brewery cave?"

"No. What did she find?"

Holmes told Mrs. Krupp about the German newspaper articles and the photographs.

"How interesting. I wonder if they were things Josef had hidden away."

"Why do you say that?"

Mrs. Krupp fixed her blue eyes on Holmes. "Josef wasn't a particularly nice man, and I didn't care much for him. But he was very smart and also very suspicious about Bern's death. He believed, as do I, that my husband did not die accidentally. I am certain he was murdered."

"I, too, am inclined to think your husband met with foul play," Holmes said. "What makes you so convinced he was murdered?"

Her answer came without hesitation. "I know Bern was murdered because it is the only way his death makes sense. You see, Bern loved the woods here and hiked through them all the time, but he wasn't a hunter. In fact, in all the years we were married, I never once saw him take his shotgun along into the forest. He was interested in plants, Mr. Holmes, not game. Do you know he discovered a dwarf trout lily—a beautiful, delicate little thing—that the botanists up at the university think may be unique in all the world to the Eisendorf forest? Imagine that! Bern called the forest his own little Garden of Eden, and he fought long and hard to make sure it would never be heavily logged, as some in the village have long wanted to do."

Something Holmes had read days earlier in one of the Rochester newspapers came to mind. "Your husband's body, as I recall, was discovered by a timber cruiser. Usually such men are sent out by lumber companies in advance of logging operations. Are there in fact plans to cut down the forest?"

"Not that I am aware of. But I wondered the same thing. I don't know why a timber cruiser would have been out there."

"We will account it as yet another small mystery for the moment," Holmes said. "I have a few more questions about your husband's tragic death. It was his own gun, was it not, that was found with his body?"

"Yes. It was an old family shotgun he'd had for years. But as I said, I'd never seen him use it. Unfortunately, I was visiting friends in Rochester on the day he died, and so I wasn't here when he left the house."

"Can you think of any reason why he might have taken the gun with him? Is it possible he was planning to meet someone, perhaps a person he had reason to fear?"

"If that was the case, he did not tell me about it. Now, Mr. Holmes, if you do not mind, there is something I would like to show you."

She left the room and returned moments later with a single sheet of yellow foolscap, which she handed to Holmes. He noted creases where the paper had been folded.

"I found this just this morning, quite by accident," Mrs. Krupp said. "It was folded up in the pocket of one of Bern's old suits I was going to give away. The handwriting is my husband's. I would recognize it anywhere. As you can see, it's dated July twentieth of this year, and the name Walter Schmidt is underlined at the top. He is a lawyer in Rochester."

"Yes, I have heard the name. There is a reference in the town annals to your husband's visit with him in July. Two days later your husband died. Do you think the events are somehow related?"

"I think it entirely possible."

"Was Mr. Schmidt your family's personal attorney?"

"No, but Bern mentioned his name a few times. It is my understanding he is the lawyer for the Eisendorf Cooperative Community."

Holmes scanned the document. Krupp's notes, arranged in bullet fashion beneath Schmidt's name, read as follows:

—dissolution 1-1-21
—vote?
—purchase shares
—forest?
—lawsuits likely

Holmes said, "Do you know what these notes refer to?"

"I wish I did. Bern was a dear man but also very secretive. He was especially reticent about business matters, which he did not like to discuss with me. I believe he thought that as a woman, I could never understand such things. Still, a wife always knows more about her husband than he knows about her, and I was aware something had come to trouble him deeply, and that it concerned the affairs of the cooperative."

"I presume you mean possible changes to the cooperative structure," Holmes said, thinking back to his recent conversation with Halbach.

"Yes."

"But your husband never revealed exactly why he was so troubled?"

"No, but I think he had talked about his concerns with Mr. Halbach and probably with the Eisens, too."

Holmes looked again at Bernhard Krupp's mysterious notes. "May I keep this document for the time being?"

"Certainly. You must believe it is important."

"I do," said Holmes, "and I will be very interested to see what Mr. Schmidt has to say about it. Now, may I ask if there is anyone in town you suspect of murdering your husband? A person, for example, who might stand to gain by his death?"

"That is the trouble. I don't really know. But I hardly think it a coincidence Bern was killed just two days after visiting Mr. Schmidt to talk about the cooperative. What do you think, Mr. Holmes?"

"I think coincidences do indeed occur," Holmes said, gazing into Katherine Krupp's eyes, "but not very often."

• • •

Later, after Holmes had asked all the questions he thought it necessary to ask, he lingered for a time in Mrs. Krupp's living room. She brought out a decanter of peppermint schnapps, and Holmes found both the liqueur and the company most pleasing.

"You will forgive me for saying so," he said, "but I wonder why you stay here, Mrs. Krupp. Surely, Eisendorf must be terribly lonely for a widow such as yourself."

"It is," she said, "but Bern and I had many friends in Rochester, and I still see them quite often. Still, you are right to wonder why I stay. I often wonder myself. Maybe staying put is what we must do as we get old and the world seems to grow ever stranger to us."

"But you are still a young woman," Holmes protested.

"I will be fifty-nine next month, and that is not young. I know, a woman is never supposed to reveal her age, but why lie about who and what you are? Besides, I don't mind being the age I am. I have learned there is such a thing as wisdom, and it offers certain deep pleasures youth cannot match. What of you, Mr. Holmes? I thought I read somewhere that you are retired. Or should I say, were retired?"

"Yes, I did retire. The world began to wear on me, and I decided some years ago to spend my days more quietly."

"But didn't you miss being a detective? What an amazing life it must have been!"

"I did not give it up entirely, Mrs. Krupp. Of late, during the Great War, I performed certain delicate assignments for His Majesty's government. And now I am here in Eisendorf, chasing my own history, as it were."

"Yes," she said softly, "now you are here. Would you care for another drink? I could talk with you all night."

12

———|● ● ●|———

olmes did not sleep that night. He thought of Katherine Krupp, her welcoming warmth, and he felt strangely stirred, as though he had visited
a secret place, long unknown to him. And he began to wonder, as he
had many times of late, whether the life he had chosen—or perhaps, it was
fairer to say, had chosen him—had been in some deep sense insufficient. He
remembered, too, what Irene Adler, she of the scandal in Bohemia so long
ago, had told him once in whispered words: "You are good at everything,
Mr. Holmes, except the thing that matters more than any other."

But what was to be done now? The heart was unfamiliar territory, un-
governed by the rule of reason, and its quaking ground made Holmes un-
steady as his mind raced in ever-tightening circles. Katherine Krupp had
disturbed his balance, interrupted the cool analytic processes by which he
normally lived, all at a time when he could ill afford to be distracted. The
Monster, prowling somewhere nearby in the darkness, still beckoned, and
he had no care for what might be troubling Holmes's heart.

Just before dawn, Holmes finally forced himself to cast Katherine Krupp
out of his mind so he could begin thinking about the Monster again. Almost
at once, an interesting idea presented itself. Holmes lit the lantern by his
bed, got out pencil and paper, and began to compose a telegram to an old
friend in Germany named Franz Musser.

They had met in 1886 when Holmes had visited Munich for the first
time to investigate the death of King Ludwig II of Bavaria. The mad king,
as he was called, and his personal physician were found dead in June of
that year in Lake Starnberg near Munich. Ludwig's death was ruled a suicide by drowning—an obvious fiction in Holmes's estimation. Hired by an
influential friend of the king, Holmes had quickly concluded Ludwig was
murdered, but his findings—suppressed by the Bavarian authorities—were
never made public, and the experience had left a bitter taste in his mouth.

Musser had been a young police investigator at the time, impressing
Holmes with his knowledge and skill. They had kept in touch over the years
as Musser, who was soon transferred to a post in Berlin, rose to become a

deputy superintendent of the German national police. As such, he had vast investigatory resources at his disposal. Holmes hoped Musser would be able to provide a crucial piece of information. If he could, Holmes would know exactly how to identify the Monster in Eisendorf's midst.

• • •

Once there was enough light, Holmes went out for his morning walk. The day was cloudy and raw, a few spits of rain coming in with the north wind, but Holmes welcomed the chance to be on the move. He went all the way out to the old mill, not seeing another soul along the way, and then stood for a time contemplating the vacant structure.

The death of Dionisius Eisen in 1893 was on his mind. The town founder met his end just a year or so after the "third immigration" to Eisendorf, an event Holmes believed also marked the arrival of the Monster in town. Although Eisen's death supposedly had been accidental, Holmes suspected otherwise. Yet if Eisen had in fact been pushed into the wheel pit, who had done it, and, why? At dinner the previous night, before Halbach fell into a drunken stupor, Holmes had managed to extract some additional details about Dionisius's demise.

"The way it's told, Dionisius was visiting the mill one day when he somehow slipped and fell into the wheel pit," Halbach had said. "There was a turbine down there, of course, and it was turning with tremendous force. Dionisius was badly mangled, and he died before they could pull him out of the pit. It was a horrible scene from what I understand."

"You say he was 'visiting' the mill. I thought he was the proprietor."

"He was, Mr. Holmes, but he didn't run the mill himself. He had other people to do that."

"I see. There was an investigation into his death, no doubt."

"Yes, but the sheriff at that time saw no reason to think it was anything other than an accident."

"Who was working at the mill that day?"

"You are testing my memory, Mr. Holmes. I really can't be certain, but I think Wolfgang was employed at the mill by then. However, you should be aware that back in those days pretty much every able-bodied man in town helped out at the mill at one time or another."

"Perhaps the Annals of Eisendorf, which you so faithfully maintain, could provide additional details," Holmes suggested.

"I'm afraid not," Halbach said. "You see, Dionisius was still in charge of writing up the annals at the time he died. It wasn't until some weeks afterward that I agreed to take on the task."

"So you are saying there is a gap in the records?"

"Yes, of about a month. It is the only such gap that exists."

"I find it strange that the death of the man who founded your town goes unremarked in the very annals he created."

"There are many strange things about Eisendorf," Halbach replied. "Don't you agree?"

"Yes," said Holmes, "and it seems I am learning more such things every day."

• • •

As he walked back from the mill past the tumbling waters of German Creek, Holmes could feel the Monster's presence, like a distillate of pure evil fouling the air. He wanted to believe he was closing in on the Monster, and yet he was plagued by uncharacteristic doubts. Perhaps it was the other way around. Perhaps the Monster was closing in on him.

So it had been in Munich on the night of his encounter with the Monster in the English Gardens. Only later did Holmes come to appreciate how foolish he had been, and how easily he had allowed himself to be deceived. He was used to pursuing criminals, but he should have realized, especially in light of how doggedly Professor Moriarty's agents were trying to hunt him down, that the tables could easily be turned.

Yet as he entered the English Gardens that night, his cab several hundred yards behind the one being driven by Paul Geist, Holmes was sure he had the upper hand. The only question was how best to proceed. One possibility was to try to pull Geist over and then question him about the murders. But Holmes had no solid proof Geist was the Monster, and even if the accountant-turned-cab driver agreed to be questioned, he would certainly deny any involvement in the crimes. It would be wiser, Holmes reasoned, to watch and wait. If Geist intended to hunt down another victim in the park, Holmes might even have an opportunity to catch him in the act.

Whatever Geist's destination, he did not appear to be in any hurry. Nor did he seem interested in picking up any passengers, since he kept his light off. Instead, he slowly meandered around the park, circling the

Kleinhesseloher See twice and trotting along the little stream known as the Schwabinger Bach, before drifting north to a path paralleling the banks of the Isar. Finally, as midnight approached, he came back to the western edge of the park, where he halted his cab on Liebergesellstrasse.

"I must go off duty now," Holmes's driver informed him when they pulled up about a block away. "Do you wish me to find you another cab?"

"Yes," Holmes said, but then instantly changed his mind. He decided he had spent enough time following Geist. Better to confront him at last. "You may go," Holmes told the driver, leaving him a handsome tip.

The street was deserted, a soft breeze stirring the big linden trees planted along its eastern edge, where darkness swallowed the park beyond. Holmes slipped behind a tree to observe. What he saw next convinced him that Geist was indeed the Monster of Munich. Moments later, Holmes plunged headlong into a trap.

• • •

Halbach was standing in front of the cottage when Holmes returned.

"He's waiting for you inside," Halbach said.

"I'm afraid I don't understand. Who is waiting for me?"

"A fellow from Rochester. Drove right up in one of those fancy cars. I didn't catch his name, but he has an envelope for you. Said it had to be hand delivered and signed for. So I told him to wait. I assumed you'd be back before long. Out for another walk, were you?"

"Yes," Holmes said, catching a hint of suspicion in Halbach's voice. "I'll talk to the man. Thank you, Mr. Halbach."

Holmes stepped inside the cottage. A strapping young man dressed in dark-gray livery—a chauffeur's outfit by the look of it, complete with billed cap—sat on the sofa in the parlor. He got up as soon as he saw Holmes.

"You are Mr. Holmes, I am sure," he said, sounding as if he was reciting a well-practiced speech. "I have been told what you look like. I have something for you from Dr. Plummer."

The chauffeur handed Holmes a manila envelope, its contents protected by an elaborate seal. "I must ask you to sign for it."

Holmes did so.

After inspecting Holmes's signature, the chauffeur bowed his head slightly, touched the bill of his cap and said, "I have been instructed to tell you, Mr. Holmes, that Dr. Plummer has reason to believe you may be in grave danger. I have also been instructed to say I am available to take you back to Rochester at once if that would suit you."

"That will not be necessary," Holmes said. "Did Dr. Plummer say why he thinks I am in danger?"

"No, sir."

"Very well. Thank you. You may leave, but tell Dr. Plummer I shall be fine."

"Yes, sir."

When Holmes read Plummer's letter, he understood why the good doctor was so afraid.

• • •

Holmes had written to Plummer to pose a vital question. How, he wanted to know, had the Monster, ensconced in his lair in Eisendorf, learned so quickly that Holmes was not only at the Mayo Clinic but being treated for emphysema? Plummer's response showed that, as a master medical diagnostician, he possessed all the skills of a good detective.

"I am quite familiar with Eisendorf, as I began my practice as a doctor in that part of the county," Plummer wrote, "and on what might be called a hunch I reviewed the clinic's records to see if anyone from Eisendorf had recently been seen as patient. I learned that on Monday, September 6, the same day you were at the clinic for tests, Mrs. Maria Eisen was also there for an afternoon appointment. I am not at liberty to reveal the specifics of her illness, but you will be interested to learn you and she have much in common from a medical standpoint."

Plummer's meaning was clear. Maria Eisen also had emphysema. Holmes was not surprised. He recalled his meeting with her at the family mansion and how obvious her symptoms had been.

The letter continued: "Mrs. Eisen underwent a test that afternoon of a kind with which you are familiar. The nurse who administered the test conducts all such tests of that type at the clinic. I am sure you understand what I am saying."

Holmes did. The nurse who had given him the spirometer test had, the same day, administered the identical test to Mrs. Eisen. Holmes read on, knowing now how he had been found out.

"I personally spoke with this nurse," Plummer wrote. "She was evasive at first, but I soon got the truth out of her. In a complete lapse of professional judgment, she mentioned to Mrs. Eisen that she had just tested you. I cannot tell you how sorry I am to report this news. I am even sorrier to report I am the real culprit in this unfortunate affair. I gave your real name to the nurse, in order to underscore how important it was for her to administer the test as thoroughly and accurately as possible. I should not have done so, of course, and I extend my sincerest apologies."

Plummer could be forgiven, especially in view of how ably he had performed his assignment as a detective. As for Maria Eisen, she must have gone back to Eisendorf and immediately spread the news of Holmes's presence in Rochester, as well as the nature of his illness. It couldn't have been long before the whole town knew the story. A day later, the Monster sent his first message to Holmes at the Zumbro Hotel.

The letter from Plummer concluded with a warning. "I implore you to take the utmost caution while in Eisendorf. You must understand, Mr. Holmes, that I have known many of the townspeople over the years. I was well acquainted in particular with Dionisius Eisen, who, as you are surely aware of by now, died a gruesome death in the mill. I found him to be a strange and, at times, frightening man. The town he founded reflects his peculiar, secretive personality. There is something dangerous and disordered about Eisendorf, and I have never felt comfortable there, nor should you. Do not let down your guard for a moment.

"P.S. I trust you have stopped smoking."

• • •

Josef Krupp's funeral was held in the Halles des Volkes, which stood on the west side of Freiheit Park, just yards from where his naked body had been found. Like the archives across from it, the People's Hall took the form of a small classical temple outfitted with a Doric portico. Inside, Holmes found a large, oblong room, painted a soft blue. A band of plaster ornament wrapped around the ceiling. Hortatory inscriptions, all in German, formed another band beneath the plasterwork. Eight tall windows brought in light. A small stage with a lectern occupied one end of the room, overlooking rows of wooden benches. Josef Krupp's body lay in a closed wooden casket near the stage.

Holmes arrived early for the services, staking out a spot in the back row of benches. He watched as the residents of Eisendorf filtered in. Most were elderly, and they seemed as old and silent as stone. Not a single child was among them. It did not require any dazzling deductions to conclude Eisendorf was a town without a future. None of the townspeople acknowledged Holmes, or sat close to him, although it was clear from their suspicious glances that they knew who he was. Holmes noticed one woman fingering a rosary, an indication that the atheistic dreams of the town's founders had not met with universal acceptance.

Katherine Krupp, wearing a stylish black dress and a black toque, entered soon after Holmes. She nodded at him as she walked past and took a seat at the front of the hall, a few steps from Krupp's casket. Peter, Maria, and Willy Eisen were among the last arrivals and also sat near the front. Willy, Holmes noted, was by far the youngest person in the room. Wolfgang Eisen was conspicuously absent, as was Georg Dreisser.

At precisely four o'clock, Frederick Halbach stepped up to the lectern, nodded toward the crowd of thirty or so people, and said, "Let us begin these services for our departed brother, Josef Edward Krupp, with words of farewell from the Book of the Dead, as written by our founder, Dionisius Eisen."

These "words of farewell" were not the most comforting Holmes had ever heard. "'The promise of a better world to come has always been a false promise,'" Halbach recited, "'and the dead rest in peace because they have no other choice. Our brother's passing is as the passing of the stars, beyond all knowing. Do not pray now to false gods or entertain foolish dreams of resurrection. Celebrate the life of he who has gone, remember him as you would remember all the good things of this world, and honor him by doing good deeds in his name. Now, let us reason together, and all will be as it should.' So it has been written, and so it shall be. Now, are there any here who wish to speak of our late brother?"

Peter Eisen stepped forward to deliver a short eulogy, to the effect that Josef Krupp was a solid citizen who worked hard and always did his best. Holmes detected nothing heartfelt in Eisen's words. The eulogy was simply a duty required of him as head of the town's most prominent family. Halbach also spoke briefly, but his observations, too, seemed perfunctory. Clearly, Josef Krupp had not been a beloved figure in Eisendorf. Halbach concluded by asking if anyone else wished to speak.

Holmes stood up. "I do," he said.

He walked to the front of the room and stood next to the casket. "You know who I am," he began, "and you know why I am here. Death is stalking your town, and yet many of you remain silent and aloof. Why? I do not pretend to know, but if it is fear that prevents you from speaking, be assured silence will not make you safer. I wish to be of help to you, as does Sheriff Thorkelson, but you must be willing to help us in turn. Will you do that?"

Holmes scanned the stout German faces that had turned to look at him, but saw no indication that his words had achieved any effect. The faces were stoic and sullen, bleached of all passion.

There was period of uncomfortable silence before Halbach said, "Mr. Holmes, I am sure your remarks were well intended, but I do not believe this is the time or place to speak of such things. We are here to honor our brother Josef's memory, not to investigate the circumstances of his unfortunate demise. I must ask you to be seated so that we can continue the services."

• • •

After the services, Holmes caught up with Peter and Maria Eisen on the portico. Willy had already made her escape.

"I am surprised Wolfgang did not attend," Holmes told Peter, "especially as he is said to have such a keen interest in Eisendorf's history. Surely, the funeral of a member of one of the town's founding families must qualify as a historic occasion."

"I must apologize for my brother," Peter said. "He can be very antisocial at times."

"Ha," said Maria, "that is quite the euphemism, husband dearest. Wolfgang in truth is barely civilized and would, I am sure, be perfectly satisfied living in a cave, wrapped in animals skins and hunting his meals with a spear."

"Now, my darling, you are exaggerating," Peter said with evident exasperation. "My brother, as I said, is simply a man who prefers his own company and so does not enjoy social occasions, as most of us do. I should not read too much into his absence, Mr. Holmes."

"I have long been inclined to think one of the best ways to judge a man is to learn what he does not do," Holmes said.

"In Wolfgang's case, that would be anything worthwhile," Maria said. "He is no doubt at this very moment wallowing in idleness at that dreadful dump he calls home. Joining us here would have been too great an effort for him."

"Perhaps your charming company simply didn't appeal to him," Holmes noted. "I can't imagine why. In any event, you look well, Mrs. Eisen, despite your condition. The doctors at Mayo are entirely first-rate, are they not? I imagine it was from them you learned I was in Rochester."

"I do not know of what you speak," she replied, her eyes narrowing into sharpened blades, "nor do I care. What difference is it to me where the mighty Sherlock Holmes goes about his dirty business of snooping into the lives of others?"

"Perhaps you should care, Mrs. Eisen. In fact, I am of a mind you have something to hide."

"What is there to hide in a place such as this, where all is pettiness and stupidity? You used to amuse me, Mr. Holmes, but now you have become impudent, and I do not like impudent people." She turned to her husband and said, "Come along, my sweets. We will leave Mr. Holmes to his silly little affairs."

"We shall talk again soon," Holmes promised as she quickly stepped away.

"That would be fine," Peter said, lingering for a moment. "We are always happy to speak with you, Mr. Holmes. And please excuse Maria. She is, well—"

"Difficult?" Holmes offered.

"Yes, I guess that would be the word," Peter said, then scurried away to catch up with his wife.

• • •

That evening, following his usual dinner with Halbach, Holmes walked over to the Eisen Block. He stood in front of Halbach's store until he saw a pair of headlights come down the street. The automobile slowed down and stopped in front of Holmes.

"You are most punctual, Mr. Boyd," Holmes said.

Tommy Boyd grinned. "Every night at seven, just like you said, Mr. Holmes. Sounds like there's plenty going on here, what with that murder. Do you need a ride out of town?"

"I will not be going anywhere tonight," Holmes said, "but I do have a job for you. Is there a good hardware store in Stewartville?"

"You bet. A couple of them, actually."

"Excellent. I have a few tools I would like you to get for me," Holmes said, handing Boyd a five-dollar gold piece. "Here is a list of what I need. Please deliver the items to me tomorrow night."

Boyd scanned the list, then said, "I should be able to get all of this stuff. What are you going to do with it?"

"I plan to commit a crime or two," Holmes said. "That will be all for tonight, Mr. Boyd."

• • •

Holmes began walking back to his cottage. The town was utterly still, its wide streets empty, its blood-red houses mostly dark. All around, the Eisendorf forest formed a mighty wall, shutting out the world. The timeless stars wheeled overhead, distant and indifferent. Holmes felt very alone.

He cut through Freiheit Park, where the town's only two street lamps struggled to produce weak pools of light. The middle of the park, where the old bandstand stood, was a black hole. The Monster could be there— waiting, watching, plotting—and Holmes would never see him.

That was the problem with the whole town, Holmes thought. At its heart it was all secrets and shadows, and in that penumbral realm the Monster flourished. But lights were slowly coming on. Eisendorf's secrets would be uncovered and its shadows dissolved. It wouldn't be long before the Monster had nowhere left to hide. Or so Holmes hoped.

He was startled out of his thoughts when he came around the side of Halbach's house. A small fire had been set with rags and papers on the cottage's front stoop. Orange flames licked at the front door. Above the flames, which rose only a few feet, a folded piece of paper had been tacked to the door.

"Fire!" Holmes shouted. "Fire!"

Halbach came out of his house. When he saw the flames, he rushed back inside. He returned with a heavy wool blanket and quickly smothered the blaze. Aside from patches of charred wood on the stoop and door, there was little damage.

"It's fortunate you spotted the fire when you did," Halbach said. "The whole place could have burned down."

Holmes surveyed the scene. The arsonist could have easily ignited a far more dangerous fire by soaking the rags in kerosene or by breaking a window and starting a blaze inside the cottage. Instead, it was clear to Holmes the fire had been staged as a warning, and he had no doubt who had done it.

"Looks like somebody left you a message," Halbach said, reaching for the paper on the door.

"Let me get that," Holmes said, grabbing the message before Halbach could.

"What does it say?" Halbach asked. He sounded genuinely curious.

"I shall examine it inside," Holmes said. "Thank you for your help, Mr. Halbach. I do not need anything more from you at the moment."

Halbach took the hint, scooped up his singed blanket, and went back to his house.

Once inside the cottage, Holmes lit the lamps in every room and made a thorough search—finding nothing—before unfolding the message.

"You are growing old and slow, Mr. Holmes," it read. "Do you really think you are a match for me? Enjoy your final hours in Eisendorf."

13

————◄ ● ● ● ►————

A sky the color of old English slate greeted Holmes when he stepped outside his cottage at dawn. If spring was a green apology, Holmes thought, autumn was a season of chastisement. The Eisendorf forest was already painted with tinges of yellow, orange, and red. Leaves were dying, and winter, always an early visitor to Minnesota, lurked like an assassin in the chilly breeze.

Holmes felt tired, his old bones weighing heavily upon him, and he expected to grow even wearier in the days ahead, in part because he was wary of sleep. Josef Krupp's murder, in the dead of night, had put Holmes on high alert. The fire set on his doorstep, and the menacing message that came with it, only served to deepen Holmes's sense of unease. The incident left no doubt in Holmes's mind that he was being watched day and night. Otherwise, how could the Monster have known Holmes had left his cottage to meet with Tommy Boyd?

It was very likely, Holmes thought, he was the Monster's next intended victim. As such, he would be especially vulnerable at night in his cottage. The Monster would have no compunction about murdering a man in his sleep. So Holmes decided he would try to take short naps during the day and keep watch at night, his meticulously cleaned and oiled Webley fully loaded and close at hand.

Holmes's weariness stemmed from more than a lack of sound sleep. He also found himself once again experiencing a vague mental fog, his thoughts as labored as his breathing. Eisendorf itself, he knew, was part of the problem. With its dark air of secrecy and its uncanny isolation, the town seemed to hold him hostage, a black hood of doubt over his head. Both Thorkelson and Dr. Plummer had recommended he leave, and the idea sounded very appealing. Yet Holmes had never retreated from a challenge, however formidable. For better or worse, he would stay in Eisendorf until the end.

● ● ●

"Tell me about your younger days in Munich before you immigrated to Eisendorf," Holmes said when he sat down with Halbach for breakfast. "What were you doing then?"

Halbach passed a plate of pancakes and sausages and looked suspiciously at Holmes. "I worked at a small clothing store in the Schwabing neighborhood, where I lived like the proverbial pauper. My mother died when I was quite young, and my father was unknown to me, so I was on my own from a very early age. My life in Munich was so miserable that I was happy to leave when the opportunity presented itself."

"Did you hold any other jobs in Munich?"

"Such a driving a cab? Come now, Mr. Holmes, I know what this is about. Do you really believe the Monster of Munich now resides in Eisendorf? Georg Dreisser seems to think you do, or so he informs me."

"Yes, I have no doubt the Monster is here," Holmes acknowledged.

"And therefore you must think he arrived with the immigrants of 1892."

"It seems likely."

Halbach said, "Well, I can assure you, Mr. Holmes, that I am not a monster of any kind, nor did I ever drive a cab, in Munich or anywhere else. And I must tell you I find it very hard to believe anyone here could be the ghastly figure who murdered those men in 1892."

"The evidence suggests otherwise," Holmes said.

"Then who is it you suspect? Wolfgang?"

"I have ruled out no one at this stage," Holmes replied, "but I am certainly interested in Wolfgang, if only because he keeps in his possession a number of old German newspaper stories pertaining to the Monster of Munich. His collection also includes some interesting photographs. He must be quite fascinated with the case. Has he ever discussed it with you?"

"No, I do not recall him ever bringing up the subject," Halbach said with unusual firmness.

"You are certain?"

"Of course. I would never mislead you, Mr. Holmes," Halbach said with a slight smile.

Or perhaps it was an inverted frown. Holmes couldn't be sure. The archivist's broad face was at once impassive and inscrutable. His mouth, pressed between thin lips, was an elongated cipher. Holmes had spent more time with Halbach than anyone else in Eisendorf, yet he remained deeply uncertain about the man and his motives. Halbach had opened up only once, on the night he'd enjoyed too many beers, but even then the gates had quickly slammed shut once Holmes became overly inquisitive.

"I am pleased to hear that, Mr. Halbach, but I must say I have not found everyone in town to be as honest as you no doubt are. Eisendorf is a place desperately in need of good, clear light, and yet all around I have found only clouds and fog. Almost everyone here seems to be harboring secrets. Why is that?"

"Do not judge us too harshly, Mr. Holmes. The simple fact is that secrets are built into the very structure of Eisendorf. Dionisius Eisen saw to that."

"In what way?"

Halbach delivered one of his smile-frowns. "It has to do with a most unusual book he compiled. I suppose you could say it's a companion piece of sorts to the official town annals. The book is called *The Secret History of Eisendorf and Its People.* You see, Dionisius believed every community has a secret history of sin and desire that never gets written up in official chronicles. He likened it to the underbrush in a forest, where sunlight doesn't penetrate. So he decided to create a book devoted to this 'shadow history,' as he called it."

"How did he go about writing such a book? Did he expect that the townspeople would all share their deepest secrets with him?"

"To be honest, Mr. Holmes, I have no idea."

"Why is that?"

"The fact is, I have never actually seen the book. I first learned of its existence at the reading of Dionisius's will back in 1893. The book, along with all of Dionisius's estate, was bequeathed to his son, Hans. Naturally, I asked him about it, thinking it would be a fine addition to the archives, but Hans did not wish to part with it."

"Who has the book now?"

"Either Peter or Wolfgang, I imagine."

"Did they inherit Hans's estate?"

"Hans died without a will—at least none was ever found—and of course he never married or had children, so I think his estate will end up going to the cousins. But it doesn't amount to much, now that the mill is closed. Hans owned that big pile of a house and not much else, or so he told me once."

"I see. By the way, are you convinced Hans died by his own hand?"

"All I can say is that I was surprised," Halbach replied with his usual circumspection. "He had never shown any signs of despondency. Then again, it is always hard to know what dark thoughts may dwell inside a man's head. But if you are suggesting he was murdered, Mr. Holmes, then what was the motive? Hans was quite harmless, he had no enemies I know of, and, as I told you, he did not possess any great wealth."

"I will not dispute your observations," Holmes said. "However, there is much I have yet to learn. In the meantime, let us return to Dionisius. He seems to have been quite the writer. Besides the chronicles of the town and the secret history, did he produce any other works before his death?"

"Well, there's his diary, of course. It's in the archives. It covers the period from his youth in Germany all the way up to his death."

"I should like to see it," Holmes said.

The mysterious smile-frown revisited Halbach's face. "Oh, I am afraid that would be quite impossible, Mr. Holmes. Dionisius in his will expressly forbade anyone except family members from reading the diary until fifty years after his death. I don't suppose you're willing to wait until 1943."

"No, I am not," said Holmes, glancing out the window of Halbach's kitchen toward the back of the archives building. Its main floor rose above a tall stone basement punctured by two heavily barred windows, which protected the vault that served as the official repository of Eisendorf's many secrets. Finding a way inside the vault, Holmes thought, might be a worthwhile endeavor.

●●●

After breakfast Holmes asked for directions to Georg Dreisser's residence, then walked over to call on Eisendorf's resident skeptic. His house, a standard brick foursquare, was at the southwest corner of town within eyeshot of the Eisen mansion. Dreisser's mother answered the door and showed Holmes into a nicely furnished parlor. There, he found Dreisser looking over a collection of coins. He was dressed in a rather foppish outfit that included a boldly colored ascot.

"You are a numismatist, I see," Holmes said, taking a seat. "Do you own any conspicuous treasures?"

"No, I am not nearly rich enough for that. But I doubt you are here to discuss my silly little hobby. You are here about the photograph Wolfgang managed to steal. Very well, I admit I lied to you."

"Why?"

"Pure vanity, Mr. Holmes. I have always thought of myself as a man of some culture and attainment. I do not like to admit I once held so menial a job as that of a cab driver. But it hardly matters because that photograph was taken in 1890 in Stuttgart, on the Königstrasse, not as you probably suspect, in Munich."

Holmes had never been to Stuttgart. Perhaps Dreisser was telling the truth. Perhaps not. "Why should I believe you?"

"Because if you were to go to Stuttgart, you could readily find exactly where that picture was taken. The fact is, I was never a cab driver in Munich. Still, I think the most interesting question about the photograph is why Wolfgang Eisen felt compelled to steal it from the archives."

"You are convinced he did so?"

"Of course. I donated it along with many other items back in May."

"If you are so embarrassed about once being a cab driver, Mr. Dreisser, why did you donate the picture to the archives, where others might see it?"

"I felt it was my duty to history," Dreisser said with an air of pretension that Holmes found almost laughable. "I trust Freddy told you all about the materials I gave to the archives."

"He did. However, he states he never actually saw the photograph."

"I told you Freddy is the prince of liars."

"Or perhaps you are, Mr. Dreisser."

Dreisser responded to this provocation with a bemused smile. "Now you see the problem, don't you? Is anyone in this town to be believed about anything? As it so happens, I am telling the truth. Whether or not you choose to believe me is up to you."

"Yes, it is. The truth has a way of coming out, Mr. Dreisser, even in Eisendorf."

"I do not fear it," Dreisser said. "I have done nothing wrong. Indeed, I am the victim of theft in this case. You really should speak with Wolfgang and chastise him for his bad behavior. Will you do that?"

"Perhaps you could do me the favor of answering questions rather than asking them," Holmes said. "Now, I presume you have a theory as to why he supposedly stole the photograph."

"Certainly. He is trying to frame me by suggesting that I was the Monster of Munich and therefore also the man who murdered Josef Krupp. It is far more likely, as far as I am concerned, that Wolfgang himself is the man you are looking for."

"And why would he want to frame you?"

Dreisser let out a derisive snort and said, "I hear from my mother that you have been talking at some length with good old Freddy. I am sure he has told you how much I am despised by certain people in this godforsaken town. It comes as no surprise to me that those people—especially the Eisens and their bootlicker, Freddy—would want to pin upon me crimes I did not commit."

"So everyone is plotting against you?"

"Yes, but they won't succeed, not so long as the mighty Sherlock Holmes is on the case. I am counting on you to clear my good name."

"Do not do any counting quite yet," Holmes said. "Only time will tell whether your name is good or not."

• • •

On his way back to the cottage, Holmes encountered Willy. She was in Freiheit Park, blowing bubbles from a jar of soapy water with a wand.

"Aren't they pretty?" she said to Holmes.

"Very. I am thinking, Willy, they are just like your secrets—here one minute and then—poof!—gone. But they are still hiding inside you. It is just that no one else can see them."

The girl nodded. "That's why they're secrets."

"I remember the first secret you told me, the one about Mr. Bones in the mill tunnel. You said you would take me to see him."

"Did I?" She blew a bubble—her biggest one yet—and watched it float away until it vanished with a pop.

"Do you know what the best thing is about having a secret, Willy?"

"I'm not sure."

"The best thing is when you finally share that secret with someone else. Don't you think so?"

"Maybe."

"That's why I would like to see Mr. Bones. We could share the secret. Do you remember exactly where he is?"

"At the bend in the tunnel, Mr. Sherlock. Maybe I'll show you tomorrow."

She screwed the lid back on the jar and put the bubble-blowing wand in her dress pocket. "Good-bye. I have to see Poppa."

Before Holmes could ask any more questions, she was gone.

• • •

Early in the afternoon, Holmes hiked to the town cemetery. He was interested in seeing the Eisen and Krupp family graves. Although Halbach had already provided a good deal of information about the village's two dynastic families, Holmes wanted to be sure the archivist hadn't left anyone out of the story.

The cemetery occupied a picturesque plot of land on the south side of German Creek beneath high bluffs. Like everything else about the little village, Holmes discovered, the cemetery was peculiar. There were no crosses, no statues of weeping virgins, no carved tree trunks symbolizing a life cut short, no gated mausoleums where the wealthy could spend eternity rotting aboveground rather than below. Instead, the cemetery was arranged with Teutonic precision, the dead lying in alphabetical order along three parallel paths. All of the headstones, with two notable exceptions, were simple slabs of gray granite carved only with the name and dates of the deceased.

Holmes soon found two Eisen family headstones, for Dionisius (1825–1893), and Hans (1858–1920). Hans's marker was of the standard variety, but Dionisius enjoyed his eternal sleep beneath a twenty-foot-high granite obelisk. The words "Founder of Eisendorf" were carved below his name. What Holmes didn't see was a gravestone for Dionisius's wife. Halbach had never mentioned her. Holmes wondered why.

The Krupp family plot proved to be even more interesting. Bernard Krupp (1861–1920) was there, beneath the usual slab, but his father, Gottfried, was memorialized by a curious, altar-like monument. A bronze plaque mounted atop it bore the inscription: "Gottfried Wilhelm Krupp, 1837–?, Vanished but not Forgotten."

Eisendorf, Holmes had come to understand, was a place where past and present were intimately intertwined. And now he had come upon a fresh puzzle from the past that might somehow relate to the town's murderous present. What had happened to Gottfried Krupp, the so-called second founder of Eisendorf? Holmes thought he knew where he could find the answer.

• • •

Holmes walked up the hill to the Krupp mansion. He was pleased when Katherine Krupp answered the doorbell. She was wearing a plain white blouse over a flaring red skirt. A pink rose was pinned near the right shoulder of her blouse. She looked, Holmes thought, remarkably fresh and beautiful. Heinrich was with her and sniffed approvingly when Holmes extended his hand.

"What a pleasant surprise," she said. "Please come in."

She escorted him to the living room where they had spent so many hours two nights before.

"Is this a social call?" she asked Holmes in a teasing tone, "or strictly business?"

Holmes wished it were a social visit, for he found it unpleasant to think about the Monster when he was with Mrs. Krupp. She was all the Monster was not, and she stood for peace and calm when everything else in Eisendorf seemed to vibrate with hidden danger.

Holmes bent over to kiss her hand and said, "It is business, I am afraid, but I shall still enjoy your company."

"How nice of you to say so," she said. "Now, tell me how I can be of help?"

"I have just been at the town cemetery, and something caught my attention. I noticed there was no date of death on the tomb of your father-in-law, Gottfried, and the inscription said he had 'vanished.' Do you know what happened to him?"

"Yes and no," Mrs. Krupp said. "I know he disappeared, but as to where he went, that remains a mystery. It's a very strange story. I am surprised Mr. Halbach didn't tell you about it."

"The archivist is not a man given to volunteering information, unless the beer is flowing freely. Besides, I would trust your account of the matter far more than his. I should like to hear the whole story, or at least as much of it as you know."

"Well, I was just a girl when it happened, but it was the talk of the town. It was in the spring of 1875. One night Gottfried Krupp left his house—this very house, which he had just built—and simply disappeared. The authorities were called in, and there was a search that lasted for days, but no trace of him was ever found."

"Do you recall where he was supposed to be going on the day he vanished?"

"Goodness, it was so very long ago. But I seem to remember something to the effect that he had business at the mill that day."

"At the Eisen Mill?"

"Yes."

"Did the authorities believe foul play was involved?"

"I think so. I know Bern always suspected someone had murdered his father."

"Did he have a particular suspect in mind?"

"I don't know, Mr. Holmes. As I told you before, Bern was afflicted with the disease of secrecy that has caused this town to rot to its core. He kept many things to himself, which is what everyone in Eisendorf does. But I will tell you it is well known Gottfried never got along with Dionisius Eisen. They were always quarreling, or so I've heard."

"Do you know what they quarreled over?"

"I'm not sure, but what do men ever quarrel over except money, power, or a woman? Power would be my guess, although a woman isn't out of the question, either. Old Dionisius, from all I've heard, was aptly named. He apparently viewed the women of Eisendorf as his harem. His wife left him, I believe, when Hans was just a child."

"Yes, I noticed she was not interred with him."

"No, she left Eisendorf as fast as her legs would carry her, or so the story goes, and was never heard from again. But Dionisius apparently continued to pursue his various affairs and that caused a lot of problems. Bedding other men's wives is a certain path to discord, especially in a place as small as Eisendorf. But as I said, it's more likely he and Gottfried fought over who would run the town."

"Why do you think so?"

"Well, Dionisius founded Eisendorf, but the town didn't begin to thrive until Gottfried came along about fifteen years later. I believe he actually had a good deal more money than Dionisius. At least, that's what Bern always told me. So I wouldn't be surprised if the two of them argued over who got to be the big boss here. You know what they say about a ship with two captains."

"Yes," said Holmes, "one of them usually ends up being tossed overboard. Perhaps that is what happened to Gottfried."

"Do you think Gottfried's disappearance all those years ago is somehow connected to Josef's murder?"

"I am beginning to think it quite likely," Holmes said. "Eisendorf reminds me of a cave with many levels. Every time I go down one passageway, I discover an opening to another one farther below. In some sense I do not fully understand yet, the Monster is intertwined with the Eisen-Krupp rivalry. There is some object he is pursuing, and he will stop at nothing to obtain it. And that is why I must ask a favor of you."

"What would that be?"

"I want you to leave town for a while. Perhaps you could stay with one of your friends in Rochester."

"You must believe I am in danger. Why do you think so? I pose no threat to anyone."

"We do not know that. Josef Krupp was murdered here, for reasons that are still murky. You are the only other person in Eisendorf with that surname, if I am not mistaken."

"Yes, that's true."

"Then, please do as I ask. I have grown very fond of you, and I want you to remain safe at all costs. Besides, you would not have to leave town for long. Matters here will come to a head very soon."

"I hope so, yet I also recall what you told me about your experiences in Munich. You were sure you had the Monster then, but—"

"But I did not. I trust it will be different this time. Now, do I have your promise you will leave Eisendorf as soon as possible?"

"Yes," Mrs. Krupp said, coming over to join Holmes on the couch, "I will do what you want. I have a good friend in Rochester I can stay with. But I will do so only on the condition you remain in contact with me. I am worried about you."

"I will," Holmes promised, thinking how nice it was to have someone in Eisendorf who worried about him. "Now, when you go to Rochester, I want you to get in touch with Sheriff Thorkelson at once. Tell him I need to know all I can about Gottfried's disappearance. I assume news stories were written about it at the time. Can you do that for me?"

Mrs. Krupp kissed Holmes on the cheek and said, "Of course. But I am still very concerned about what will happen to you. Surely, you are in more danger here than anyone else."

"True" Holmes said, "but if I did not know how to conduct myself in dangerous situations, I should have been dead long ago."

•••

That night, as he sat in his cottage, Holmes wrestled with all manner of questions jostling for attention in his brain. The biggest of them all—the one that stabbed at him like a razor-sharp blade—was also the most difficult: What was the Monster's ultimate motive, beyond the sheer pleasure he seemed to derive from the act of murder? There had to be an enormous prize at stake. But what was it? And how many more lives was the Monster ready to snuff out in order to claim it?

As the night wore on, Holmes found himself inevitably drawn back to Munich. He had a vivid recollection of everything that had happened when he followed Paul Geist into the English Gardens.

Geist had stopped his cab at the edge of the gardens along the Liebergesellstrasse, in a spot where a huge tree bent down over the street and sopped up much of the light from the nearest lamp. Watching from less than a hundred yards away, Holmes decided to confront Geist in his cab. Holmes still couldn't be sure Geist was the Monster, but he thought it very likely. And then Holmes's suspicions were confirmed.

Geist, whose face remained obscured, stepped down from the driver's seat, patted his horse on the hindquarters, and came back to the side of the cab, where he paused to take a long, slow look around. Then he opened the door to the back seat and, with considerable effort, began pulling out what at first looked to be a rolled-up carpet.

"My God," Holmes whispered to himself, realizing at once what Geist must be doing. It was no carpet he had slung over his shoulder, but rather something long and heavy wrapped in a blanket. It had to be another victim. Holmes watched with grim fascination as Geist hauled his awful cargo into a thick clump of bushes. Moments later, he was back up on his cab.

Holmes knew he had to act before Geist could make his escape. But the man who had just tossed away a body as though it was mere trash appeared to be in no hurry. Apparently well satisfied with his work, he lit a cigarette.

Drawing out his revolver, Holmes made his way toward the cab, the big linden trees that bordered the street screening his movement. His footsteps were as soft as the warm summer air, and Geist—still smoking, his back toward Holmes—gave no evidence he heard them. Moments later, still undetected, Holmes darted from the woods and swung up into the back seat of the cab. He put his revolver to the driver's head.

"Das Monster von Munchen," he said. "Ich habe dich gefunden."

14

———◖● ● ●◗———

"Sorry I couldn't get here yesterday," Osgood Thorkelson said, settling his expansive bulk into a chair in the parlor of Holmes's cottage. "Had a big deal over near Byron. Some crazy farmer took a potshot at his neighbor, then holed up in his barn. Took the whole damn day to smoke him out. But I did manage to get that telegram off. Never sent one to Germany before. Let's hope this Musser fellow has what you're looking for. It could break this whole thing open."

"Yes, but it could be a week or more before we receive a reply," Holmes noted. "That may be too late to do us any good."

"I guess we'll see. Now, before I forget, I have some news about that revolver you found in Halbach's store. We couldn't lift any fingerprints, but our ballistics fellow is pretty sure the gun was fired within twenty-four hours of the time you found it. He says he can tell by the way the barrel smells. Too bad we don't have the fatal bullet. As soon as we're done here, I'm going to have a long talk with Halbach. He has some explaining to do as far as I'm concerned."

"By all means, have at Mr. Halbach. He is a shifty character, in my estimation. However, without a bullet to match to the barrel, we have no hard evidence the gun was used to kill Josef Krupp, despite that mocking note attached to it. Nor can we put the weapon in Mr. Halbach's hand. His store, I fear, is an open invitation to thievery. A child could open the front door lock. It is not impossible that someone could have taken the gun, used it, and then returned it."

"Why go through the trouble?"

"Presumably to implicate Mr. Halbach in the murders. Or, conversely, as a clever counterstroke on Mr. Halbach's part. He could argue that he would never be so stupid and careless as to use a gun kept for all to see in his own place of business as a murder weapon. In either case, questions remain."

"They always do in this damned town," Thorkelson said. "It's crazy when you think about it. The town looks as simple and straightforward as can be, but once you step inside, you're in a maze."

"So I have discovered," Holmes said, "but I am beginning to find my way through it. Tell me, Sheriff, do you know an attorney in Rochester named Walter Schmidt?"

"Yes, I've met him a couple of times. What about him?"

Holmes showed Thorkelson the notes Mrs. Krupp had found from her husband's consultation with Schmidt.

"Hmm, what do you make of it?"

"The notes clearly refer to something involving Eisendorf's cooperative. I don't know the specifics yet, but I intend to speak with Mr. Schmidt."

"I wish you luck. Lawyers don't like to talk about matters involving their clients. I doubt he'd tell me a thing, but maybe you'll be able to pry something out of him."

"Prying is one of my specialties," Holmes said with a smile.

"And you are very good at it. What else have you learned since we last met?"

Holmes provided a synopsis of his conversations the day before with Dreisser and Halbach.

"Do you think Dreisser was telling you the truth about where he drove that cab?" Thorkelson asked.

"His story is plausible, but I am unable to verify it, and a trip to Stuttgart is not on my agenda at the moment. Mr. Dreisser remains very much a question mark, as does Mr. Halbach. By the way, I also had another talk yesterday with Willy Eisen concerning Mr. Bones."

"So you're still interested in that skeleton, or whatever she found. Well, I still wouldn't be surprised if she dreamed up the whole thing."

"I believe her," Holmes said. "Willy is not a liar. Indeed, she would not know how to lie."

"Well, let's hope you're right," Thorkelson said. "Seems like you've got lots of angles to pursue at the moment."

"Perhaps too many," Holmes said. "However, I have made progress on another front. Dr. Plummer sent me a most revealing letter."

After Holmes had described the contents of the letter, Thorkelson said, "I guess that solves one little mystery. Maria must have blabbed the news to everyone in town."

"So it would seem. And yet I have been thinking about it, and I am not so sure she spread the story around town. She appears to have little contact with anyone outside of her household, and she clearly hates everything and everyone in Eisendorf. I do not picture her as the town gossip."

"Maybe she mentioned it to Peter, and he spread the word."

"That's possible. Or perhaps Wolfgang overheard her talking about my presence at the clinic. In any case, let us turn to other matters. Did you find the newspaper stories I requested?"

"Yes, Mrs. Krupp came by the office," Thorkelson said. "She said you'd asked her to leave town for a while. She also told me you wanted to find out as much as you could about Gottfried Krupp's disappearance. I didn't know anything about it, so I sent my secretary over to the newspaper offices. One of the librarians there dug out a bunch of old stories." Thorkelson handed Holmes a folder containing yellowed editions of the *Bulletin* and *Post* newspapers from Rochester.

"Ah, these are exactly what I wanted," Holmes said. "Did you find anything of interest?"

"That's for you to decide, Mr. Holmes. I'm not sure what you're after. We're talking about things that happened way before my time."

"The usual rules of time, Sheriff, do not seem to apply to Eisendorf. What happened here a half century ago may well have a direct bearing on what is happening now. Time saturates this town like blood flowing from a deep wound. In any case, let us see what the press can tell us."

The newspapers offered a series of stories about Krupp's sudden disappearance, which had provoked a storm of publicity. Holmes quickly read through the accounts, then stood up and began pacing about the parlor, clutching a newspaper in his hand.

"You must be a very fast reader," Thorkelson noted.

"In my line of work, it is a useful skill."

"Did you find something?"

Holmes nodded. "I call your attention to the following paragraphs, from the Rochester *Post*, dated October sixth, eighteen seventy-five, one day after Gottfried Krupp's disappearance:

"'Mr. Krupp was last seen at his house at six o'clock Tuesday evening, telling his wife he had business to attend to with Dionisius Eisen. However, Mr. Eisen told authorities he never saw Mr. Krupp that evening or at any time thereafter.

"'Stated Mr. Eisen, "I was much surprised to learn Gottfried said he wished to meet me at the mill. I cannot believe such was his real destination, as the mill has been closed for the past two days to repair a broken shaft and does not operate in any case after dark." Authorities thoroughly searched the mill, but found no evidence Mr. Krupp had been there.'"

Holmes continued to pace, leaving Thorkelson to ponder the significance of the two paragraphs. The sheriff did not mull over the matter for long. "Well, Mr. Holmes, I suppose you think Dionisius Eisen might have been involved in Krupp's disappearance."

"It is a distinct possibility. What I am certain of is that Gottfried Krupp was murdered."

"And you're certain because—?"

"Because stolid burgers like Gottfried Krupp are not the sort of people who simply disappear of their own accord. Something happened to him, and when we find out what that was, we may at last be in a position to grasp the full dimensions of this case."

As Thorkelson was preparing to go, Holmes explained why he had asked Katherine Krupp to take refuge in Rochester. "I insisted upon it because I believe she could be in jeopardy. She left yesterday. I would greatly appreciate it if you could stop by her friend's house in Rochester—I have the address—and let her know I am well."

Thorkelson gave Holmes a sidelong glance and said, "Be happy to. I must say, Mr. Holmes, it sounds like you and the lady have become fast friends. Well, that's good. She's very nice, from all I can tell."

"Yes," said Holmes, "and I want to be sure nothing bad happens to her."

• • •

After the sheriff left, Holmes sat for a while and reviewed the progress of his investigation. He had established that at least five men from Eisendorf—Peter and Wolfgang Eisen, Frederick Halbach, Josef Krupp, and Georg Dreisser—could have been in Munich in 1892 during the Monster's killing spree. Josef was now dead, and Holmes was certain he had not been the Monster.

Holmes lacked definitive evidence against any of the four remaining suspects. He had hoped to eliminate one or more of them simply by observing how they used their hands. The Monster, Holmes had learned in Munich, nearly at the cost of his life, was right-handed. But so, too, were all of his suspects in Eisendorf.

Holmes considered the pros and cons of each suspect. Wolfgang Eisen was at the top of the list. He had a violent temperament, as Holmes had discovered firsthand. He had a secret stash of German newspapers recounting the Monster's crime spree in Munich. He had been uncooperative during interviews with Holmes and the sheriff. He had possibly tried to frame Georg Dreisser. Everything about him, in short, seemed to invite suspicion. But was he smart and devious enough to be the Monster?

Then there was Peter Eisen, the town's leading citizen. Like his brother, he had strong connections to Munich. He wasn't quite as large and strong as Wolfgang, but his general build was similar to that of the Monster. He also struck Holmes as a very intelligent and crafty man who knew how to evade uncomfortable questions. Yet at times, especially around his wife, he seemed rather weak willed. Was he really capable of committing a series of brutal crimes?

Halbach presented even more question marks. He was a canny operator, and a man well used to keeping secrets. A gun from his store had very probably been used to kill Josef Krupp. Like the other three suspects, he also had no real alibi for the time of Krupp's murder. Yet, as with Peter Eisen, Halbach did not appear to possess the sheer ruthlessness needed to murder in cold blood. Then again, it was hard to say what passions might lurk behind Halbach's carefully constructed facade.

Finally, there was Georg Dreisser. The most obvious mark against him was that he had once been a cab driver, possibly in Munich. His employment at the Mayo Clinic meant he could have learned very quickly of Holmes's presence in Rochester. The timing of his return to Eisendorf, only months before Hans Eisen and Bernard Krupp met their violent ends, was also suspicious. But his cool, skeptical manner was not that of a conniving killer, and he seemed to have no real motive for murder.

Holmes also had to consider other possibilities. Perhaps the Monster was someone other than one of his four suspects. What if Halbach or someone else had doctored the town records, thereby putting the real killer in the clear, at least as far as the murders in Munich were concerned? There was also a chance—a long one, as Holmes saw it—that the killer in Eisendorf had no connection to the Munich murders, but had simply piggybacked on that case in order to attract Holmes's attention. But that begged another question. Why would the killer want to complicate his plans by dragging Holmes into the investigation?

Identifying the Monster, Holmes saw, had turned into a feast of possibilities. The problem was, he needed to put some real food on the table, and he needed to do it quickly. There would be more deaths in Eisendorf, he was certain, if the Monster was not stopped soon.

• • •

The young man at Holmes's doorstep was fresh faced and eager, and carried a small notebook in his hand. It required no miracle of deduction to identify him as a newspaper reporter. When Holmes opened the door, the man said he was indeed a correspondent for the Rochester *Bulletin*. He wished to know if Holmes cared to comment on the investigation into Josef Krupp's murder.

Holmes did not. "I would encourage you to speak with Sheriff Thorkelson," he told the young man.

"I have, sir, but I would like a statement from you. Surely you must be looking into Mr. Krupp's death."

"No, I am merely enjoying a brief respite here before returning to England."

"But why would you want to stay in a place such as this?"

"It is delightfully quiet," Holmes said, "and the people are most interesting."

• • •

That afternoon, as it so often did in spare moments, Holmes's restless mind wandered back to Munich, and he thought of that unforgettable night outside the English Gardens when he confronted the Monster.

Revolver in hand, Holmes had climbed up into the Monster's cab, certain he had his man. He was sure, too, that he had surprised his quarry. Then came the moment when everything turned around, certainty dissolved into doubt by the Monster's stunning statement: "I am happy to have found you, Mr. Holmes. It is a great pleasure I am sure to meet such a famous man. Shall we go for a ride?"

The cab's big black horse, as if by some secret command, then reared up so violently that Holmes was thrown back in his seat, barely keeping a grip on his revolver. Holmes managed to fire off a shot, but it went well wide of the Monster, who had spun around and leaped down from his seat. Most of his face was obscured by a black scarf. Holmes had no time to look into the Monster's eyes. Instead, he was fighting for his life.

The Monster was a powerful man, and he grabbed at Holmes's revolver with his left hand, pushing it up and away. Then Holmes saw the long blade in the Monster's right hand, shimmering in the lamplight. The cab's horse saved Holmes. Before the blade could descend in its deadly arc, the cab lurched forward, and the panicked horse went off at a gallop. Caught off balance, the Monster reached for one of the cab's doors, but it swung open, and he tumbled out to the pavement.

Holmes now went on a wild journey through the park as the horse raced along a series of winding pathways around the lake. After a near tip-over, Holmes was able to crawl up to the driver's seat and grab the reins. He turned the cab around and retraced his route back to the quiet street where he had confronted the Monster. But the Monster was gone, vanished into the dark immensity of the city. Holmes had never seen his face.

• • •

"Do you have a drawing of the mill tunnel?"

The question was put to Frederick Halbach as he sat at his desk in the main reading room of the archives. Holmes had gone to see Halbach after shaking free from his Munich reveries.

"We do," Halbach said. "Dionisius Eisen made it himself. He was very proud of that tunnel. I imagine you would like to see it."

"I would," said Holmes.

Halbach retrieved the drawing from a large file cabinet and then directed Holmes to a long table in front of the reading room's loudly ticking grandfather clock. "We can spread the drawing out there, if you like."

"That would be excellent," Holmes said. The drawing, accomplished very skillfully in pen and ink at a scale of twenty feet to the inch, spread out across a three-foot-long sheet of paper. It showed the tunnel in both plan and section. What caught Holmes's eye at once was a slight bend near the center of the tunnel, just as Willy Eisen had said.

"Is there some reason for the bend?" Holmes asked.

"Not that I know of," Halbach said. "I assume Dionisius intended it to be straight. But as I mentioned to you before, he had men blasting and digging from either end. My guess is that when they met in the middle, they discovered the tunnel wasn't perfectly aligned."

"Yes, I can see how that might have happened. I know the tunnel is no longer in use, but I presume it remains accessible."

"I'm not really sure. I believe Peter Eisen mentioned to me some months back that a portion near the mill had caved in. But I suppose a person could still get in from the far end where the dam used to be. Are you planning an underground tour, Mr. Holmes?"

"No, I am simply curious," Holmes lied.

"Well, you wouldn't find anything in there as it is, except for a lot of rock and seeping water."

"Is that Sherlock Holmes hard at work?" a voice boomed out. Holmes turned around to see Peter Eisen just inside the entrance to the reading room. "Maria and I were just talking about you."

"Favorably?" Holmes asked.

Eisen said, "How could anyone speak ill of so great a figure as yourself, Mr. Holmes?"

"You wife has never had any trouble doing so. Besides, I have found it is when people begin to speak well of a man that he should be most on guard."

"So flattery will get me nowhere," Eisen said. "Do you mind if I join you?"

"Please do," Holmes said. "It would be a pleasure to talk with Eisendorf's leading citizen."

Once Eisen was seated at the table, Halbach said, "Mr. Holmes has been examining Dionisius's drawing of the tunnel."

"So I see," Eisen said. "Looking for something in particular?"

"Not really," Holmes said. "I simply wish to learn a bit more about your town's most famous feature. It is quite impressive, although Mr. Halbach informs me a portion of the tunnel has collapsed."

"Yes, earlier this year. Not sure what happened. But it makes no difference now. The mill will never reopen as far as I can see, and with no mill there is no need for the tunnel. It's really too bad. There was a time when this town was a going place, and the mill was very successful. Ah, but tempus fugit, as they say. The world changes, and we must change with it. Now the mill is just another relic of Eisendorf's glory days."

"I heard that," said Georg Dreisser, who had slipped into the reading room while Holmes, Halbach, and Eisen were hunched over the drawing. "I was not aware Eisendorf had any glory days. But perhaps Mr. Eisen can enlighten me. That is, if he can spare the time. Trying to frame me for murder must keep him and his brother very busy."

Eisen glared at Dreisser and said, "I really have no idea what you're talking about, Georg, but as you can see, we're occupied at the moment."

"Ah, you've got out that old drawing of the mill tunnel. Are you planning a grand reopening, Peter? I would think the mill has cost the Eisen family enough money by now."

Halbach said, "Georg, is there something I can do for you? Otherwise—"

"Otherwise, I should get the hell out, is that it, Freddy? Well, I did have a question for you, but it can wait. As for you, Peter, you and Wolfgang had best stop telling lies about me. Mr. Holmes knows what I mean. Just because you're the Eisens, that doesn't mean you can do whatever you goddamn well please in this town."

With that parting shot, Dreisser went out the door as quickly as he had come in.

"Now you know why Georg is not a popular figure in town," Eisen said. "He can be quite nasty, and he thinks everybody is against him."

"Perhaps they are," Holmes said. "Mr. Dreisser believes Wolfgang is trying to implicate him in certain crimes."

"Well then, he should take up the matter with my brother," Eisen said. "It is not my business. And since we seem to be talking about crime, I would be very interested to learn, Mr. Holmes, if you have any suspects yet in poor Josef's murder."

"I always have suspects," Holmes replied, "but I can say no more at present. However, I would note that in the course of my investigation I have found myself drawn into Eisendorf's unusual history. It is quite remarkable how many violent deaths and disappearances have occurred in so small a community."

Eisen said, "I fear you are right, and I have no explanation for it. Perhaps we are just unlucky here."

"I doubt luck has much to do with Gottfried Krupp's disappearance," Holmes observed.

"Now, there's a piece of ancient history. Don't tell me you're digging into that, Mr. Holmes?"

"I have found Eisendorf is rich ground for all manner of excavating. Do either of you know anything about the matter?"

Halbach claimed to know little about the case. "For some reason, it's not very well covered in the town annals."

"I doubt I can be of much help, either," Eisen said. "It happened long before I arrived here."

"Did your uncle, Dionisius, ever speak of Mr. Krupp's disappearance?"

"Not that I recall. Why do you ask?"

"Idle curiosity. I am wondering about something else as well. Mr. Halbach has informed me of a book, written by Dionisius, called *The Secret History of Eisendorf and Its People.* He tells me it remains in the possession of your family."

Eisen glanced at Halbach before telling Holmes, "Freddy is a font of information, isn't he? Yes, there was such a book. I paged through it once, and it was gibberish, pure and simple. My uncle was a most peculiar man. He had dreams and visions, and he put them into the book. They made no sense."

"You speak of the book in the past tense. Do you no longer have it?"

"All I can tell you is that Wolfgang took charge of the book some years ago. Hans gave it to him, I suppose, because Wolfgang has such an interest in family history. What my brother did with it I can't say. You can ask him about it, though, if you're so inclined."

"I have found that your brother is rarely amenable to inquiries of any kind," Holmes said.

Eisen raised his hands in a gesture of futility. "I know, I know. He can be so difficult at times. If you wish, I could ask him if he still has the book."

"Please do," Holmes said.

Before Holmes left—Eisen intended to stay to discuss some "routine administrative matters" with Halbach—he asked about the state of the town's cooperative.

"I have heard rumors a big change is in the wind," he said, not mentioning that Halbach himself had been one source of such reports. "Is that true, Mr. Eisen?"

Eisen's affable manner gave way at once to the courteous but distant formality Holmes associated with bureaucrats of all stripes.

"I am afraid such matters must remain confidential for now, Mr. Holmes. There are some very delicate issues under discussion, and to speak of them at this point would be inappropriate. However, I have no reason to believe they pertain in any way to your investigations here. Would you concur, Freddy?"

Halbach nodded. Still, Holmes wondered whether the archivist honestly agreed with Eisen's assessment. Perhaps he did. Or perhaps he was abetting a cover-up. There was no sure way to tell. Even so, Holmes was beginning to suspect that the cooperative's fate might lie at the heart of the Eisendorf enigma.

• • •

A little before seven, Holmes walked over to the Eisen Block to meet Tommy Boyd. The cabman, as usual, arrived right on schedule.

Holmes, who had a distinct sense of being under surveillance, looked all around before going up to the taxi. Boyd rolled down his window as Holmes approached.

"How's it going, Mr. Holmes? I've got the stuff you wanted."

Boyd handed Holmes a paper bag imprinted with the name "Stewartville Hardware." Its contents consisted of a half-dozen lock-picking tools.

"You must be planning on breaking into something," Boyd said.

"I like to think of it as an unorthodox form of inquiry," Holmes replied.

"Well, I guess that's one way of putting it. Is there anything else I can do for you?"

"Yes. I want you to pick me up here at ten o'clock sharp tomorrow morning. Can you do that?"

"Sure thing."

"Excellent. I also want you to make another visit to the hardware store. I need two of the best torches you can find with fresh batteries."

Boyd looked puzzled. "Torches with batteries, I don't—"

"Flashlights, as you Americans call them. I will also need some other tools. A hammer, a crowbar, a pickax, a shovel, and a bolt cutter would be good." He handed Boyd a twenty-dollar gold piece. "That should cover everything."

"It'll be more than enough. Say, can you tell me where we're going tomorrow?"

"To a dark place," said Holmes, "with a bend in the middle of it."

15

———◄●●►———

The next morning Holmes walked over to the Eisen Block just before ten to wait for Tommy Boyd. He found Willy Eisen standing outside Halbach's store. She wore a red dress with an outsized white bow at the waist. Her tiara, tilted at a precarious angle, looked as though it was about to tumble off her head.

"Can I go with you to see Mr. Bones?" she asked.

"What makes you think I'm going to see him, Willy?"

"I just know. He lost his head."

"Mr. Bones did?"

The girl nodded. What a strange marvel she was, Holmes thought. How did she know he was about to explore the mill tunnel? Or was it a mere coincidence she'd met him in front of the store?

"I am sorry to hear about Mr. Bones," Holmes said. "Do you know where his head went?"

"It's a secret."

"I see. When did you find Mr. Bones?"

Willy began counting on her fingers but soon gave up. "I don't remember."

The girl, Holmes had come to understand, was unanchored from time, a ship drifting back and forth across endless waters. It could have been a week ago or a year ago that she'd found Mr. Bones. Regardless, Holmes wanted to verify there really was a skeleton, or parts of one, in the tunnel. The bones, if they existed, might well be proof of what Holmes had come to suspect was Eisendorf's original sin—an act of violence that had initiated the town's long descent into secrecy and darkness.

"Does your uncle Wolfgang ever talk about Mr. Bones?" Holmes asked.

Willy adjusted her tiara and said, "No, but he knows. He came to breakfast."

"At your house today?"

"He was mean to me. He said I'm stupid. He should die."

"You should not say such a thing about your own uncle, Willy."

"I don't care," she said before suddenly veering off in another direction. "Momma says you're bad. She told Georgie."

"You mean, Georg Dreisser?"

"They talk a lot. I listen when I'm invisible."

"What do they talk about?"

"Silly things. He kisses Momma."

"Ah, and does your Poppa know?"

"Poppa knows everything," she said. "I love Poppa. Oh, oh, here comes the taxi man."

Holmes looked up to see Tommy Boyd's Model T approaching.

"Are we going now?" Willy asked.

Boyd pulled up next to Holmes. "All set?"

"In a minute." Holmes looked sternly at Willy and said, "You must stay here. The tunnel could be dangerous. I would not want you to be hurt."

Halbach, wearing his shopkeeper's apron, emerged from the store. "Ah, there you are, Willy," he said. "I saw you out front and thought you'd be coming in for candy."

"Yes," she said, "I like candy. Good-bye, Mr. Sherlock. Be nice to Mr. Bones."

After Willy had gone into the store, Halbach said, "I trust you're not leaving us, Mr. Holmes. I would miss our daily meals."

"Do not worry," Holmes said as he slipped into the taxi's front seat. "Mr. Boyd and I are just going for a little ride in the country."

• • •

"Where to?" Boyd asked once they were under way.

"Back toward Stewartville."

Holmes was pleased to be on the road, paroled from the prison that was Eisendorf. From the moment of his arrival in town, he'd felt a cloud come over him, as though he were inhaling some invisible toxin, and it had affected his work. In 1892, in the span of only a few days, in a city of a third of a million people, Holmes had reached the Monster. Now he'd already spent a week in a town of forty people, and what did he have to show for himself? The Monster was right in front of him, malevolent and taunting, and yet Holmes had not yet managed to identify him.

Holmes began to wonder if the sharp edge of his deductive genius had grown dull from long retirement. Or had age and illness done their inevitable, erosive work? Was he simply not the detective he once had been? Had he become a weaker version of his old self? Holmes did not want to believe it, but neither had he wanted to believe his lungs were failing him.

It had been one thing to hunt down the Monster in Munich, when Holmes was in his prime, his mind a steely wonder, his energy never flagging, his courage undaunted. And, of course, there had been tobacco then. The sure stimulant of nicotine had always been a welcome ally, and he remembered many long nights of lucubration with his pipe, each bowlful igniting a fire of ideas in his head. Now, he was beginning to feel as though the fire were slowly going out, embers where there had once been vigorous flames.

How he wanted now to talk with Watson, who knew better than anyone else his black moods! Perhaps, Holmes thought, that was his real problem now. Perhaps he had fallen prey to a despondency born of frustration and doubt. Perhaps he was imagining his own decline. It had happened before. But once his state of mind improved—

Holmes suddenly became aware that Boyd was speaking to him. He roused himself from his unhappy thoughts. "Would you repeat that, Mr. Boyd?" he asked. "I fear I am having a little trouble hearing you."

"I was just wondering if you have any more directions for me, Mr. Holmes."

They had made the twisting climb out of Eisendorf and were back on top of the world, cruising due west beneath a starched blue sky across sunny uplands ripe with waving fields of wheat and corn. The sight of bright sunshine and open land lifted Holmes's spirits. It truly was invigorating to be out of Eisendorf.

Holmes said, "I do, Mr. Boyd, but first I want to make sure we have everything we need. Did you bring the flashlights?"

"Two of them, just like you said. Best ones I could find at the hardware store. Plus I've got shovels and all the other gear you asked for in the back."

"Excellent. Now, Mr. Boyd, how well do you know the roads in this vicinity?"

"Pretty well. Where do you want to go?"

"Do you know where the old Eisendorf mill dam is, on the west side of Table Rock?"

"Can't say that I've ever been there, but I'm guessing I could find it. The rock is hard to miss."

•••

They were barely a mile out of Eisendorf when they saw a sign for Olmsted County Road 2.

"Go south on that road," Holmes said.

Boyd slowed down and turned left. A half mile down the gravel road, a small farmhouse came into view. Just past it, the road jogged sharply to the west.

"Maybe we should ask the farmer for directions," Boyd said. "I'm not really sure where we are."

"Or perhaps we should try another road."

"OK, I'll look for a place to turn around," Boyd said just as Holmes spotted a narrow set of wheel ruts, more a path than a road, veering off toward the east.

"Stop for a moment, if you would," Holmes said. "That path up ahead intrigues me." Holmes knew that German Creek was somewhere to their east, circling past Table Rock. The path might lead them there.

"Let's see where it goes," he told Boyd.

"You're the boss," Boyd said. He put his taxi in gear and turned onto the path, which wound through a pasture, then began a steep descent after entering heavy woods. The Model T bumped along for several hundred yards before the path ended in a small clearing. Boyd braked to stop, and he and Holmes got out of the car. A long, ocher-colored cliff, its eroded face rising in a series of pinnacles and battlements, loomed up straight ahead. It was crowned by a dark band of trees.

"Table Rock, unless I am mistaken," Holmes said. "You are a most able navigator, Mr. Boyd."

"I do my best."

Holmes heard rushing water just beyond the clearing. "We'll have to reconnoiter," he said. "I would appreciate it, Mr. Boyd, if you could come along with me. We can go back for the equipment once we know we're in the right place."

"Oh, I wouldn't miss this for the world. You lead, and I'll follow."

A faint trail meandered away from the clearing, through a stand of towering cottonwoods, toward the water. Holmes and Boyd followed it. Before long they found German Creek, tumbling briskly through a field of boulders. The cliff forming the west face of Table Rock rose from its opposite side.

"What a pretty little spot," Boyd said.

"Quite charming," Holmes agreed, "but also very secluded."

They walked a hundred yards or so downstream into another small clearing. The air was cool and still, the sky still a startling autumnal blue. The world seemed at peace.

"Ah, here we are," Holmes said. "Behold, Mr. Boyd, the old Eisen Mill dam."

The dam's stone abutments rose from either side of the creek. They were surprisingly massive, at least fifteen feet high and nearly as wide. Holmes marveled at the work it must have taken, in so remote a place, to haul in all of the limestone, cut it, and lay it up block upon mighty block. Dionisius Eisen had indeed been quite a builder.

The dam itself was gone, swept away—as Halbach had told Holmes—by a flood some years earlier. Gone too was the millpond that had stored water behind the dam. The pond had once provided a steady source of water for Dionisius Eisen's ingenious tunnel, visible across the creek.

Holmes walked up to the near abutment, resting one hand on its rugged stonework as he took a good look at the boarded-up entrance to the tunnel, which was cut into the base of the cliff. The opening was about six feet square, easily big enough to accommodate visitors. Holmes noticed that the boards blocking the entrance were nailed together in haphazard fashion. They hardly looked to be a formidable barrier, and Holmes foresaw no trouble prying them apart with the help of the tools Boyd had brought along.

"Well, we have found the tunnel," Holmes said. "Are you up for a little exploring. Mr. Boyd?"

"Sure, I'm game, Mr. Holmes, but is it safe in there?"

"I have been told most of the tunnel is accessible. Naturally, we will have to watch ourselves."

"Do you mind telling me what we'll be looking for?"

"An old secret," Holmes said.

• • •

Holmes was about to send Boyd back for their equipment when he caught a glint of light atop Table Rock. A spray of pebbles began clattering down the cliff as a red-tailed hawk, on the hunt, came knifing down from the heavens. Holmes felt a deadly presence, like the sharp passage of a cold front.

The first bullet raced past Holmes's left ear with a supersonic buzz. "Get down," he shouted and dove for cover behind the abutment. Another shot rang out. The bullet crashed into the side of the abutment, sending out shards of stone and mortar.

Boyd scurried up and crouched next to Holmes. "God almighty, somebody's shooting at us."

"So I have noticed," Holmes said as he slid over to the edge of the abutment and poked out his head, just before a third bullet whistled by. Holmes was an able geometrician and in his retirement had written an interesting little monograph on how to calculate the trajectories of bullets. He did some calculating now, based on the shooter's likely perch on Table Rock.

He patted Boyd on the shoulder and said, "Just stay where you are. I believe geometry is in our favor."

"I hope you're right," Boyd said. "That sounds like a mighty big rifle up there."

Two more shots followed, both thumping into the ground well past the abutment.

"He cannot hit us from where he is," Holmes said, "but I have no doubt he will start looking for a better position." It was not in Holmes's nature to panic, but he had begun to breath heavily, and his lungs were starting to sting. He drew his Webley from his jacket pocket. It would be of little avail, he knew, in bringing down the hidden gunman. But the revolver might at least be useful in making a demonstration.

"We're trapped, aren't we?" Boyd said, desperation edging into his voice.

Holmes craned his neck to look around. The line of cottonwoods rose only ten yards behind them. If he and Boyd could reach the trees, they would quickly disappear from the shooter's view.

More pebbles began sliding down the cliff. As Holmes had predicted, the shooter was on the move.

"We're pinned down," Boyd said. "He's going to get us!"

"Yes, which means we cannot stay here," Holmes said. "We need better cover. Here is what we must do."

Boyd listened intently to Holmes's brief instructions. "All right," he said, "I guess it's do or die. Just say the word."

"You're going to be fine," Holmes said. "I am the prime target, not you. Remember what I said. Be quick and decisive, and don't stop moving until you're well into the trees."

Holmes edged around the abutment, and from a crouch, fired two quick rounds toward the top of the cliff. He then handed the revolver to Boyd and said, "Go!"

The cabman took off toward the trees. Keeping as low as he could, Boyd zigzagged like a darting bird, hoping a bullet wouldn't hunt him down. But there was no gunfire. Boyd raced into the grove of cottonwoods and got behind the biggest specimen he could find.

"I'm OK," he shouted to Holmes.

Holmes knew his dash to the shelter of the cottonwoods would be more perilous than Boyd's. The gunman cared nothing about a cab driver from Stewartville. Holmes was the target, and he was sure he would draw fire once he made a dash for the cottonwoods. The fact that he was older and slower than Boyd did not improve his chances.

After Boyd caught his breath, he peeked around the tree, scanning the clifftops across the creek. Then he saw it—the glint of a rifle barrel propped over the trunk of a fallen tree at the cliff's edge. Crouched behind the rifle was a man, his face hidden behind a black executioner's hood. The sight of the gunman, ready for the kill, sent an icy jolt down Boyd's spine. He had never been so afraid in his life.

But Boyd was determined to follow Holmes's instructions. He brought up the revolver and began firing in the general direction of the hooded figure. Out of the corner of his eye, Boyd saw Holmes coming toward him, stooped over but running with surprising speed. Rifle shots rang out, echoing across the valley. By the time Boyd had emptied the revolver, Holmes was almost in the trees. Bullets kicked up dust around him.

"Come with me!" Holmes shouted as he reached the line of cottonwoods.

Boyd, feeling a sudden surge of exhilaration, aware he was in the midst of the great adventure of his life, turned to follow Holmes deeper into the woods. Then, in an instant, everything changed. Tripped by a fallen branch, Holmes lost his balance and went down hard. There was a sharp cracking sound as he hit the ground.

Boyd rushed over and saw at once that Holmes was badly hurt. Blood was spreading like spilled ink across one of his trouser legs. Even more blood was gushing from a wound on the side of Holmes's head, which had struck a sharp-edged boulder when he fell.

"Mr. Holmes, are you all right? Can you hear me?" Boyd asked.

Holmes heard a voice, far away. Feeling vaguely confused, he managed to roll over onto his back. He opened his eyes and gazed up through an intricate tangle of cottonwood branches at the far blue sky. The world felt as if it were moving away. Or perhaps he was moving away from it, toward darkness. "I fear I have been shot," he said, before passing out.

• • •

When Magnus Swenson saw the two men at the door of his farmhouse, one carrying the other over his shoulder, he knew at once someone had been hurt.

"We need help," Tommy Boyd said. "My friend has been badly injured."

Swenson, a lumbering man with a droopy mustache and blond hair that tumbled down in long bangs over his forehead, nodded. "Ja, sure, you come right in. What has happened? Were you the ones I heard shooting?"

"We were being shot *at*," Boyd said emphatically. "Let's put him down on that sofa over there. We must get this man to a doctor as soon as possible. Do you know who he is?"

"It does not look like he is from around here," Swenson observed.

"This is Sherlock Holmes," Boyd said.

"That famous detective who has been over in Eisendorf? Well, I'll be."

Swenson's wife, a broad woman with round cheeks and jolly eyes, came into the room. "Oh, my," she said. "What has happened here?"

"A shooting, I guess," her husband said. "This fellow who got hurt, Mother, is Sherlock Holmes. He is a famous man. He came here all the way from New York."

"London," Boyd said as he and Swenson carefully set Holmes down on the sofa. Holmes, who was passing in and out of consciousness, let out a small cry of pain. Blood had caked on the left side of his head. There was more blood on the thigh of his right trouser leg. Holmes looked terrible, Boyd thought, but at least he was still breathing.

It had taken Boyd a half hour to get Holmes to the farmhouse, and he would later say that he was not sure how he had found the strength to do it. His first instinct, when he saw Holmes had been wounded, was to put Holmes over his shoulder and head back to his taxi a few hundred yards away. But he quickly realized that might be a fatal mistake. The gunman, who had already demonstrated some level of marksmanship, would have an easy shot at the taxi from his perch.

So Boyd had decided on a different plan. He wrapped a makeshift tourniquet around Holmes's leg wound, slung Holmes over his shoulder and started walking, as fast as he could, through the woods. He remembered the farmhouse they had seen earlier and determined he would try to reach it. He was nearly exhausted by the time he stumbled out of the woods and spotted the house. "Stay with me, Mr. Holmes, stay with me," he repeated time and again, but Holmes gave no response.

Now, as he looked down at Holmes, whose long body had sunk into the old sofa, Boyd knew there was no time to waste.

"Do you by any chance have an automobile?" he asked Swenson, whose wife was mopping Holmes's forehead with a damp cloth.

"Ja, just got it last year. I suppose you will be wanting to bring this famous fellow to a doctor."

• • •

Holmes finally regained consciousness as Boyd and Swenson were about to take him out to the farmer's elderly Model T.

"What is going on?" Holmes asked, staring up at the two men. "Who are you?"

Boyd said, "It's Tommy, Mr. Holmes, your cab driver, and this is Mr. Swenson, who's helping us. You've been hurt. We're going to take you to a doctor."

Holmes tried to focus his thoughts, but something was wrong. The bright, clear light that usually filled his mind had gone dim and cloudy. When he closed his eyes, powerful strokes of lightning flashed through the clouds, but he still couldn't find his thoughts.

"Where are we?" he asked, struggling to make sense of his surroundings. His mind was a flickering chaos awash in confusion and dread.

"It will be all right," Boyd assured him. "Can you stand up, Mr. Holmes? We must get you to the doctor."

Holmes tried to lift himself off the couch, but a wave of nausea and vertigo left him reeling. Darkness overtook him again.

• • •

Holmes dreamed of Munich. Or at least it seemed like a dream. He was in the English Gardens, by himself, at night. There was sign, under a street lamp, that said Liebergesellstrasse. A cab was parked nearby, its big black horse foaming with sweat. Holmes walked through a grove of trees until he came upon a rolled-up blanket in the grass. Something was in the blanket. Holmes began unrolling it. He expected to find a grotesquely mutilated body. Instead, he found a straw man. Pinned to its chest was a message: "Du Bist ein Dummkopf."

"A fool. I was a fool," Holmes murmured before he opened his eyes and winced in pain. He was no longer in Munich.

• • •

"It's all right, Mr. Holmes," Tommy Boyd said. "We're not too late. You're going to be OK."

They were in the back seat of Swenson's sputtering Model T, on their way to Stewartville. The ride was a strange agony for Holmes, who slipped in and out of consciousness. Even when he was awake, he felt asleep, the world a moving dream, his mind struggling to grip reality. It was as though he were trying to turn a greased doorknob, but his hand kept slipping, and the door simply wouldn't open. What was happening? Had he gone to a different place? He couldn't tell, and every time the Model T hit a bump, his head seemed to detonate.

"We're almost there," a voice said, and Holmes went back to sleep.

Boyd had tried the whole way to keep Holmes awake. But Holmes was not very responsive, and he couldn't maintain a conversation. The gravity of the situation was not lost on Boyd. He hoped he had done the right thing by carrying Holmes to Swenson's farm rather than trying to make a faster escape in his taxi. If Holmes did not pull through, Boyd knew he would be haunted by his decision for the rest of his life.

"Can you drive any faster?" Boyd asked Swenson.

"Ja, if you want me to go off the road and kill us all. I am going as fast as I can."

Boyd looked down at Holmes and said softly, "Just hang on. We won't let you die."

• • •

Dr. Daniel Swift, Stewartville's only physician, wasn't especially concerned about Holmes's leg wound. It was a through and through shot, near the outer edge of the thigh, little more than a graze. Most important, it had not come anywhere close to the femoral artery. Otherwise, Swift would probably be looking at a corpse.

The blow to Holmes's head was, the doctor knew at once, far more worrisome. There had almost certainly been a concussion, the brain banging against the skull like the clapper of a bell. Holmes—lying on the examination table in Swift's office—had now entered a state of delirium.

Swenson and Boyd had arrived with Holmes at Swift's office just before noon. The doctor, stunned to learn his patient's identity, set to work at once examining Holmes. Head injuries were always something of a guessing game. Swift had seen patients with apparently slight bumps to the head suffer grave consequences. A few had even died. Swift had also seen a young hunter, shot straight through the head with a .22 caliber rifle round, make a complete and startling recovery. How Holmes would fare the doctor couldn't say, but he knew that some of the best medical care in the world wasn't far away.

"What does it look like, Doc?" Boyd asked when Swift came out to the waiting room.

"It is hard to say. Mr. Holmes's vital signs are steady, but he clearly has suffered a tremendous blow to the head. That is never a good thing. The town ambulance is on its way, and I have already called Mayo to tell them we will bring him there as quickly as possible. We can only hope his condition doesn't deteriorate before we can get him to Rochester."

16

————⟨• • •⟩————

"**M**r. Holmes, can you hear me?"

Sherlock Holmes opened his eyes in response to the voice. He saw a man, dressed in a white coat, leaning over him. The man's face was long and narrow, his blue eyes peering out from behind owl-rim glasses. Who was this man? The face, like the voice, was familiar, but Holmes couldn't quite place it. Holmes tried to concentrate, to no avail. It was as though a gauzy sheet had been drawn across his mind.

"I hear you," Holmes said.

"Do you know where you are, Mr. Holmes?"

Holmes looked around. He was in a white room, staring up at a powerful light mounted to the ceiling. He heard other voices murmuring in the background.

"I am," he began, "I am . . ." His voice trailed off.

"You are in the hospital," Dr. Henry Plummer said. "You have been injured. There is a minor bullet wound to your leg that should heal up nicely. But you also received a strong blow to the head. Do you remember what happened?"

"Do I remember?" Holmes repeated. Yes, something had happened. But what? Holmes closed his eyes and tried to penetrate past the gauze, its diaphanous folds fluttering like a flag in the breeze. Sometimes he could see a little beyond. There were shapes, movements, shadows, tantalizing hints. But nothing came into focus.

Holmes was aware that his memory, always a powerful instrument capable of moving back through time with uncanny precision and clarity, did not seem to be working as it should. Instead, everything was jumbled and indistinct. He saw a glint of light, a high yellow wall, dark-green brushstrokes above it. He heard sharp cracking sounds. Then he was running. But where was he running, and why?

"What time is it?" Holmes asked. "Is it morning?"

"No, not yet," Plummer said. "It is just after three o'clock in the afternoon, and you are at St. Mary's Hospital in Rochester. Do you recall how you got here?"

Holmes tried to remember. He was in a big box of some kind, and he was being jostled. There was a whining sound, like a siren. A man was with him. Then he was out of the box, moving, on his back. A hallway. Harsh lights. Women in white. More voices.

"I am not sure," Holmes said. "Am I sick?"

"Yes, but we will make sure you get well. Now, why don't you rest for a while, Mr. Holmes. We will talk again later."

"Rest," Holmes said as he drifted off. "Yes."

• • •

Sheriff Osgood Thorkelson had planted himself like a wide-spreading oak in the biggest chair he could find in the hospital's main waiting room. He intended to stay put until he could talk to Holmes. That plan changed when Plummer came out to report on Holmes's condition.

"It's a concussion, and a serious one," Plummer said, not bothering with any preliminary pleasantries. "The good news is that there does not appear to be any swelling of the brain, although it still could occur."

"Will Mr. Holmes be all right?"

"I am optimistic that will be the case, but only time will tell. At present, however, Mr. Holmes remains in a confused and agitated state, as is to be expected after such an injury."

"So I won't be able to talk with him?"

"No, not for a while. His head may begin to clear by tomorrow, or it may take more time. There is no way to predict these things. Even when he does recover, he may have no memory of the events that brought him here. Speaking of which, Sheriff, what did happen today?"

Thorkelson, who had already talked with Tommy Boyd, gave Plummer a brief account of the events by the old mill dam. "I think Mr. Holmes is lucky to be alive. Somebody clearly was trying to kill him."

"Well, I am happy they did not succeed," Plummer said. "The death of Sherlock Holmes would be a great loss to the world."

Thorkelson nodded. "Yes, I could not imagine it. Well, thank you, Doctor. I will be back tomorrow to see how Mr. Holmes is doing. In the meantime, I am putting a deputy outside his door around the clock, just in case."

• • •

Thorkelson had learned of the shooting in a telephone call from Boyd. The cabman phoned from Dr. Swift's office in Stewartville. Boyd had wanted to go to Rochester with Holmes, but Thorkelson asked him to stay put. The sheriff then dispatched two deputies to Stewartville to take Boyd's statement and search for evidence at the scene of the shooting.

With Boyd leading the way, the deputies reached the site of the old dam by late afternoon. They soon found several bullets lodged in the ground behind the abutment where Holmes and Boyd had taken cover. Boyd felt a shudder as he thought back to the moment when shots had begun to ring out. It was a wonder he and Holmes hadn't been killed.

After a bit of reconnoitering, the deputies located a winding path up to the top of Table Rock. Boyd stayed by the abutment while the deputies climbed. He directed them by shouts and hand signals to the spot where he had seen the masked gunman. It didn't take long for the deputies to find shell casings of the type commonly used in a .44-40 caliber Winchester rifle. But the rocky ground yielded no shoe prints or any other evidence that might help identify the shooter.

That night, after reading the deputies' reports, Thorkelson felt a familiar sense of discouragement. The bullets and shell casings could be linked to a specific rifle, but finding the right weapon would not be easy. The Winchester was probably a Model 1892, a very common weapon used by hunters. There were undoubtedly hundreds of them in Olmsted County alone.

Aside from the ballistics evidence, Thorkelson had little to go on. The thickly wooded eastern slope of Table Rock overlooked Eisendorf, and the shooter could easily have climbed to the top without being detected. From there, it was only a short walk to the cliff at the rock's western edge. The old dam lay a hundred feet almost directly below. Thorkelson was very familiar with Winchester rifles, and he was surprised the shooter had missed Holmes at such short range. Maybe the Monster, for all of his lethal talents, wasn't much of a marksman.

Both the Eisen mill and the family's mansion stood in the shadow of the rock, as did Wolfgang Eisen's house. It would have been a simple matter for Wolfgang to sneak up to the top of the rock and attempt to assassinate Holmes. Trouble was, anyone else in Eisendorf could have done the same thing because of the thick woods that ringed the town. The woods provided ready cover, and a man with a long gun could easily have circled through the forest from almost anywhere in Eisendorf and reached Table Rock without being seen.

Thorkelson wanted to search Wolfgang's property to see if he could find a Winchester like the one used in the attack on Holmes. But he doubted he could obtain a search warrant. The good judges of Olmsted County were sticklers when it came to probable cause, and Thorkelson lacked compelling evidence Wolfgang was the shooter.

As he pondered the shooting, Thorkelson found himself wrestling with another problem. How, he wondered, had the Monster known when and where to stage his ambush? At first, Thorkelson thought Boyd might have inadvertently given away Holmes's plans. But the cabman insisted he didn't know their destination in advance when he picked up Holmes in Eisendorf. It was a puzzle. Holmes, of course, might have an explanation, but who knew when, or if, he might begin to remember the day's events?

• • •

Holmes was still in no condition to talk the next morning, so Thorkelson decided to go to Eisendorf. Holmes, he knew, had four suspects in town, and the sheriff intended to speak with each of them. He wanted to find out who did or did not have an alibi for the time of the shooting. He also wanted to know if any of the four would admit to owning a Winchester rifle.

Thorkelson's first interview was with Frederick Halbach. The sheriff found him at the archives, laboring over his the latest additions to the Annals of Eisendorf.

"I trust Mr. Holmes is doing well," Halbach said when he sat down with Thorkelson. They were seated at the same table where Halbach and Peter Eisen had talked with Holmes two days earlier. Georg Dreisser had also made an appearance then. When Halbach remarked upon this circumstance and mentioned that Holmes had been examining a drawing of the mill tunnel, Thorkelson was intrigued.

"So, the three of you must have known Mr. Holmes was going out to look at the tunnel," he said.

Halbach's response was, as usual, a model of circumspection. "I did not know that to be the case, Sheriff. I assumed Mr. Holmes might want to have a look at the tunnel at some point, but he did not reveal any specific plans to me. As for what Peter and Georg might have known about his intentions, I cannot say. It would be best to ask them."

"Did you see Mr. Holmes yesterday before he went out to the tunnel?"

"I spoke to him very briefly when Mr. Boyd picked him up outside my store. But all he said was that they were going for a ride in the country."

"With picks and shovels and flashlights in the back of the taxi. Not your usual ride in the country, I would say. And yet you claim you had no idea as to their destination. Seems strange to me."

"I did not notice the equipment, Sheriff, so there was nothing to arouse my suspicions. I took Mr. Holmes at his word."

"Of course you did. What time did you speak with Mr. Holmes?"

"Ten o'clock or thereabouts."

"And where were you for the next two hours, Mr. Halbach?"

"I was at my store."

"Did you have many customers during that time?"

"Just Willy Eisen, but she left not long after Mr. Holmes did. I closed the store at noon, on the dot, and went home."

"But no one other than Willy actually saw you in the store?"

"No. However, I assure you, Sheriff, I am not the person who tried to kill Mr. Holmes, if that is what you are thinking."

Thorkelson made some quick calculations. Boyd had reported he and Holmes reached the site of the tunnel at about half past ten, thirty or so minutes after leaving Eisendorf. Would that have been enough time for Halbach to grab a rifle, circle up to the top of Table Rock, and try to assassinate Holmes? Maybe, the sheriff thought, but it would have been tight.

"Do you own a rifle, Mr. Halbach?"

"I have a twenty-two at the house."

"Anything of larger caliber?"

"No."

"Would you object to a search of your house and store?"

"As a matter of fact, I would. The idea of strangers pawing through my personal property does not appeal to me. You will need a search warrant if you wish to disrupt my life in that way."

"Nothing in this town is every easy, is it?" Thorkelson said. "All right, Mr. Halbach, we'll see about a warrant. I expect we'll speak again."

"I look forward to it," Halbach said.

• • •

Thorkelson's next stop was at Wolfgang Eisen's house. He found Wolfgang in the yard, taking target practice with a pistol. A direct hit shattered one of the yard's many stray liquor bottles as Thorkelson pulled up and got out of his sedan.

Eisen gave the sheriff a cold stare before putting his pistol—a small automatic—in his back pocket. "What do you want?" he asked. "Are you here to accuse me of something as you always do?"

"No need to be defensive," Thorkelson said. "I just have a few questions about what happened yesterday."

"You mean the shooting, I suppose. I know nothing about it."

"Perhaps we can go inside and talk," Thorkelson suggested.

"We can talk here. I don't need you nosing about in my house."

The conversation went downhill from there as Eisen complained of being "persecuted." He answered questions grudgingly. He said he was home by himself at the time of the shooting and for most of the rest of that day. He did admit to hearing gunfire but assumed it was hunters.

"I have to wonder what someone with a high-powered rifle would be hunting at this time of year," Thorkelson noted.

"You'd have to ask them."

"Do you own a rifle, Mr. Eisen?"

"I don't see where that's any business of yours. Everyone around here has guns. So what?"

"Just asking, Mr. Eisen. But I do need to know if you own a Winchester rifle."

"No," he said. "Anything else?"

"Did you have any visitors here yesterday?'

"I don't get visitors. People know better than to bother me."

"I imagine they do."

The conversation was going nowhere, and both men knew it. Eisen was rough and crude, but he was also canny. He had no alibi for the time of the shooting, but he was smart enough to realize he didn't need one. Spending time alone at his miserable little house was what he did every day. Unless someone came forward to testify Eisen was lying as to his whereabouts, there was nothing to put him at the scene of the shooting. Thorkelson held out little hope of finding such a witness in Eisendorf, where, as he'd once remarked to Holmes, "the ostrich is the municipal bird."

"Well, I can see there's no sense in going on with this," the sheriff said.

"No sense at all," Eisen said. "Don't take your time leaving."

• • •

Thorkelson's interview with Peter Eisen at his mansion proved to be friendlier but equally unsatisfactory. He'd hoped to find Maria and Willy there as well, but both were gone. Maria, Peter explained, was off on a shopping spree in St. Paul. As for what Willy was up to, he had no idea. "She just roams," he explained.

"I have a few questions regarding the incident with Mr. Holmes," Thorkelson began. "Can you tell me where you were yesterday morning from about nine o'clock until noon?"

"Ah, so once again I am a suspect. Well, I can tell you I was right here, as was Maria. She can vouch for me. She'll back this evening if you wish to speak with her."

"I will," Thorkelson said, but he had no doubt Maria would confirm her husband's alibi, and she his. The sheriff had never figured out what the two of them saw in each other, but they always seemed to stick together. "By the way, was Willy with you?"

"I don't think so. As I said—"

"She roams. Now, did either you or your wife hear any gunfire yesterday morning?"

"Yes, but that's not uncommon. I thought it was a hunter or possibly someone taking target practice."

"Do you own a rifle, Mr. Eisen?"

"An old .22. Would you like to see it?"

"Perhaps. Would you mind if I had a look around the house?"

"As a matter of fact, I would. Privacy is highly valued in Eisendorf, and I am no exception in that regard. But if you return with a search warrant, I will of course cooperate fully."

"Of course. So you have no rifle bigger than your .22?"

"Correct. I'm not a hunter. Wolfgang handles the chores in that department."

"I see. Do you know if he owns a large-caliber rifle such as a Winchester?"

"He might. He likes his guns. But I don't really pay much attention to that sort of thing."

Thorkelson then quizzed Eisen about the mill tunnel. Clearly, Holmes had expected to find something in the old tunnel. If Willy's story about "Mr. Bones" was to be believed, Holmes must have been looking for a skeleton. Eisen, however, thought that was a ridiculous idea.

"It's another of Willy's fantasies, I'm sure," he said. "There really is nothing to see in the tunnel."

"When was the last time you were in it?"

Eisen let out a long breath. "Goodness, it's been years and years. I know Wolfgang went in there fairly regularly when the mill was operating. Sometimes debris would cause a backup in the channel, and he'd have to clean things out."

"Would you have any objections if I sent in a couple of my deputies to have a look?"

"Probably not, but let me check with my attorney. To be blunt, Sheriff, it's a liability issue. A small section of the tunnel gave way earlier this year, and I'm not sure I want anybody nosing around in there. If Mr. Holmes had told me about his plans, I would have tried to discourage him. It's just not safe."

"Didn't you have a chance to warn him when he was at the archives looking at that drawing of the tunnel?"

"I did," Eisen admitted, "and I just wasn't thinking. I'm afraid I didn't really put two and two together. I thought Mr. Holmes was just curious about the tunnel. But it didn't occur to me that he intended to go in there. I couldn't see any reason why he'd want to."

"And yet someone went to the trouble of trying to kill Mr. Holmes, presumably because he intended to go into the tunnel."

"But do we really know that, Sheriff? If you ask me, the tunnel probably had nothing to do with the whole business. Whoever tried to kill Mr. Holmes simply saw a good opportunity to attack him, in a remote place well outside town, and so they did. Still, it's a frightening thing to think about. I certainly hope Mr. Holmes will be all right."

"As do I," said Thorkelson.

• • •

Thorkelson made his final stop of the day at Georg Dreisser's house. Dreisser, formally dressed as always, plied the sheriff with tea and platitudes but offered nothing in the way of useful information. He denied knowing of Holmes's plan to inspect the tunnel. He also said he owned no firearms, finding them to be "too dangerous and noisy for any civilized man." And like everyone else the sheriff had interviewed that day, he would not consent to a search of his property without a warrant. Just to make Thorkelson's life more difficult, Dreisser reminded him that since his house was owned by the cooperative, it would have to sign off on a search as well.

Dreisser, who was cordial in all of his responses, claimed to have been at home when the shooting occurred. His mother was away, however, and there was no one to support, or disprove, his alibi. It was plain to Thorkelson he had arrived at another dead end.

Even so, the sheriff did make one interesting discovery. Dreisser's house was at the west edge of town not far from the wooded slope of Table Rock. Like the Eisens, he would have had an easy time reaching the rock's summit from his house. But had he actually done so? Thorkelson had no way of knowing.

• • •

A reporter from the Rochester *Bulletin* with a source at the Mayo Clinic learned of Holmes's arrival at the hospital, and the story went out on the national wires an hour later. Although Holmes had largely kept out of the limelight since his retirement, his name remained known throughout the world. The news he was seriously injured quickly made its way across the Atlantic, where one of the more sensational London dailies offered the headline: "Famed Detective near Death."

It was the sort of headline Dr. John Watson would have seen almost immediately, had he been in London. But he wasn't. He had gone to the Scottish moors to hunt red grouse, and the remote lodge where he was staying did not provide its guests with newspapers or a telephone. The hunting, however, was excellent.

• • •

"Ah, I am thinking you would be the sheriff," said a big man who hobbled up to Thorkelson in the waiting room at St. Mary's early in the evening. "'Twould be a fine thing if you could tell me how Mr. Holmes is doing."

The man looked to be well into his seventies and walked with the aid of a cane. He was tall and heavy, with a wild white beard, a broad Irish face marked by a scar over the left eye, and the kind of voice that seemed to invite instant friendship. His attire included a gaudy red jacket that might once have done service in a marching band.

"I do not believe we have met," Thorkelson said.

"Shadwell Rafferty," the man said with a slight bow. "Mr. Holmes and I go back a ways, I suppose you could say, and it is awfully disturbing to hear he's been hurt."

The name sounded familiar, but it took Thorkelson a few moments to place it. Then he had it. Rafferty was the detective from St. Paul who had worked with Holmes and Watson on a series of cases in Minnesota. In fact, there'd been one only a few years earlier—a strange, locked-room mystery on the top floor of a skyscraper. Thorkelson had read about it in the newspapers, which depicted Rafferty as a brilliant fellow, but he didn't look all that brilliant at the moment.

Thorkelson stood up to shake his visitor's hand. "A pleasure, Mr. Rafferty. You are the fellow who owned the saloon up in St. Paul, are you not?"

"Yes, and Prohibition has now done its dirty, destructive work. I suppose do-gooders have their place, but trying to reform humanity is, in my opinion, a task best left to the angels, who have eternity to accomplish it. As it is, we now have a country where a man cannot get an honest drink. God save us all! But I digress. It is Mr. Holmes who concerns me. I saw the story in the *Pioneer Press* this morning and came right down, only to discover the nurses in this fine institution seem to think they are in possession of a state secret when it comes to Mr. Holmes's condition. They will tell me nothing. I am hoping, Sheriff, that you can illuminate me."

"Well, I wish I had good news for you," Thorkelson said, "but I do not. The doctors tell me Mr. Holmes is still struggling. His concussion was a very serious one."

"And has it affected that magnificent brain of his?"

"That is what worries the doctors most. He is not coming around the way they had hoped."

• • •

Katherine Krupp also stopped by the hospital that evening. The news that Holmes had been seriously injured left her feeling sick and anxious. If only he had left Eisendorf with her! Yet she knew it was not in Holmes's nature to flee from danger. Now, she could only pray his stout, stubborn courage would not cost him his life. The nurses wouldn't let her in to see Holmes— she wasn't on the "approved" list of visitors—but she came to the hospital every day anyway. It was the least she could do.

• • •

As a boy in Yorkshire, Holmes had sometimes gone swimming in a small pond near the family home. It was a shallow pond, and Holmes amused himself by diving to the mucky bottom in search of discarded objects. Even at a depth of only three or four feet, the water was so murky nothing could be seen, and so Holmes had been forced to proceed entirely by feel, dredging with his fingers. He had found old bottles, the rusted barrel of a shotgun, biscuit tins, and even the occasional article of clothing left behind by swimmers.

Lying in his hospital bed, his head a gigantic nail being pounded by an even larger hammer, Holmes began to dredge again, only now he was searching for memories at the bottom of his mind. The muck was thick and persistent, but as time wore on, nurses coming and going, doctors shining bright lights in his eyes, words passing back and forth like distant echoes, Holmes slowly started retrieving what had seemed lost. It was hard, frustrating work, and there was no moment of grand revelation, no sudden burst of clarity.

Instead, the way back began with images pulled at random from the murk. An automobile, going uphill on a winding road. Holmes in the front seat. Who was the driver? There was a name, but Holmes couldn't remember it. A boy? No, not a boy. Something else.

A loud noise like the crack of a whip. Plumes of dirt exploding from the ground. Where was he? What was happening? Bullets! Someone was shooting. Running now across rocky ground. More cracks of the whip. Falling.

"Open wide, Mr. Holmes."

Holmes looked up. A woman in white stood over him, a thermometer in her hand.

"What?" he asked.

"Time to take your temperature. Mr. Holmes."

"Yes," he said, and felt the little glass tube slide into his mouth before he fell asleep.

• • •

Dr. Henry Plummer studied Holmes's chart. The first twenty-four hours after his injury had gone well enough. Holmes was drowsy and confused—common symptoms after a concussion. But now, four days later, he had a fever of 101, not a good sign. Could Holmes have an infection, perhaps as a result of his bullet wound? Or was something else going on, possibly swelling of the brain, or worse? Plummer wasn't certain. But he was beginning to worry. The longer Holmes remained in his current condition, the less likely he was to make a full recovery.

Before he left the hospital, Plummer placed a telephone call to the Western Union office in Rochester. "I wish to send a message to London, England," he told the operator, adding, "It is most urgent."

From the Journals of Dr. John Watson

———◄•••►———

17

—◄●●●►—

In my long association with Sherlock Holmes, two events stand out as the happiest of all occasions. The first occurred on a spring day in London, in 1894, when my friend—thought to be lost forever after his plunge over Reichenbach Falls with Professor Moriarty—reappeared so suddenly that for one astonishing moment I was prepared to believe he had literally come back from the dead. The second return of Holmes, as it were, took place on a late September afternoon in 1920, at a hospital in Minnesota. After a journey of eight days from London, every second of it fraught with agonizing worry, I was ushered into Holmes's room, having been told to prepare for the worst, only to see him sit up in bed, smile, and say in a firm and welcoming voice, "My dear Watson, how good to see you!"

I had undertaken my journey after receiving a telegram from Dr. Henry Plummer, a physician at the Mayo Clinic. It arrived on September 20, only hours after I had returned to London from a hunting trip in Scotland. From this message I learned Holmes had sustained a serious head injury after an attempt was made on his life and that his prognosis was poor. Feverish and drowsy, he seemed unable to remember any details of the events leading up to his injury, while his acute intellect had been rendered dull and torpid. Seeing the face of an old friend, Plummer thought, might help Holmes come out of the fog into which he had fallen.

My response was immediate. Despite the protestations of my dear wife, who thought I could scarcely afford to leave my medical practice on such short notice, I booked passage at once on the *Olympic*, which by a fortuitous circumstance was poised to sail from Southampton to New York the next day. While on board, I remained in touch with Plummer via telegraphic messages, learning that Holmes continued to languish in a dreamlike state. After a twenty-four-hour train trip from New York, I finally reached Rochester, a city with which I was very familiar, on September 29, and went immediately to see Plummer at St. Mary's Hospital.

I had first met Plummer, as well as Drs. Charles and William Mayo, when I underwent surgery at the Mayo Clinic in 1904. Holmes had accompanied me on that difficult trip, during which I was often in great pain, and had kept a long vigil at my bedside. My failure to do the same for Holmes on his trip to Rochester to be treated for his own medical problems is a decision I shall always regret. Had I been with Holmes, he might well have avoided his terrible injury.

At the hospital, I fully expected to hear bad news regarding Holmes's condition. Instead, Plummer greeted me with a look of profound relief. "I cannot explain it," he said, "but this morning Mr. Holmes was a changed man. It was as though a strong wind suddenly dissipated the fog inside his head. His fever is also gone, and he is very eager to return to his investigations. There is one more thing you should know. Mr. Holmes informed me he has not used tobacco in three weeks and that it is his intention never to smoke again. It will do wonders for his health."

"That is excellent news," I said, "though I am quite amazed he was able to stop. By the way, does he know I am here?"

"No," Plummer said. "I thought it would be a nice surprise for him."

And so it was when I walked into his room, where I found him shaving off the last of his beard. He was indeed surprised to see me, but what struck me at once was the deep affection evident in his voice as he came over to greet me. The conversation that followed was one of the most remarkable I ever had with Holmes.

"It is quite extraordinary what goes through one's mind when one is in the grip of a long delirium," he said. "Time becomes elastic, Watson. Distances vanish. Memories mix and collide, and there are strange perceptions. And now, for reasons that I do not pretend to understand, I feel as though I have emerged from a kind of deep sleep, a deadness of the spirit, that lasted for years."

"What do mean?" I asked, for I had never heard Holmes—a man usually given to the most concrete and logical utterances—speak with such intensity about his own emotions.

"Do you know why I retired so many years ago, my dear Watson? It was because I had grown weary of the world of men. Indeed, there were many days when I found myself at the black bottom of a pit, struggling to see the light of the sun. And so I went off to the Sussex Downs to lead a solitary life. Only my bees and my research sustained me. I became an exile from humanity."

"My God, Holmes, I had no idea you had a fallen into such a state."

"Nor did anyone else. It is the nature of despondency to keep its own counsel."

"And yet what of the work you did for the government during the Great War? You undertook the most difficult assignments and carried them out with the utmost skill and daring."

"Yes, because England called, and I knew I must do my duty. But I took no satisfaction from it. Indeed, the war and its vast bloodletting served only to further depress my spirits. Then came my breathing problems and the diagnosis here in Rochester. Hope seemed lost. I should have gone back to England, a hollow man, had it not been for a note slipped under the door of my hotel room."

Holmes then briefly described how he had been drawn to the tiny town of Eisendorf in search of the Monster of Munich.

"I became a detective again, and for a time my spirits rose. But the town, with all of its secrecy and strangeness, exacted a toll on me. It was as though I was ingesting a slow poison. Weariness and doubt became my companions, and I wondered if I was up to the task of hunting down the Monster. And then—"

"You took a bad knock to the head."

"Yes, and after lo these many days of delirium, I now find—quite to my astonishment—that I have become a new man. I have climbed out of the pit. How it happened I shall never know. But it has happened, and that is the important thing. I am ready to bring the Monster to justice, and you, Watson, shall be with me the rest of the way."

• • •

"Well now, here are a couple of schemers if I ever saw 'em," said the man whose voice I would have recognized anywhere. I turned around to see Shadwell Rafferty, as outsized as ever, standing in the doorway.

"My God," I said, rushing up to shake his hand. "How wonderful to see you, Mr. Rafferty!"

"And likewise," he said, squeezing my hand with his powerful grip. "Why, it is like old times, or perhaps I should say very old times, for the three of us are not getting any younger."

"Speak for yourself. I am feeling younger than I have in many years," said Holmes, who rose from the rocking chair where he had been seated next to me. He went over and submitted himself to the usual mauling by Rafferty, who was fond of bear hugs.

"Ah, then you are ahead of the game, Mr. Holmes," said Rafferty. "As for me, I've gotten fatter, slower, and altogether untidier since we last met, but as Wash likes to say, if a man is still sucking air, he has no cause to complain."

"And how is your partner?" I asked Rafferty, who had for years operated a popular saloon in St. Paul with George Washington Thomas.

"Wash is a wonder. He is past seventy, now, but he is still chasing the ladies as fast as his old legs will carry him."

"Dr. Watson has been known to do a little chasing as well," Holmes said, "although he is once again a proper married man."

"Really, Holmes, I have never 'chased' women," I protested.

"Well, no matter how enthusiastically you may have pursued the fair sex, Dr. Watson, congratulations are in order," said Rafferty, who produced a flask from somewhere inside his large red suitcoat. "Would anyone care to do something illegal?"

"Most certainly," said Holmes. We found three glasses and enjoyed a taste of the excellent brandy in Rafferty's flask.

"I managed to preserve a few treasures when we closed the saloon," he said. "Say what you will about the French, they know their brandy, God bless 'em. Well, now that we have all enjoyed a decent libation, perhaps you can tell us, Mr. Holmes, about your run-in with that fellow you call the Monster down in Eisendorf."

And so he did, recounting in precise detail all that had transpired since his arrival in Minnesota. He also told us about his first encounter with the Monster in Munich.

When Holmes had finished his tale, Rafferty and I agreed it was most remarkable. "So, if I have followed you correctly, you have four prime suspects in the matter, and the task now is to figure out which one is the Monster," Rafferty said. "Or do you already know?"

"I have an idea," said Holmes, "but I will need to learn more before I can be certain."

• • •

Although Holmes was desperate to leave the hospital, Dr. Plummer insisted that he stay one more night to make sure he suffered no relapse. I concurred with that opinion. So it was that Rafferty and I ate dinner with him in his room, after which Holmes was permitted to take some exercise by walking the hospital's long corridors.

We had hardly left his room when a most remarkable scene occurred. A woman sitting in one of the waiting rooms fairly leapt to her feet when she saw us come around the corner.

"Mr. Holmes," she said. "How happy I am to see you are recovering at last!"

Holmes went to her at once and kissed her on the cheek. Both Rafferty and I were quite surprised by this gesture, as Holmes was usually very formal in his relations with the fair sex.

The woman was in her late middle age, tall and well built, with strong but elegant features, a fine head of dark hair, and intense blue eyes. I found her quite infatuating. Clearly, Holmes did as well.

"I must introduce you to Mrs. Katherine Krupp," he said, bringing her over to us. "She is the one person in Eisendorf in whom I could place my complete trust, and she has been of great help to me."

After all the usual niceties were completed, Holmes said he wished to speak to Mrs. Krupp in private. Rafferty and I then retired to Holmes's room, where we reminisced about our many adventures together. A half hour later, Holmes rejoined us.

"Mrs. Krupp has informed me of a most intriguing development in Eisendorf," he said. "It explains many things, and I think I may finally be in a position to unravel the Eisendorf enigma."

"And what is this 'development?'" I asked.

"You will learn soon enough, my dear Watson. In the meantime, we all have much work to do."

Rafferty gave Holmes a shrewd glance and said, "Spoken like the Sherlock Holmes of old! You will keep us in the dark as long as you can. But I do have one question. Am I right in thinking it was not entirely a matter of business between you and the lady?"

Holmes smiled as broadly as I had ever seen him smile. "I would never be foolish enough," he said, "to question the wisdom of Shadwell Rafferty."

Later that evening, Plummer stopped by, and I spoke with him for a time while Rafferty huddled with Holmes in his room to discuss the case. When Rafferty emerged from their meeting, he grinned and said, "I have my marching orders, Doctor. You will be pleased to know the game is afoot."

• • •

Holmes was released from the hospital the next morning on Plummer's orders. We immediately booked a suite at the nearby Zumbro Hotel, then met with Rafferty for breakfast in the dining room.

Over hotcakes, sausages, and eggs, Holmes discussed his theory of the case at some length, and it became clear to me that one man in Eisendorf had emerged as his prime suspect. "However, certain knotty questions remain, and that is why I have asked Mr. Rafferty to undertake a mission for me in St. Paul. I am hoping what he finds will serve to confirm my ideas."

"It won't take long," Rafferty said. "There is no footprint a man can leave in St. Paul that I cannot trace. Wash and I will find out what you need to know, Mr. Holmes."

"Splendid," said Holmes. "I will make arrangements with Sheriff Thorkelson so that you can stay in touch with him by telephone or telegraph. He will pass on any information you and Mr. Thomas have garnered."

"So you will be in Eisendorf?"

"Yes, Watson and I will go there tomorrow, and my intention is to stir things up. The Monster needs to know we are closing in. Faced with this prospect, he will become doubly dangerous. But I believe it will also force his hand."

"Then I suppose you know what my advice will be, Mr. Holmes."

"I do. We shall be careful, but we cannot avoid certain risks. We must allow the Monster to think he still has the upper hand. There will be another attempt on my life, I assure you. But this time, I shall have Watson with me."

• • •

Late that morning, we went to see Sheriff Osgood Thorkelson at his office. Despite his more than ample girth, Thorkelson was, as Holmes put it to me, "surprisingly light on his feet, and with a far better mind than one is accustomed to find among the rural constabulary." It also became clear to me that Holmes was fond of the sheriff, who had been a confidant during his trying time in Eisendorf.

"Mr. Holmes, I can't tell you how good it is to see you up and about," Thorkelson said after we were ushered into his office. "You had me very worried for a while. And now you have Dr. Watson with you as well."

"Yes, and I am determined to bring this business to an end. Perhaps, Sheriff, you could begin by informing us of any significant developments that have occurred since I suffered my injury."

"There are two, Mr. Holmes, beginning with this," Thorkelson said, handing a telegram to Holmes. "It just came in a few hours ago from Musser, that policeman friend of yours in Germany. Have a look."

I peered over Holmes's shoulder as he scanned the message, which read: "PAUL GEIST ILLEGITIMATE STOP MOTHER KATRINA GEIST BORN MUNICH 1841 STOP FATHER LISTED AS DIONISIUS EISEN BORN MUNICH 1827 STOP LOOKING FOR PHOTO STOP WILL SEND IF FIND MUSSER."

Thorkelson said, "You'll have to refresh my memory a bit, Mr. Holmes. Paul Geist was the fellow you were chasing in Munich back in 1892, correct?"

"Yes. He was the accountant suspected of stealing a great of money. But he was also a cab driver and the man I followed into the English Gardens. He was, in other words, the Monster of Munich."

"And now this Musser fellow in Germany is saying Dionisius Eisen was Geist's father. Well, that puts an interesting slant on things, doesn't it."

Holmes nodded. "Indeed it does, and we may be certain Paul Geist, using a different name, is now in Eisendorf."

"Do you know who he is?"

"I have a strong suspect," Holmes said, revealing the name to Thorkelson. The sheriff looked stunned.

"Are you absolutely certain, Mr. Holmes?"

"No, I cannot yet prove beyond all question he is the Monster. However, if Mr. Musser is able to find a photograph, all doubt will be removed. Now, Sheriff, what is your other news?"

"See for yourself," Thorkelson said. He showed Holmes a copy of the Rochester *Bulletin* dated four days earlier. "You'll find the story quite interesting, I'm sure."

Holmes perused the story with his usual alacrity, then gave it to me. It read as follows:

"The fifty or so remaining residents of the village of Eisendorf in south Olmsted County will vote on Oct. 1 whether to dissolve the cooperative arrangement upon which the town was founded 65 years ago. Under the terms of the proposed dissolution, the community's assets would be distributed on an equitable basis to its members. The assets include the village itself as well as some 5,000 acres of surrounding farmland and forest.

"Frederick Halbach, the town's administrator, said the cooperative is 'no longer viable' because of the town's dwindling population and the closing of its two main businesses—Eisen's Tunnel Mill and the Krupp Brewery. 'The unfortunate fact of the matter is that Eisendorf is dying,' Mr. Halbach stated, 'and we must deal with this reality.'

"Mr. Halbach added he believes the vote in favor of dissolution will be 'nearly unanimous. It is really the only choice we have.'

"The town has frequently been in the news of late because of a recent series of violent events. Last week, just outside Eisendorf, the famed detective Sherlock Holmes was shot and wounded by an unknown assailant. He has been hospitalized in Rochester since then.

"Holmes was investigating the murder on Sept. 11 of one of the town's residents, Josef Krupp. It is believed he was also looking into two other suspicious deaths that occurred in Eisendorf this year.

"However, Mr. Halbach said these incidents bear no relation to the impending vote on the cooperative. 'Our community leaders have been looking at the condition of the cooperative for several years now,' he said, 'and we simply decided that the time had come to act.'"

"Now you know what Mrs. Krupp told me," Holmes said. "I do not think it a coincidence the vote was set for a time when it was assumed I would still be incapacitated. There is something very suspicious, I assure you, about the plan to dissolve the cooperative. It is in all likelihood a motive for murder."

"How so?" the sheriff asked.

"I have a rather peculiar idea in that regard. Do you recall, Sheriff, who discovered Bernhard Krupp's body in the Eisendorf forest?"

"Yes, it was a timber cruiser. I think he was working for a lumber company over in Winona."

"His name, I presume, is in your reports."

"Sure. Why do you ask?"

"I should like you to contact him," Holmes said. He began jotting down something on a notepad atop the sheriff's desk. When he was finished, he handed the note to me. I read it with a mixture of wonder and surprise, then passed it on to Thorkelson.

"I have written down several questions I would like you to put to the cruiser," Holmes told the sheriff. "Please let me know as soon as you have the answers."

Thorkelson read the questions and let out a low whistle. "Well, Mr. Holmes, I'm not quite sure where you're going with this, but I will get you the answers as quickly as I can. Anything else I can be of help with?"

"Not at the moment. Dr. Watson and I will attend to the next matter of interest ourselves. We need to talk to a lawyer."

• • •

Walter Schmidt was a tall, portly man of about fifty, with a jowly face, shrewd gray eyes, and a manner of speaking that suggested the most studied consideration lay behind his every word. He was, in short, very much like the solicitors of my acquaintance in London. Holmes and I paid a call on him after lunch, at his office just a block away from our hotel.

"It is a great privilege to meet you, Mr. Holmes, and you as well, Dr. Watson," he said as we took seats across from his desk. His wood-paneled office, well-stocked with law books, was ample but not grand. "To what do I owe the pleasure of your visit?"

In years past, Holmes might have performed various feats of deduction to impress the lawyer, but he did not do so now. Instead, he went directly to the point. "It concerns Eisendorf," he said. "I understand you represent the cooperative there."

Schmidt gave a judicious nod. "I do. Is there a particular matter of interest to you?"

"There is, Mr. Schmidt. As you know, a vote will be held tomorrow regarding the fate of the cooperative. My question for you is very simple: Who will stand to gain the most if the cooperative is dissolved?"

"I fear I am not at liberty to discuss the affairs of the cooperative, Mr. Holmes. It is a matter of client confidentiality. I am sure you understand."

"Your discretion is commendable, Mr. Schmidt. Were you equally reticent with Bernhard Krupp? You talked to him earlier this year, did you not, about the state of the cooperative?"

"I may have," Schmidt said.

"Come now, you must remember. Two days after your meeting with him, he died under highly questionable circumstances. I do not believe his death was a coincidence. He learned something from you, and it cost him his life."

Schmidt, a sudden chill in his eyes, stared at Holmes and said, "I have no knowledge about what may or may not have led to Mr. Krupp's death. As to the subject of my conversation with him, I will state only that he raised certain concerns with me regarding the cooperative. Beyond that, I can say nothing.

The questions you are asking, Mr. Holmes, would be better put to the cooperative's governing board. I represent them, but I cannot speak for them."

"Ah, and who are the members of the board? Or is that, too, a state secret?"

"It is not a secret. The board has three members: Peter Eisen, Wolfgang Eisen, and Frederick Halbach. Perhaps you met them during your stay in Eisendorf. Any of them could speak to you about the vote tomorrow and the reasons for it, if they so choose."

"Yes, and I suspect they will choose not to, just as you have, Mr. Schmidt."

"I am bound to honor my clients' wishes," Schmidt said, rising from his chair. "Now, if you will excuse me, I must be in court soon. As I said, it was a great honor to meet both of you."

As we were being shown the door, Schmidt paused and said, "By the way, have you had a chance to visit the archives in Eisendorf, Mr. Holmes? It's a veritable treasure trove of fascinating historical documents. One you might find to be of particular interest is called the '1870 Amendment to the Cooperative Agreement.' Of course, you didn't hear this from me. Good day, gentlemen."

After the lawyer had left, I said, "Mr. Schmidt, I gather, dropped a little hint for us."

"Indeed he did," said Holmes. "Yet I somehow doubt Mr. Halbach will be eager to show us the document in question, in which case we shall have to consider other options."

"Such as?"

Holmes smiled and said, "I have always found, my dear Watson, that locks are far less complicated than people."

• • •

"The most mysterious feature of the Eisendorf enigma is time," said Holmes at dinner that evening. The Zumbro Hotel's dining room was not crowded, the food was passable, and Holmes was in an expansive mood as he went over the case. I felt a deep sense of satisfaction to serve once again as his confidant.

"And why is time more important in this affair than in any other?" I asked.

"Because, Watson, the timeline of the case, to which I have devoted considerable thought, is at once very long and quite short."

"How pleasing it is to hear that you are still speaking in riddles, Holmes. There can now be no doubt you have fully recovered your faculties."

"And I am pleased that advancing age has not diminished your pawky sense of humor, my dear Watson. But consider the following: The first of Eisendorf's many enigmatic events occurs in 1875, when Gottfried Krupp vanishes, never to be seen again. Think of this as a prologue of sorts. Then, seventeen year later, the Monster—fresh from butchering four men in Munich—arrives in Eisendorf as part of the 'third immigration.' A year later, Dionisius Eisen, the town's founder, dies in an 'accident' at the mill. I cannot prove it, but I think it very likely he was murdered by his illegitimate son, the Monster.

"And then, insofar as we know, the Monster ceases his murderous ways, and nothing of consequence happens in Eisendorf for the next twenty-seven years, until there are two more supposedly 'accidental' deaths, followed by the brazen killing of Josef Krupp. What can we conclude from this singular series of events? Why the long hiatus?"

"Perhaps the Monster simply felt no need to murder anyone during that time."

"Yes, that is one possibility. The other is that the Monster left Eisendorf after Dionisius's death. We know both Peter Eisen and Georg Dreisser did so, while Wolfgang Eisen and Frederick Halbach remained in town. But regardless of what may have led to the Monster's long hiatus from mayhem, something clearly caused him to resume his murderous activities this year."

"And you think it must have something to do with the fate of the cooperative?"

"I do. The Monster, remember, does not kill out of passion, even though he misled the authorities in Munich into believing so. No, he murders in order to obtain something of great value."

"But what could that be in a place such as Eisendorf, which you have described as a dying town?"

Holmes smiled and said, "I think, my dear Watson, we are the verge of finding out, and I have no doubt you will find the answer quite surprising."

18

———•••———

The first day of October 1920 is one I shall never forget. It was the day I went with Holmes to Eisendorf, and in that strange little village locked away in its deep valley, the Monster demonstrated the full depths of his depravity. Yet not even Holmes, I believe, was prepared for the stunning act of destruction that brought the case to its extraordinary conclusion.

We left Rochester at eleven o'clock that morning on the Chicago and Great Western's daily train to Stewartville. Holmes had told me to pack for a visit of "three days and no more. If we have not concluded the affair by then," he added, "I shall be forced to regard it as the greatest failure of my career."

Upon our arrival in Stewartville, Tommy Boyd met us at the station. Holmes dropped his characteristic reserve and all but hugged Boyd, who was equally pleased to see us.

"Wait until I tell the wife I've now met not only Sherlock Holmes but Dr. John Watson as well," the cabman said, flashing a broad smile. "Yes, sir, this is a day I will always remember. I assume Eisendorf is our destination."

"It is," said Holmes, "and this time, Mr. Boyd, I promise you will not have to carry me out of town on your back. Do you have the items I asked you to bring along?"

"I do. Everything is in the back."

"Good. Then let us be on our way."

The day was cool and damp, the sun gone into hiding, and spectral wisps of fog sailed across the open countryside outside of town. It was a bleak and lonely scene, ripe with foreboding. This sensation only increased as we plunged into the thickly wooded valley where Eisendorf lay. The forest, show-ing its autumn colors, seemed to envelop the road in its own dense mystery as the fog grew ever thicker. By the time we reached Eisendorf, the fog had become oppressive, clamped over the village like a heavy gray shroud.

"It would seem nature itself wishes to impress upon us the mystery of Eisendorf," Holmes noted as we drove down the main thoroughfare.

The town gave no sign of vitality, its streets devoid of activity, its central park a vacant wasteland, its crimson houses posed like lifeless sculptures. I understood now why Holmes had found the town so dreary and dispiriting. I understood, too, what he meant when, during our ride, he had spoken of "a cloud of dread" hanging over Eisendorf. I felt it now—a sense of unspeakable menace lurking in the fog—and I gave an involuntary shudder. After we had passed several buildings, one of which Holmes identified as the Eisen Block, he directed Boyd to a cottage near the edge of town.

"Home, sweet home," Holmes remarked as we got out of the cab. Boyd, meanwhile, removed a large canvas bag from the rear seat, along with our valises.

"Just leave the bag by the door," Holmes said. "Now, Mr. Boyd, would you do us the favor of returning to town at seven o'clock tonight? Meet us at the usual place. Before you come, please check at the telegraph office in Stewartville. There may be a message addressed to you. If there is, bring it along."

"Will do," Boyd promised.

●●●

Once the cabman left, I asked Holmes about the message and the canvas bag.

"The message, if it arrives, will be from Mr. Rafferty. As for the bag, you will find out tomorrow what I have in mind."

I was about to question Holmes further when a man emerged out of the gloom.

"Mr. Holmes, what a pleasant surprise," the man said as he drew near. "I heard you had finally gotten out of the hospital, but I was not sure whether you would be coming back. And this must be Dr. John Watson. I am Frederick Halbach. Welcome once again to Eisendorf."

"Thank you," Holmes said. "Am I safe in assuming the cottage is still available?"

"Certainly. As you know, I had all of your belongings sent up to Rochester after your, well, your misadventure here, but the cottage itself is just as it was."

"Good. I am sure Dr. Watson and I will find it most comfortable."

"You seem to have some gear with you," Halbach said, glancing at the canvas bag. "Are you planning another little expedition? I trust it will have a more satisfactory conclusion than your first one."

"Our plans are our own business," Holmes said rather curtly as Halbach showed us into the cottage's parlor.

"Will you be here for long?" Halbach asked.

"Just long enough. Now, Mr. Halbach, what can you tell us about today's vote? It will be held at six o'clock in the town hall, as I understand it."

"I see you have been reading the newspapers. Yes, it will be a vote on whether to dissolve the cooperative."

"How long have you known that this was going to happen?"

"Well, the possibility has been discussed for some time, but it was only last week, while you were in the hospital, that the date for a vote was finally set."

"And yet before my unfortunate injury, you never told me the cooperative was on the verge of dissolution. Why is that?"

"I did not think it germane to your investigation, so I felt no need to mention it."

"I must wonder what else you have withheld," Holmes said, staring at our host. "Be that as it may, I shall await with interest the outcome of the vote. In the meantime, I should like to show Dr. Watson your archives. I have no doubt he will be quite intrigued."

"Of course," Halbach said. "Come by anytime, and I will be happy to give the doctor a tour."

As we sat for a few moments in the cottage's parlor, I was struck by how vital Holmes seemed despite his medical condition. His breathing was by no means normal, but he did not act in a way suggesting he suffered from any great deficiency of breath. I was struck as well by the absence of tobacco in his life. I myself had given up the habit some years earlier, but I had never believed for a moment Holmes would be able to function without his pipe and cigarettes.

When I told Holmes what I was thinking, he said, "I fear I shall always miss tobacco, but I also know I am done with it forever. It is a discipline with me now, and not doing what one wants provides a certain kind of cruel pleasure. But we are not here to talk of my trials and tribulations. It's time you had a look at Mr. Halbach's archives."

• • •

We found Halbach in the archives' ample reading room, and he was quite eager to show me around. I noticed at once the unusual grandfather clock, which ticked loudly at the rear of the room.

"Perhaps Mr. Holmes has told you about the clock," Halbach said. "That row of numbers beneath the face was intended to count every day since the village's founding in 1855. It's broken now, but if it were still working, it would register exactly twenty-four thousand days tomorrow."

Holmes, who has been listening to Halbach, said, "As I recall, that is when Dionisius predicted an 'astonishing event' in Eisendorf. It would appear he was off by one day, if the cooperative is indeed dissolved by tonight's vote."

"Well, who can say what surprises tomorrow may bring?" Halbach said. "Dionisius was a peculiar man, but I believe he possessed certain rare gifts of foresight."

"Did he also envision the end of Eisendorf?" I asked. "Your village hardly looks as though it can go on much longer."

Halbach responded with a thin smile. "You are right, Doctor. The saga of Eisendorf is coming to an end. Our days here are numbered."

Holmes had drifted away, and out of the corner of my eye I saw him paying particular attention to a room at the rear where an open staircase led down to the basement.

"We must be going," he abruptly announced. "Dr. Watson and I would like to get settled in."

Instead of returning directly to our cottage, however, we walked around to the back of the archives building. Because the building stood on a slope, its basement was accessible at the rear, where Holmes showed me a metal door.

"Here is the situation," he told me, bending over to examine the door's lock. "The vault for the archives is in the basement. Mr. Halbach usually leaves the vault door open when he is working upstairs. There are certain documents in the vault I should like to examine. Therefore, I need to get into the basement. To do so, I must pick this lock, which I have already examined at some length. It is one of the Yale Company's tumbler mechanisms, and it presents certain challenges."

"So you are not certain you can open it?"

"Oh no," said Holmes, showing me a set of lock picks he had obtained from Tommy Boyd, "I do not think Mr. Yale's handiwork will defeat my efforts. But it may take a bit of time. Now, Watson, come along and I will tell you what we must do."

When we returned to our cottage, Holmes explained his plan.

"But don't you think Mr. Halbach will become suspicious?"

"Not if you are your usual charming self. I will need a half hour, no more. I believe you can keep Mr. Halbach occupied for that period of time."

I promised I would do my best.

• • •

At quarter past two, as instructed by Holmes, I returned to the archives, where Halbach was still at his desk.

"Ah, Dr. Watson. What brings you back so soon?"

"Holmes is resting—I fear he is not yet quite fully recovered from his injury—and I thought I might learn a bit more about your archives. Holmes mentioned in particular the annals you maintain. Would it be possible to look at one of the volumes?"

"Certainly, though I must warn you that the bulk of them are in German."

"I confess I know hardly ten words in that language, but I am sure you will be an able translator. The very first year of the annals would be especially interesting, I should think."

"Volume one is indeed quite fascinating," Halbach said, a touch of pride in his voice. "Let me show you."

As I turned to follow Halbach, I let my hat drop to the floor. When I bent down to pick it up, I glanced back at the front door. It had two small windows, and in one of them I could see the face of Sherlock Holmes. In an instant, he was gone, and I knew our plan had now been set in motion.

So it was I spent the next half hour with Halbach discussing the minutiae of life in Eisendorf. Meanwhile, Holmes was busy down below, rummaging through the secret files in the basement vault. Or, at least, I presumed he was.

• • •

It was nearly three o'clock by the time I left the archives, after profusely praising its many wonders to Halbach. He asked me to stay longer—I suspected it had been some time since anyone had shown such an interest in his work—but I told him I had to arouse Holmes from his nap.

"Come back anytime," Halbach said, and I promised that I would try to do so, though in truth I had found my excursion into the quotidian life of the town exceedingly dull.

"Did you find what you are looking for?" I asked Holmes as soon as I returned to the cottage.

"Not everything," Holmes said, "but enough. It required more time than I anticipated to defeat Mr. Yale's ingenious mechanism, so I managed to spend only fifteen minutes inside the vault. But since its contents have been impeccably organized by Mr. Halbach, I was able to quickly locate two treasures."

"One of them, I take it, is that 1870 amendment to the cooperative agreement mentioned by Mr. Schmidt."

"Yes. It is only a page long, but it is most telling."

"How so?"

"Let us just say it provides a powerful motive for murder, Watson. As I suspected, this business is, at bottom, all about trees. I have no doubt the timber cruiser will provide confirmation once Sheriff Thorkelson talks with him."

"And what was the second treasure you discovered in the safe?"

"This," said Holmes, handing me a leather-bound chapbook. "It is Dionisius Eisen's diary."

"My God, Holmes, was that a wise thing to do? Won't Mr. Halbach miss it?"

"Perhaps. But it was not stored in a readily visible place, so it will be some time, I suspect, before he notices the diary is missing, and by then, it will not matter."

Since the diary was in German, I could not read it. "What does it reveal?" I asked.

"It reveals that Dionisius harbored terrible secrets," Holmes said, "but there is no time now to go into the details. We still have much to do today. I should like you to meet some members of the Eisen family."

•••

Just after four o'clock, we found ourselves at the front door of the Eisen family mansion. The house would hardly have impressed in England, but in Eisendorf it qualified as a castle, albeit a crumbling one. Vines clung to its deteriorating stone walls, from which much of the mortar had been scoured away, and an air of melancholy oozed out its high, shuttered windows.

"Not the most charming place I've ever seen," I noted as we climbed up the steps to the front doors.

"More charming than our hostess is likely to be," said Holmes.

Willy Eisen answered our knock. Holmes had described her to me in great detail, and so I was not taken aback to see her dressed in a long gown with angel wings affixed to her shoulders. Her blue eyes sparkled.

"Mr. Sherlock," she said, "I knew you'd come back. Poppa said so. I can show you Mr. Bones now. Don't tell Wolfie."

"My dear Willy, it is good to see you," Holmes said. "Yes, I would like to see Mr. Bones. But first I would like you to meet my friend, Dr. John Watson."

The girl gave me a curious look and said, "Do you operate on people?"

"Sometimes."

"Do you take their bones and hide them?"

Before I could reply to this strange question, I heard a voice from inside the house asking, "Who is it?" A moment later a woman I assumed to be Maria Eisen appeared. She did not greet us warmly.

"Hah, the great detective," she said, glaring at Holmes. "I thought I was done with you. Well, I have nothing to say. You and your short little friend may leave at once."

Although Holmes had warned me of Mrs. Eisen's imperious manner, I was nonetheless shocked by the harsh vehemence of her words. Nor did I think of myself as particularly short.

She tried to slam the door, but Holmes put his shoulder to it. "We must talk, Mrs. Eisen. By the way, this is my friend, Dr. John Watson."

"Ah, your paid liar. How nice it must be to have someone whose only job is to puff you up before the world. Now, go away. As I said, I do not wish to talk."

"I am not a liar," I remonstrated as Holmes, ignoring Mrs. Eisen's taunting words, pushed her aside and strode into the front hall. I followed him through the hall and into a large parlor. There, Holmes planted himself like a statue, arms crossed. Mrs. Eisen rushed in behind us.

"Out!" she said. "You have no right—"

"I have every right," Holmes said, cutting her off. "I have come here to tell you I know the truth. The truth about you, the truth about what is happening here. I know the lie you have lived. I know all of your foul secrets."

"Go away," she repeated, "and take this stupid man—" she delivered a venomous stare in my direction—"with you."

Holmes paid no heed to this provocation. Instead, he said, to my utter surprise, "Please tell Mr. Dreisser to join us."

"Whatever are you talking about? You are—"

Her denial was interrupted by the sudden appearance, through a door from the dining room, of a man I took to be Georg Dreisser.

"I presume you noticed my cane in the hall stand," he said with an air of nonchalance. "Very observant on your part, Mr. Holmes. I was simply paying a call."

"One of many such calls, no doubt," remarked Holmes, who then turned to Mrs. Eisen and asked, "And where might your husband be?"

It was Dreisser who replied. "Peter is busy supervising the vote today. Now, as I have business of my own to attend to, I shall be on my way."

"By all means," said Holmes. "We would not want to keep you here."

Dreisser delivered a small bow in our direction before taking his leave.

When he was gone, Holmes did something quite surprising. He went straight up to Mrs. Eisen, grabbed her rudely by the shoulders, and whispered into her ear.

As Holmes stepped away, there was a flash of terror in Mrs. Eisen's dark, mordant eyes.

"If I were you, I should take a trip," Holmes told her. "Perhaps catch a train to St. Paul. The sooner the better. It would be good for your health."

I expected some curt, rude reply, but instead she looked at Holmes and said, "Yes, perhaps I will."

"Good. Now, Dr. Watson and I shall say good-bye to Willy."

The girl was waiting for us in a swing seat on the front porch. A shawl covered her angel wings, and a small white purse rested in her lap.

She said, "I heard the ghost again, Mr. Sherlock."

"In the apartment building?"

"Yes."

"When was this?"

"In the dark."

"Last night?"

"Maybe."

"Did you hear what the ghost said?"

"No. Ghosts only whisper."

"I see. What were you doing in the building?"

"Looking at secret things."

"What kinds of things?"

"I can't tell you."

She stood up and said, "I have to go. Momma doesn't like me. Good-bye, Mr. Sherlock." She ran down the porch stairs and was soon out of sight.

"Do you have any idea what she was talking about?" I asked Holmes.

"Yes," he said, "and I would very interested in seeing her secret things."

$\bullet \bullet \bullet$

"We are nearing a dangerous moment," said Holmes as we walked back to the cottage. "The Monster is preparing to set a trap, and I believe Willy will be his agent. He manipulates the poor girl just as he manipulates everyone else. Indeed, that is how he was able to stage his ambush at the old mill dam. Willy told him, in all innocence, that I would be going there to explore the tunnel. Now, I have no doubt he intends to set another ambush. We must be very vigilant."

The rest of the afternoon went by uneventfully. Holmes pored over Dionisius's diary while I napped. For dinner, Halbach provided us with cold sandwiches and a quart of the Krupp Brewery's cave-aged lager, which I found to be excellent. Prohibition, it seemed, had not yet turned Eisendorf dry. When we had finished, Holmes said, "It is nearly seven, Watson. Time for a little constitutional."

We walked to the Eisen Block. Automobile headlights soon appeared. The taxi pulled up in front of us, and Tommy Boyd rolled down his window to speak to Holmes.

"Got the telegram you're waiting for and also got this from the sheriff," he said, handing over two messages to Holmes. "The sheriff says you'll know what it's about."

"Very good," said Holmes. "Now, here's a message for the sheriff. Can you deliver it yet tonight?"

"Consider it done, Mr. Holmes. Do you want me to come back tomorrow night?"

"No, I think not," Holmes said. "We have other plans."

When we returned to the cottage, Holmes opened the telegram, scanned it with evident satisfaction, then handed it to me. The message read: "HE IS YOUR MAN STOP FRAUD THEFT LINK TO TWO MURDERS NEVER PROVEN STOP LEFT HERE UNDER CLOUD STOP MORE TO COME RAFFERTY."

The message from the sheriff proved equally significant. Thorkelson said he had reached the timber cruiser by telephone and asked him the three questions posed by Holmes. The answers, as summarized by the sheriff, were most revealing.

"We now know with certainty the Monster's ultimate motive," Holmes said.

"And are you equally certain as to the Monster's identity?"

"Yes, but questions remain, especially regarding how much help he may have had from an accomplice. And irrefutable proof is still lacking. Everything will depend on what happens tomorrow."

Our next stop was at Halbach's house. Holmes wanted to know the results of the vote.

"It was thirty-six in favor and only four against," he told us. "The cooperative will be dissolved. I knew it would happen, but it is still a sad day."

"And also a very profitable one for certain members of the community, if I am not mistaken," Holmes noted.

Halbach shrugged. "Perhaps. Time will tell."

Back at our cottage, Holmes said, "Get some rest, Watson. I will wake you when it is time."

"Time for what?"

"A visit to one of Willy Eisen's secret places."

• • •

True to his promise, Holmes shook me from my sleep at two in the morning.

"No lights for the moment," he said softly. "Someone may be watching, and it is possible we are heading into a trap."

We were soon out the door. The night was cold and windy. The fog had dissipated, and a half moon dangled amid the stars.

"Where are we going?" I whispered.

"Shhhh," Holmes said, picking up his pace. We slipped past Halbach's house, crossed the main road then circled behind the Eisen Block. As usual, the town appeared to be absolutely deserted. Soon, we were at the side door of a two-story wooden building.

"Welcome to the Wohngebäude," said Holmes, taking a long look around before lighting the lantern he had brought along and handing it to me. Once inside, we climbed a set of stairs to the second floor, then proceeded down a long hallway lined with doors to small apartments, all of which proved to be utterly empty. Halfway down the hall, we reached a door numbered 210.

"Wolfgang's secret office," Holmes said. "There is no need to go in. It will tell us nothing now."

"Then what are we looking for?" I asked.

"Willy Eisen's hideaway," Holmes said. "It's where she heard the 'ghost' she told us about this afternoon. I suspect it was Wolfgang. Indeed, I may have seen his shadow behind one of the windows in this building on the day I arrived in Eisendorf. In any case, I think Willy likes to spend time here. The question is where."

A little farther along the hall, Holmes stopped before a door that was narrower than the others we had passed. He pulled it open to reveal a steep staircase. It led to a large attic set beneath rows of heavy rafters. Boxes, old pieces of furniture, and racks of moth-eaten clothes lay scattered about the floor. The smell of dust, old wood, and animal droppings permeated the air, which was heavy and unpleasant. As I followed Holmes, I noticed several small dormer windows set between the rafters.

"Ah, what have we here?" Holmes asked.

Our lantern illuminated an alcove with a small window covered by portions of an old gingham dress serving as a makeshift curtain. A stool sat next to the window. Beside it was a jar containing peppermint sticks and other candy. A sheet hung from the rafters on one side of the alcove.

"This is Willy's perch," Holmes said. "She can watch the whole town from here."

"I can't imagine there is much to see."

"To her eager eyes, it must all be a wonder," said Holmes, a note of wistfulness in his voice. "Such is the privilege of youth and innocence. Now, let us see where she stores her treasures. I am sure she has collected many things on her forays through town. Look behind that sheet, Watson."

I pulled back the sheet to reveal a battered humpback trunk lodged between two sloping rafters. Straps secured its lid. I slid the trunk out into the center of the alcove, unbuckled the straps, and lifted the lid. At first, I saw nothing remarkable. Willy Eisen's trove included beer bottles, tarnished silverware, costume jewelry, two pocket watches, a woman's shoe, a fountain pen, and a tin of talcum powder. A large portion of the trunk, however, was taken up by a flour bag bearing the name "Eisen's Tunnel Mill." I lifted out the bag, which clearly did not contain flour, and its contents tumbled out.

"My God!" I said, utterly startled, for I found myself staring at a human skull.

Holmes did not look at all surprised. "It appears we have found him at last," he said.

"Found whom?"

"Gottfried Krupp, if I am not mistaken. And you will note, Watson, there is a hole in his forehead. Someone shot him."

• • •

After our visit to the Wohngebäude, I fell fast asleep on the couch, hoping to enjoy several hours of uninterrupted repose. This hope was quickly dashed, for it seemed as though I had barely put my head on the pillow when Holmes shook me awake. His face was ashen.

"Read this," he said. "It was left on our doorstep."

The message, in block lettering, said: "I have the girl. Best do as I say, Mr. Sherlock. Mr. Bones awaits. Send the sheriff away when he arrives. I will be in touch at the sound of the three. I look forward to our final meeting."

19

—⦗● ● ●⦘—

"What are we to do?" I asked Holmes as I sat up and rubbed sleep from my eyes. "Do you really think he would kill an innocent like Willy?"

"Without hesitation," said Holmes. He was the pacing the parlor floor, his hands balled into fists. "I should have seen this coming, Watson."

"Maybe the Monster is bluffing," I said.

Holmes shook his head. "No, I have no doubt he has her. And he knows I will do everything in my power to rescue her. He has planned how it will all end. I will die, and so will Willy."

"But we know who he is, Holmes," I protested. "We must call the sheriff at once and have him arrested. He will be forced to tell us what he has done with the girl."

"No, Watson, that will not do. He already has the girl secreted away somewhere, probably under the control of his accomplice. I am sure he left instructions to murder Willy if he is taken into custody. I cannot allow that to happen."

"I am sorry to say this, Holmes, but how do we know he hasn't killed her already?"

"He has not," Holmes said with surprising force. "I have come to know the man. He will want to gloat, to revel in the final consummation of his plans. I believe he intends to murder Willy in my presence. It will be a delicious pleasure for him."

"Then we must find her, Holmes. But how?"

Holmes stopped pacing and sat down. His great gray eyes had become the eyes of a wolf on the hunt.

"The Monster will tell me where she is, Watson."

"Why on earth would he tell you? And even if he did, what could his purpose be other than to lure you into a trap?"

"You are right. It will be a trap. And I know where it will be set. Remember what his message said: 'Mr. Bones awaits.' The Monster wishes to lure me to the scene of Eisendorf's original sin, as I have called it. There, he intends to write the final chapter of his cruel story, which he is convinced will end with his triumph and my demise. And why should he not feel confident? Thus far he has anticipated my every move. I have been his plaything."

Holmes went over to the window. It was still pitch black outside, Eisendorf as dark and quiet as a cave. "The Monster will be resting now," he said, "and nothing will trouble his sleep. Everything is in place, or so he believes. But he is wrong, Watson! For once, he is wrong! It is time now to turn the tables."

"What do you mean?"

"We are going to the Eisen mill, Watson. There is something I must do."

• • •

I was hungry, having consumed not one morsel of food since our early dinner, but Holmes refused to entertain the sensible idea of looking for something to eat. "You are slave to your stomach," he told me while I threw on my clothes.

"We are all slaves to our stomachs," I noted, but as the cottage appeared to be bereft of anything edible, I saw no choice other than to sally forth without sustenance. Holmes, meanwhile, handed me the canvas bag Boyd had brought along when he delivered us to Eisendorf. Inside, I found a pair of small miner's picks, two nickel-plated flashlights, extra dry-cell batteries, several flares of the kind used in railroading, and—to my delighted surprise—four chocolate bars. A note attached to the bars said, "Something for you in case you get lost in the dark. Tommy."

"I now share your high opinion of our cabman," I said, unwrapping one of the bars and devouring it.

"Just bring the flashlights and batteries," Holmes said. "And also put that new revolver in your coat pocket."

At Holmes's insistence, I had purchased a short-barreled but powerful Smith and Wesson revolver in Rochester. "You must be expecting trouble," I said.

"Yes, and I pray it occurs at the right time and in the right place. Are you ready, Watson?"

"I am," I said after testing the flashlights. "Lead the way."

We were out the door moments later. It was four o'clock in the morning, and dawn was still a good two hours away. Not a breath of wind stirred in the dense silence of the town. Above, the heavens offered a magnificent pageantry of glittering stars, and I took comfort in their timeless presence. Better yet, I was with Holmes, and I could think of no braver nor better companion.

We walked south from the cottage to Mill Avenue, where we turned west. I soon heard German Creek frothing along nearby but could not see its fast-moving waters. Holmes all the while kept a careful watch, pausing now and then to listen for footsteps or any other indication we were being followed. But we neither heard nor saw anything suspicious. Before long, we reached a point directly below the Eisen mansion, which was illuminated by a single lamp in the uppermost window of its tower.

"It reminds me of a lighthouse," I said to Holmes.

"Yes, and we are sailors, Watson, heading into uncharted seas."

• • •

A few minutes later, we stood outside the massive wooden doors that gave entrance to the Eisen mill. Holmes had told me about the mill and its curious tunnel, but when I saw the hulking structure, illuminated by a single electric light above the entrance, I was struck at once by its gloomy aspect. Its walls were of rough-faced stone, laid without pattern or course, and they rose straight and solid, with no windows to interrupt them. A medieval dungeon, I thought, could not have presented a more formidable appearance. Carved into an archway above the doors were the words "Eisen's Tunnel Mill, 1874."

Holmes went up to the doors, which were secured by a stout iron bar and a heavy padlock. "The lock," Holmes informed me as I shined my flashlight on it, "is one of Mr. Corbin's models and quite simple." Taking out his set of picks, Holmes opened the lock with his usual brisk dexterity.

Once inside the mill, we made our way toward the rear, zigzagging through a mechanical wonderland of shafts, gears, cogwheels, belts, and pulleys. Although the mill had been closed for several years, its machinery— rollers, sifters, separators, and other devices—still stood in place, linked by an intricate tangle of spiderwebs. Despite its long period of dormancy, the mill still smelled of grain. There was dust as well, dancing in the beams of our flashlights.

Near the back of the mill we reached the rim of a deep pit excavated into bedrock. We stopped to peer down into the pit, which at its bottom held a turbine connected to a shaft. Water diverted from German Creek had once poured with great force into the pit, turning the turbine and thereby providing power for all of the machinery.

"Here is where Dionisius Eisen met his end," Holmes said. "It must have been a horrible death, sliced to pieces by the turbine blades. I am certain now it was no accident. But it was perhaps a grisly form of justice. In any case, the tunnel cannot be far."

Leading away from the wheel pit was a wooden sluice. We followed it to the far rear wall of the mill. There, we found a wooden gate, mounted vertically much like the blade of a guillotine. Holmes had begun to gasp and cough in response to the dust in the air, and I too found the atmosphere most disagreeable. Setting down my flashlight, I managed to push the gate far enough open so that Holmes could slip under. I quickly followed. We were in the tunnel at last, and its cool, moist air—largely free of dust—came as a welcome relief.

The tunnel was six feet high and equally wide. Its profile was that of a parabolic arch. The mind works in strange ways, and the sight of this arched passageway instantly sent me back to my service in Afghanistan, where I had once watched an artilleryman draw out the steep parabolic trajectory of a mortar shell.

Holmes had to bend over slightly to keep from scraping his head on the ceiling. Being several inches shorter, I had no such problem. Almost at once we encountered an area of fallen rock, but there was a narrow path around the obstruction, and we slipped past without difficulty.

Navigating the rest of the tunnel turned out to be more of a challenge. Its rough floor was littered with jagged chunks of fallen rock. The floor was also wet, and quite slippery, as a result of water seeping down from the ceiling and walls. A channel, about two feet deep, ran down the center of the floor. It had once carried water from German Creek to the mill, but it contained only a trickle now. We had hardly walked ten yards before I nearly lost my footing.

"Careful, Watson, careful," Holmes whispered. "I cannot afford to have you break a bone."

As we moved farther into the tunnel, guided by our flashlights, I saw no evidence of shoring, even in places where the ceiling appeared unstable. I must confess I felt a growing sense of unease. Indeed, I could not help but think of what would happen should a portion of the ceiling suddenly collapse, as seemed entirely possible.

Before entering the tunnel, Holmes had informed me our destination would be a slight bend near its center point. It was there, he said, that Willy Eisen had discovered Mr. Bones.

"We are getting close," Holmes said as the beams of our flashlights penetrated the darkness. "Do you see the bend, Watson?"

I did. Only twenty or so feet ahead, the tunnel made its turn, and as we came upon this spot, I saw something curious—a side chamber, about ten feet deep, partly filled with loose rock that looked to have been left over from the original excavation long ago. Even more curious were the decorations adorning this chamber. Toys, teacups, canning jars, a bracelet, and even a ragdoll were arrayed with evident care on a high ledge cut into the chamber's walls. It was as though we had stumbled upon the artifacts of some strange burial cult.

"Can you make any sense of it?" I asked Holmes as he played his light across the ledge and its strange collection of objects.

"It is Willy's handiwork," he replied. "This is her most secret place, the one she intended to show me. I believe she left these items as a sort of offering to Mr. Bones, her name for the skeleton, or part of one, she found here."

"You mean Gottfried Krupp, I presume."

"Yes. This is where she discovered his skull. Perhaps she dug it out by accident while searching for hidden treasure, or perhaps it simply fell out of the loose rock one day, and she came across it. I have no doubt, Watson, that if we were to dig through the rock in this chamber, we would find the rest of Gottfried Krupp's remains. He was entombed here in 1875 after Dionisius Eisen murdered him."

"How can you be sure?"

"It fits the facts. Gottfried Krupp and Dionisius Eisen were known to have quarreled over money and power. Gottfried had injected a great deal of new money into Eisendorf after his arrival, and he may well have thought he was thus entitled to take control of the town from Dionisius, its founder. Dionisius did not agree. There is something else, and it may be the most potent motive of all. I have had an opportunity to read through a good deal of Dionisius's diary, and it is clear he was the Don Juan of Eisendorf. He pursued almost every woman in town, and Gottfried's wife was among them. It appears that in her case his pursuit was successful."

"And Gottfried found out?"

"Yes, and he threatened to expose every evil and devious thing Dionisius had ever done. Dionisius even said so in his diary. In any event, I am convinced Dionisius came to the conclusion his only course of action was to murder his rival. Newspaper accounts from 1875 make it clear Gottfried was on his way to see Dionisius at the mill when he disappeared. I believe he did see Dionisius and that Dionisius shot him dead, then hid the body here in the tunnel. And here it stayed until Willy found the skull."

"I am curious. Did Dionisius also admit in his diary that he had murdered Gottfried?"

"No. Remember, he saw his diary as an important piece of the history of Eisendorf. As such, he expected it would ultimately be enshrined in the town archives. Admitting to affairs and other sorts of wrongdoing was one thing. Admitting to murder, however, was quite another. That was a secret he intended to take to the grave."

"And yet, if you are correct, Dionisius himself was later killed. Do you think the Monster did it to revenge Gottfried's murder?"

"Yes, I believe the Monster committed the crime. But if revenge was involved, I am not sure it had anything to do with Gottfried. The Monster had other, more personal reasons for killing Dionisius."

"Well, it is a confounding business, Holmes, that is all I can say."

"Do not feel bad, Watson. I, too, have been confounded at times by Eisendorf. The town wears a mask of order and reason, but a beast lurks underneath and always has. Dionisius was the town's first monster. He in turn spawned another one. Now, a long, long game is nearing its end, and I am all that stands between the Monster and the fulfillment of his dark dreams."

"Do not forget I am with you, Holmes. We will confront this madman together."

Holmes reached out and touched my hand. "I shall never forget you have always been and will always be the best friend a man could have. But I fear I must face the Monster alone."

Before I could protest, Holmes added, "There is no use arguing, Watson. No use whatsoever." Then he stood back for a moment, studying the objects Willy had placed on the ledge. Finally, he picked up the rag doll and said, "Yes, this should do nicely."

I was mystified. "Whatever are you talking about?"

When he told me, I was astounded. "Holmes, you cannot be serious. It is an awful risk to take."

"Ah, Watson, one of the few advantages of growing old is that risk becomes a constant companion, for every day is the day the curtain might fall at last, is it not? So, I will take this risk, because I can and because I see no other way to save Willy."

I knew that once Holmes had made up his mind, he could not be dissuaded, no matter how dangerous the course of action he intended to take. So I did as I was asked. But as we walked back through the tunnel, I wondered if I might soon become complicit in the death of the greatest man I have ever known.

• • •

Events now moved with astonishing speed, rushing toward a strange and violent conclusion. It was almost dawn when we returned to the cottage, and in a mere eighteen hours Eisendorf would be changed forever. The Monster would see to that, but not before receiving the surprise of his life from Sherlock Holmes.

I lay down for a nap after our visit to the tunnel. When I awoke, I was mortified to find that I had slept four hours and that Holmes and Sheriff Thorkelson were in the midst of an intense discussion in the kitchen.

"You should have awakened me when the sheriff arrived," I told Holmes when I joined them.

"I did not see the need," Holmes replied. "I have been telling the sheriff about my plan. Unfortunately, he is of the Watsonian persuasion and thinks I am taking an absurd risk."

"Good," said I. "The sheriff is absolutely right."

"I believe I am," Thorkelson said, "and God knows I have been doing my level best to persuade Mr. Holmes of the error of his ways. But I am having precious little success."

"Nor will you," said Holmes. "My mind is made up. It is that simple."

"I could arrest the Monster and his accomplice right now," Thorkelson offered. "Maybe we could make a case, maybe not. But we could sure as hell—pardon my language—put the screws to them. One of them might just crack and tell us where the girl is."

"They are not men to be cracked like walnuts, Sheriff. They are both hard and deadly characters, and they would happily take the first available handbasket to hell, as the saying goes, before giving you one ounce of satisfaction."

"What makes you think you can take on the two of them alone, Mr. Holmes, if they are such tough customers?"

"I am of a mind, Sheriff, that in the end I will have to deal with only one of them. You must trust me when I say this. And you must also trust my plan. I am grateful for your concern, but the time has come to act, and I will not be deterred. Can I count on your support?"

Thorkelson was a man I had come to like, despite knowing him for only a few days. He had strong, honest eyes—the surest sign of character—and I knew he had developed the utmost respect for Holmes. The sheriff was looking at Holmes now, searching that magnificent face for assurance. He found it.

"Of course you have my cooperation, Mr. Holmes. But I swear to God, if you get yourself killed, I will never forgive myself."

"Nor will I," I said.

"Then I must not get myself killed," Holmes said. "Very well, Sheriff, here is what we must do."

• • •

The first step in Holmes's plan was to pay a visit to Halbach. The three of us went at once to the archives, where we discovered Halbach had company. A man I soon learned was Peter Eisen had joined the archivist for a cup of coffee.

"Please, gentlemen, sit down and share a cup," Eisen said. "By God, Mr. Holmes, this must be the famous Dr. John Watson with you. Sorry I missed you at the house yesterday. Willy said you were there."

"Yes, we had a few minor questions for your wife," Holmes said. "I may want to speak with her again today."

"Good luck with that. She went up to St. Paul yesterday. Some sort of last-minute thing."

"I see. By the way, Mr. Eisen, when did you last see Willy?"

"She was around last night, but I haven't seen her yet this morning. She usually gets up at first light and does her wandering."

"What about you, Mr. Halbach?" Holmes asked. "Have you seen Willy today?"

"No."

"I am afraid, then, I have some very bad news," Holmes said. He went on to explain he had good reason to believe Willy had been kidnapped by a person or persons unknown and was in grave danger.

Eisen's face turned white. He stood up, accidentally knocking over his cup of coffee. Ignoring the spill, he said, "My God, are you sure, Mr. Holmes? Who would want to take my dear child? We must find her. We must gather everyone in town and begin a search at once. I assume you have men on the way, Sheriff, and if you—"

Holmes interrupted. "There can be no search," he said, showing Eisen and Halbach the note he had received. "There is only one hope for the girl. I must do as this madman asks. The sheriff agrees, and he intends to leave town immediately. Willy is just a pawn. I am the real target."

"Is it wise for the sheriff to leave?" Halbach asked. "How do we know Willy is even alive?"

"Of course she's alive," Eisen snapped. "She has to be. Isn't that right, Mr. Holmes?"

"Yes. I believe she is alive and unharmed. But she will almost certainly be harmed if we act foolishly. Here is what I want you to do, even though it will be very hard. Go about your daily business as though nothing is amiss. Let me find Willy. I will do all in my power to save her. She is as dear to me as she is to all of you."

"When will you hear from this villain again?" Eisen asked.

"Soon," said Holmes. "I do not think he is a patient man. By the way, do you suppose there is any chance Wolfgang might have run across Willy?"

"I have not seen my brother today, but I will go right away and ask him. Would that be all right, Mr. Holmes?"

"Certainly. And if you learn he or anyone else in town has seen her, let me know at once."

"Of course. Now, if you will excuse me, I must try to get in touch with Maria. It is all so unbelievable. I really do not understand. Promise me you will get my lovely girl back, Mr. Holmes?"

"I will do all I can."

• • •

Afterwards, we walked with Thorkelson back to his sedan. He got behind the wheel, started the engine, and said, "You must stay in touch with me, Mr. Holmes. You have the phone number where I'll be in Stewartville. Two of my men will join me there shortly. We can be here in less than a half hour if you need us."

"Thank you, Sheriff. I know I can rely upon you."

"Well then, Godspeed, Mr. Holmes," Thorkelson said. "I hope to see you again very soon."

"You shall," Holmes promised.

It was a promise I most fervently prayed Holmes could keep.

• • •

The remainder of the day, spent largely at our cottage, went by at a glacial pace. I was very much on edge, wondering how events would play out. Holmes, on the other hand, seemed to be perfectly at peace, giving no sign of the nervous anticipation he had often displayed in years gone by.

"When do you think the Monster will contact us?" I finally asked.

"When he is ready, Watson."

"That is not very helpful, Holmes. And what of the 'sound of the three' he mentioned in his message? How are we to know what that means?"

"We will know it when we hear it," Holmes said. "You must be patient, Watson. The curtain will rise soon enough on the final act."

Late in the afternoon, Halbach brought us bread and cheese, along with two quarts of Krupp's beer. By six o'clock, as darkness took Eisendorf in its grip, I saw nothing to do but eat. Holmes ate a few slices of cheese but drank no beer.

More hours ticked by, and I began to fear the Monster had no intention of contacting Holmes again. When I mentioned this thought to Holmes, he gave a vigorous shake of his head.

"He will be in touch, Watson. It is something he is compelled to do, just as I will be compelled to go to him."

As my watch came up on eleven o'clock, I found I was barely able to keep my eyes open. I was about to get up from the couch and pace around the room when I heard the loud toll of a bell from somewhere outside. The bell rang twice more, then stopped.

"It is time," Holmes said. "Come, Watson."

We left the cottage at once, and Holmes knew exactly where to go. We crossed Freiheit Park at a quick step and came up to the vacant building that had once been a school.

"He rang the bell in the tower," Holmes said. "There will be a message for us inside."

The building's front doors were wide open, despite the chill night air.

We went into a small vestibule. Posted there was the message we had been waiting for.

It said, "Come to the bend in the tunnel at midnight. Come alone, or I will have to cut up the girl just like those fags in Munich. This will be your only chance to save her. Are you up to it, Mr. Holmes?"

"You were right, Holmes," I said. "You have what you wanted, but I am still very worried. Much could go wrong. Why don't you let me at least go with you to the mill?"

"No," Holmes insisted, "I must do this myself. There can be no other way."

20

— ❙ • • • ❙ —

The story of what transpired that night in the tunnel of Eisen's Mill is one I must leave to Holmes himself. He wrote it all out ten days later, as we sailed on the *Mauretania* to England. It is an unusually frank document, using in several instances words not acceptable to polite society. Yet it is also thorough and unblinking in its depiction of Holmes's final confrontation with a truly monstrous criminal, and I do not see how I could improve upon it in any way.

• • •

An account of the Events of October 3, 1920, Beginning at Midnight, in the Tunnel of Eisen's Flour Mill in Eisendorf, Minnesota, and Concerning the Man Known as the Monster of Munich, by Sherlock Holmes.

The sky harbored no moon, and the little town of Eisendorf was as black as a colliery pit on the night I went to confront the Monster for the last time. I brought along a powerful light, as well as my revolver, but I had no expectation of surprising so ruthless and cunning a villain. Once I entered the tunnel of the Eisen Mill, he would have me at his mercy, or so he believed. Yet I was willing to bear any risk if I could save little Willy Eisen—the purest spirit I have ever known—from a terrible fate.

The mill's double doors were open when I arrived, inviting me into the Monster's lair. I stepped inside and immediately encountered a most obnoxious situation. When I had gone to the mill earlier in the day with Watson, there had been some dust in the air but not enough to greatly impede my breathing. Now, however, the atmosphere within the mill seemed as thick as a bowl of meal, so great was the concentration of grain dust. I knew what this portended. The Monster was preparing for a mighty act of destruction in which I, and Willy, would perish.

I soon learned he had already claimed another victim. As I made my way through the choking air to the rear of the mill, I came upon its deep wheel pit. I shined my light to the bottom and saw the battered body of a man dressed in overalls and a flannel shirt. He lay face down, sprawled across the pit's turbine. A bloodstain bloomed from the back of his head, suggesting he had been murdered by a heavy blow. This horrible scene was not unexpected. The Monster, I knew, intended to wipe out everyone who lay between him and the fortune he coveted. I could not see the dead man's face, but I had no doubt as to his identity.

There was nothing to be done for the man, and I moved on, all the while coughing and struggling for breath. For a moment I feared I might collapse for want of air, but I was able at last to make my way into the mill's long tunnel. There, the air became much clearer. Even so, I could not avoid coughing in an effort to clear my lungs. The Monster thus knew I was at hand, yet I saw no point in trying to disguise my presence, and I walked as quickly as I could down the tunnel. I had taken out my revolver, although I had little reason to think it would be of use. I saw no one, nor did I hear a sound other than my own breathing.

Just before reaching the bend at the middle of the tunnel, I paused, watching and listening. All was still quiet. I assumed the Monster was waiting for me in the side chamber at the bend. I edged up to it and announced my presence.

"It is Holmes," I said. "I am alone."

There was no response.

I peered around the corner, into the chamber. Willy Eisen, her hands and feet bound with ropes and a gag in her mouth, lay on the floor. I got down on one knee to help her. She was breathing, but her eyes were closed, and she appeared unconscious. I began to untie the ropes.

"Good evening, Mr. Holmes," the Monster said. He had come up behind me, from some unknown hiding place. "How nice of you to join us. Please drop that pistol of yours, or I will have to blow you to kingdom come, and I would actually rather wait, if you don't mind." His voice purred with menace.

I let my revolver fall to the floor and slowly stood up. I turned around to see Peter Eisen. He had a double-barreled shotgun pointed at my chest. A flashlight was in his other hand. He turned it on, shining the beam in my eyes, and told me to back up. Then he kicked away my revolver.

"Put your light down, too," he instructed, "and hold up your hands." I did as I was told, my right hand almost touching the ledge where Willy had mounted her collection of objects. Eisen slowly bent down and set his flashlight on the floor, its beam shining straight up, leaving the sides of the chamber in shadow. The light cast an eerie glow on his cruel, eager face, which looked as Lucifer's must have when he first saw hell.

"What did you do to Willy?" I demanded.

"Oh, she'll be fine—for the moment. Just a little ether to keep her from getting rambunctious. Children can be such a problem."

"To the contrary, I think of Willy as a lovely girl."

"How very touching," he said. "I must say I wasn't sure you would come, Mr. Holmes. I salute your courage, if not your intelligence. It's only fitting we meet here. I assume you've uncovered Willy's little secret by now."

"Yes, I know who is buried behind us."

"'Alas, poor Gottfried,' to misquote the Bard. Eisendorf's first murder victim, but far from the last."

"You have seen to that."

"Yes, I have, and my long labors are about to bear fruit. Say, how about a smoke, Mr. Holmes, just for old time's sake?" He took a pack of Lucky Strikes from his shirt pocket and waved it in front of me. "Still tempted?"

"I quit."

"Very wise of you, especially with that nasty emphysema. On the other hand, who knows how much time you have left to enjoy one last smoke? Why, it could only be a matter of minutes."

He was clearly enjoying himself, as sadistic men always do when they think they have the upper hand.

"You know, Mr. Holmes, when Maria informed me last month you were at the Mayo, I could scarcely believe my good fortune. You were a loose end, dangling for almost thirty years, and it bothered me. Now, I will be able to clip you off at last. Incidentally, I imagine you are surprised to see me. You were expecting Wolf, weren't you?"

"No, I have known for some time Wolfgang was merely your tool. You led, he followed. And now you have killed him. I found his body in the pit. I presume he will be blamed for my death, and that of Willy."

"Yes, it all works out quite nicely, especially given all of his suspicious behavior of late. I've even ginned up some additional evidence against him, which will be 'discovered' by the sheriff in due time. As for Wolf's death, it will be assumed he got careless and accidentally blew himself up with the mill."

"You are delusional," I said. "Sheriff Thorkelson knows you are the murderer."

"Does he? I don't really care. The fat fellow can think whatever he likes, but the fact is he can't prove a thing. I am sure you understand."

"Yes, I understand a great deal about you, Mr. Eisen. Or should I call you Mr. Geist? That is you real name, is it not?"

"Does it matter? A name is just a mask behind which a man can hide and do as he pleases."

"And what pleases you above all else is the thought of great riches, isn't it? I imagine you and Wolfgang were very poor growing up in Munich, especially after your father abandoned you."

Eisen's cold insouciance gave way to a scowl. "I would bring the old man back from the dead if I could just to spit in his face," he said. "I suppose you know the story. He returned to Germany after Eisendorf failed the first time around. He got a good job in Munich, probably by lying and cheating his way into it. He bought a nice big house. Then he started dicking around—that was all he was ever really good at—and sired two bastards by his housemaid."

"Your mother."

"Yes, my dear, ox-dumb mother. No doubt Dionisius promised to marry her, but he never did. Instead, he latched on to Gottfried Krupp, who had money to burn, and returned with him to reestablish this miserable town."

"Leaving you and Wolfgang behind in abject poverty."

"Not a pretty story, is it?" Eisen said, his sardonic tone of voice returning. "No wonder I'm such a bad human being."

"You must have felt betrayed."

"I am of the mind that most of us are betrayed in one way or the other, Mr. Holmes. Still, once I was old enough to be on my own, I vowed I would never spend another day in poverty."

"But honest enterprise never appealed to you, did it?"

"Let's just say I'm not attracted to the virtuous life. The trouble with goodness is that it's boring, and I bore easily."

He was indeed the perfect monster—a man without conscience or remorse. But he was also a man who very much enjoyed crowing over his murderous exploits, and I intended to keep him talking as long as possible.

"Speaking of Munich," I said, "did you conceive of your scheme to kill young male prostitutes before or after you began embezzling money from Martin Treuer?"

"After. You see, I could remove only so much money from his business without giving myself away. I therefore began looking for another way to fatten my wallet."

"And so you turned yourself into the Monster of Munich."

"It wasn't difficult, Mr. Holmes. Indeed, you might say it came naturally. I'm sure you get my drift."

In that instant I realized I had been wrong in thinking money alone had motivated the murders in Munich. Perverse sexual thrills had also been part of the equation.

"Ah, a light has gone on in that great brain of yours, hasn't it?" he said. "Yes, Mr. Holmes, I'm what they call a pervert. I fagged around in Munich, so it was easy to find *Strichjungen.* Once I identified a suitable candidate, I bought a big insurance policy in his name, with a straw man as the sole beneficiary, and then all I had to do was kill the pretty young fellow to collect. I'll admit it was grisly work, cutting up those tender bodies, but I enjoyed every minute of it."

He spoke these words with pride, as though the murder and mutilation of his fellow human beings should somehow earn him my admiration.

"Did you kill the men yourself, or did your assign that task to Wolfgang?"

"You know the old adage, Mr. Holmes. If you want a job done right, do it yourself. Wolf never had a taste for blood. But he helped out as needed. Brotherly love is a wonderful thing."

"And then you managed to kill two birds with one stone, as it were, by murdering Martin Treuer and making it appear he was just another of the Monster's victims."

"Yes, the timing couldn't have been better. I found out he was going to file a theft complaint against me, so I had to get rid of him. The police never had a clue. I intended to go on with the insurance scheme—it was a real moneymaker—but then you came along, Mr. Holmes, and began to interfere."

"Your scheme wasn't nearly as clever as you thought," I said.

"Perhaps, but you weren't very clever either, were you? With any luck, I would have killed you in the English Gardens. And then I missed you again at Table Rock. That was very depressing. I used to be an excellent shot, but I fear age has diminished my eyesight. No matter, here we are now, enjoying each other's company."

I looked down at Willy, who was beginning to stir. Once she was fully awake, I believed, Eisen would kill us both.

"Every moment with you is a delight," I said, striving to maintain the conversation. "I confess I have many more questions. For example, how did you come to leave Munich? Did you meet Dionisius there quite by chance?"

"Yes, and it was a gift from the heavens. By the late summer of 1892 Munich was becoming untenable—I will give you credit for that, Mr. Holmes—and I began looking for greener pastures. That's when I stumbled on one of the fliers Dionisius had put up in beer halls extolling the wonders of Eisendorf. Mother had told me about him, but I hadn't laid eyes on him since I was a small child. So I went to see him. He didn't exactly greet me with open arms. Even so, I managed to convince father dearest that Wolfgang and I should return with him to America. The fact I had plenty of cold harsh cash to dangle in front of him proved to be very persuasive."

"But he didn't want to acknowledge having two illegitimate sons, so you were presented in Eisendorf as his nephews."

"Yes, and no one in town ever figured out the truth. Even our half brother, Hans, was in the dark until right before I killed him. How shocked he was! But I believe a man should not die in ignorance, which is why we're having this conversation, Mr. Holmes."

Eisen kept on talking, happily unfurling his tale of murder, deception, and greed. He told me how, not long after arriving in Eisendorf, he discovered Dionisius's terrible secret—the murder of Gottfried Krupp; how he blackmailed his father until he refused to pay any more, and then murdered him at the mill, with help from Wolfgang; how he wooed and married Maria Krupp in order to avail himself of her family fortune; how in 1894 he left Eisendorf, seeing no further prospects there, and moved with Maria to St. Paul, where Willy was born; and how the family lived for twenty years in a mansion on Summit Avenue, only blocks from the home of my late friend and patron James J. Hill.

Later, I would learn from Shadwell Rafferty's investigations that Eisen worked as an insurance broker in St. Paul, eventually becoming a suspect in two murders there. Charges, however, were never brought. Then, during the Great War, Eisen went bankrupt because of improvident investments and was also accused of embezzlement in several civil lawsuits. So it was he, Maria, and Willy returned in 1919 to Eisendorf, where Wolfgang had remained all along.

"It was the prospect of a new fortune that brought you back to Eisendorf, wasn't it?" I said. "How did you find out about the opportunity here?"

"Good old Freddy told me. He saw what was coming with the potential dissolution of the cooperative, and he wrote me a letter. I imagine he expects to be rewarded for his loyalty. He will be disappointed."

"I am sure he will be," I said. "What do you suppose the Eisendorf forest is worth?"

"My, my, Mr. Holmes, I am impressed. How did you figure that out? I suppose Freddy told you."

"No, it wasn't Mr. Halbach. It had to do with the timber cruiser who discovered Bernhard Krupp's body. I wondered what a cruiser was doing in the forest, and I made inquiries. He said you had hired him to survey the forest and assess its value. He determined that the forest, which has no equal in the Midwest, would yield high-quality hardwood lumber worth hundreds of thousands of dollars. Naturally, you wanted to take control of the forest, which is why you and Wolfgang went on your murderous spree here."

"Very good, Mr. Holmes. May I assume you've seen the 1870 amendment to the cooperative agreement?"

"Yes."

"Then you know that once the cooperative is dissolved, ownership of the timberland reverts to surviving heirs of Gottfried Krupp and Dionisius Eisen. Shall I spell it out for you, Mr. Holmes?"

"No need. You have been murdering all the other heirs so that you alone will benefit from the sale of the forest. Hans Eisen was the first, and you arranged his death to look like a suicide. Then came Bernhard Krupp, who loved the forest and undoubtedly would have fought any plan to log it. His death was made to appear accidental. Josef Krupp was next. Not only was he a potential heir, but he had also become suspicious about his cousin's death."

"Yes, he was nosing around, so Wolf and I took care of him. Besides, I wanted to make sure you'd have a nice juicy crime to investigate in Eisendorf."

"How thoughtful of you. And you also kept Wolfgang busy trying to cast suspicion on Georg Dreisser. After all, it is hard to like a man who is sleeping with your wife."

"Ha, so you dug out that old chestnut! Congratulations, Mr. Holmes. Yes, I've known about their affair for a long time, and I don't care. It gave Maria something to do, and I count that a blessing. But Georg is such a smug, unpleasant man I thought I should have a little fun at his expense with that old photograph Wolf found in the archives."

"And yet Wolf, despite all his loyal service to you, is now dead, murdered like all the rest."

"Yes, poor Wolf had to go, I'm afraid. All those souvenirs he kept from Munich were becoming problematical, especially after Willy got her hands on them. Wolf even kept an autopsy photo of my last two victims there. Oh, and I suppose you saw that photograph of me in front of the Treuer Mill. I knew Wolf had it and would never part with it, but at least I got him to scratch off my face."

"When did you kill him?"

"This afternoon. It was simple. 'Oh, Wolf, what's that over there on the wall?' 'Where?' 'Right over there.' And then, as he turned away, a heavy wrench to the back of the skull. Killing is so easy, Mr. Holmes, it is a wonder people don't do it more often."

"Your whole life has been killing people or using them, hasn't it? Even Willy became your toy. You sent her out to spy for you, and she reported back everything she'd seen and heard because she loved you and thought you were her father."

For the first time, Eisen's cold eyes betrayed a hint of surprise. "Ah, so you have excavated yet another secret, Mr. Holmes. Yes, Maria carried on with a fellow in St. Paul who must have sired my little idiot girl. Not that it matters. As you know, I prefer men myself. Indeed, Maria and I never consummated the marriage bed."

"And yet you have stayed with her, no doubt as a matter of convenience," I said. "Divorcing Maria would have left you without her family money, which you relied upon for many years. As for Maria, I imagine she found you to be an amusing companion. Does she know what you've done?"

"That's a very good question, Mr. Holmes. You'll have to ask her. I must tell you I've always been rather fond of Maria. Unlike most women, who are stupid cows, she is not the least bit nice, and that makes her interesting. Maria was my daily dose of gall, and I found it bracing. But now—"

"Now, you have no further use for her. Here is where I am afraid your plans will not work out. You see, I warned her Friday she would be your next victim. That is why she left so abruptly. She won't be back. You're on your own now, and that cannot be a comfortable feeling, can it? Despite your life of murderous scheming, you have squandered away every cent you ever made. The truth is that you are a pathetic failure."

"No," he said, his cool, taunting manner flashing into anger. "You lie!"

He stepped forward, his cheeks reddening. He pointed the shotgun directly at my face. "Do not ever say I have a failed. I have always been a very good businessman. I have just had bad luck, through no fault of my own."

"My apologies," I said. "Perhaps I was misinformed."

"Ha, you have been misinformed about many things. You think yourself very clever, and yet you are a fool. I have outsmarted the great Sherlock Holmes at every turn. Every turn! It will make me famous, don't you think, when the world knows what I have done?"

"No, you will not be famous," I said, hoping to make him even more agitated. "Indeed, as a criminal you are of the lowest type. Compared to Professor Moriarty, you are—"

"Do not speak to me of Moriarty!" he shouted. "He is dead. I am alive, and it is I who will go down in history as the man who killed Sherlock Holmes."

"I doubt that," I said. As I spoke, Willy let out a groan and began to open her eyes. The time had come to act, but first I had one more question to ask. "Tell me, what time did you set the detonator for?"

"Ah, I knew you would notice the dust in the mill. It must have made it hard to breathe for a man with your—how shall I put it?—limitations." Eisen looked down at his watch, the barrels of the shotgun dipping toward the floor as he did so. "We have fifteen minutes, and then—"

He did not finish the sentence.

Hidden behind Willy's rag doll on the ledge, inches from my raised hand, was Watson's revolver. I had placed it there during our earlier visit to the tunnel. Watson had thought it a terrible risk, but I had correctly assumed that the Monster, a man proud of his every evil act, would choose to confront me in the side chamber.

He saw the sudden movement of my hand and began to raise the shotgun, fear suddenly lodged like two dark stones in his eyes, but he was too late. My first shot caught him in the neck. The second one tore into his chest.

"You," he said, before he fell dead.

There is no cause for pride in killing a man, and I took none in Eisen's death. But I felt no remorse, either. It had to be done.

The shots, which rang out so loudly I was momentarily deafened, roused Willy into full consciousness. I unbound her hands and feet. "We must go quickly," I told her.

"Mr. Sherlock," she said, staring at her father's bloody corpse, "what happened to Poppa? Did you hurt him?"

"Yes," I said, "but I had no choice. He was going to kill us both. He was a bad man, just like Wolfie."

"Wolfie tied me up. Poppa came, but he laughed at me. Didn't he love me?"

"No," I said, "but I love you, Willy, and I will make sure you are taken care of. Now, we must leave this place. Your Poppa did a terrible thing, and we are in great danger."

I gave Eisen's flashlight to Willy and instructed her to run to the far end of the tunnel, away from the mill. I followed behind at a considerably slower pace. She was waiting for me when I reached the tunnel's portal, which was blocked by a makeshift arrangement of boards. I put my shoulder to them and was soon able to clear an opening. I sent Willy out first. I had just stepped out myself when I heard, from the other side of Table Rock, a thunderous blast.

"What was that?" Willy asked as we scrambled down toward the abutment of the old dam on German Creek.

"The end of Eisendorf," I said.

• • •

Holmes proved to be right, although the demise of the cursed little town did not occur immediately. Even so, the mighty explosion, which utterly destroyed the Eisen Mill, wreaked much havoc. Massive blocks of stone from the walls were hurled all across the western side of town. One crashed through the roof of the Peoples' Hall. Others caused heavy damage to houses, including the Eisen mansion.

When I heard the blast, I knew it must somehow be the work of the Monster, and I rushed to the mill, fearing Holmes might be buried in the ruins. Soon, everyone in town had arrived with their flashlights and lanterns. The scene was chaos, the mill reduced to a scattering of stones and the twisted remains of machinery. I wanted to go into the tunnel to look for Holmes but could find no clear entrance amid the smoking ruins. My stomach became a churning hollow as I began to fear the worst.

After a time, I heard someone shout, "There's a body down in the wheel pit."

Tortured by dread, I made my way through the ruins to the pit. Flashlights shone down on the body, which lay amid much debris. I could not see the man's face, but I could tell at once by his thick head of hair and broad shoulders that it was not Holmes. I let out a long breath.

By the time the first fire trucks from Stewartville arrived, at half past one, Holmes was still missing, and my anxiety grew more intense. The firemen, who had high-powered lamps, searched the ruins for additional bodies but found none. I located the fire captain and told him of my fears regarding Holmes. He agreed to send two men around to the other side of the tunnel to see what they could discover.

As we were talking, I saw the lights of a car weaving past the line of fire trucks parked at the scene. The car drew near, and Thorkelson stepped out. I went at once to speak with him.

He greeted me with a smile and said, "You'll never guess who I found walking on the roadway into town."

At that moment, Holmes and Willy Eisen emerged from the backseat, and I felt a surge of joy. I rushed to embrace Holmes. "My God, the two of you made it!"

"Yes, Watson, but it was a near thing. It is over now, and the Eisendorf enigma will no longer haunt my days and nights. The time has come to go home."

EPILOGUE

I t has been twenty years now since the Eisendorf affair, and war is once again consuming Europe. Yet even though the desperate fight against Germany commands much of Holmes's attention, he still speaks from time to time about what happened in that curious little village hidden away in the hill country of Minnesota. Both the town and its strange lot of Germans are gone now, but Holmes's memories of the place and its people remain remarkably vivid, an indication of how deeply the events there affected him.

Indeed, it would be no exaggeration to state that the relatively short time Homes spent in Eisendorf changed the course of his life. It was there he finally came to terms with his illness by forsaking tobacco. Since then, he has remained free of the "demon weed," as he jokingly calls it, and his emphysema has not gotten appreciably worse. It was in Eisendorf as well that he achieved a kind of spiritual renewal. To this day, Holmes maintains that the concussion he sustained helped him emerge from the state of quiet despair into which he had fallen. I know of no medical reason why such should have been the case, but it hardly matters now. For whatever reason, Holmes became a different man after his experiences in Eisendorf.

After we returned to England in late October 1920, Holmes kept up a steady correspondence with Sheriff Thorkelson and Katherine Krupp. The sheriff's very first letter provided an interesting footnote to the case. He reported that Holmes's police friend in Germany, Franz Musser, had finally sent a photograph of Paul Geist, the man Holmes had come so close to capturing in Munich in 1892. The picture revealed, as we knew it would, that Geist and Peter Eisen were one and same person.

Mrs. Krupp, of whom Holmes was exceedingly fond, eventually made a visit to London. Willy Eisen came with her. The girl was utterly enchanted, discovering many "secrets" as she toured the city with Holmes and Mrs. Krupp, who by then was in charge of Willy. Mrs. Krupp had petitioned to become the girl's legal guardian when she turned twenty-one. Maria Eisen, who had abandoned Eisendorf for St. Paul, readily agreed. She was all too happy to be rid of Willy.

In her many letters to Holmes Mrs. Krupp kept him well informed about developments in Eisendorf. The town's fate, as it turned out, was sealed by a series of events that began after the dissolution of the cooperative and the deaths of Peter and Wolfgang Eisen. Maria, through her lawyers, moved at once to take control of the cooperative's lands, despite allegations—never proved—that she had in some manner been a party to her husband's crimes.

The prize Mrs. Eisen sought was the magnificent forest surrounding the town. Two years of litigation ensued, as other townspeople—among then, Frederick Halbach and Georg Dreisser—made claims upon the land. In the end, however, Maria's right to the forest, as the heir of the Eisen and Krupp families, was upheld by the courts.

Once Maria won her case, she immediately sold off the forest at great profit to two logging companies, who soon set about their work. Mrs. Krupp described the devastation in a letter to Holmes in 1923: "My heart is broken," she wrote him, "by the destruction of our beautiful forest. The green hillsides and deep hollows grow more bare by the day, and when the axmen are finally done, Eisendorf will occupy a wasteland. My only hope is that after the village is gone—and that day cannot be far off—the forest will reclaim the land and the birds will return to sing their sweet songs."

With the forest reduced to stumps, Mrs. Krupp saw no choice but to leave Eisendorf, as did most of its few remaining residents. Only Halbach, she reported, stayed on, still going daily to his beloved archives, even though there was no human history left to document in Eisendorf except his own. "He has become a king presiding over ruins," Mrs. Krupp wrote of Halbach. "It is a sad thing to see."

The end came in 1927, a year in which heavy spring rains sent the rivers and streams of southeastern Minnesota pouring over their banks. With its forest gone, Eisendorf proved especially vulnerable to flooding as water surged with unstoppable force down the steep, denuded hillsides encircling the town. In May of that year, a flash flood "rolled down the valley of German Creek and into Eisendorf like a great ocean wave," as Mrs. Krupp described it.

The flood swept away some of town's vacant houses and left others buried in mud and debris. The apartment building known as the Wohngebäude was utterly destroyed, as was the abandoned Eisen mansion, which was torn from its foundations by a massive mudslide. The torrent also caused so much damage to the Eisen Block that it had to be demolished. Even the mill ruins were not spared, the flood scouring away all traces of the structure and its foundations.

Only one person perished in the flood. Frederick Halbach's body was found three days later in the mud-filled basement of the archives. Oddly, the basement safe, which would have protected the contents of the archives, was found with its door open, and all of the records Halbach had maintained so faithfully over the years were destroyed. "I believe," Mrs. Krupp later wrote, "Freddy decided he would take Eisendorf's history with him to the grave. Perhaps it was the right choice."

One small piece of the town's history did survive, however, although in a most curious way. In 1925 a novel appeared called *Secrets of a Small Town*, by a writer named Geoffrey Dean. The book created something of a sensation in the popular press because of what one critic described as its "hothouse scenes of marital infidelity" in the fictional midwestern community of Germantown.

Only later did we learn, from Mrs. Krupp, that the author was in fact Georg Dreisser, and that the novel was based on incidents recorded in Dionisius Eisen's *Secret History of Eisendorf and Its People*. "The story I'm told," Mrs. Krupp wrote, "is that Dionisius's rather earthy history was found in Wolfgang Eisen's house after his death. Georg somehow got his hands on it and turned it into a novel. Strange to think, is it not, that a community founded on the highest ideals may in the end become best known for lurid sexual escapades?"

Dreisser's authorial career did not last for long. He was killed in an auto accident in Rochester in 1926. Many of the other players in the Eisendorf saga are also gone. Osgood Thorkelson, who provided so much help to Holmes, was felled by a heart attack in 1930. Dr. Henry Plummer died of a stroke in 1936, an event that prompted front-page coverage in the Rochester newspapers. Maria Eisen met her end in 1928, consumed by emphysema. It was said her funeral drew few mourners.

Such was not the case with another funeral in St. Paul that year, for our dear friend Shadwell Rafferty, whose death culminated a remarkable case that shook the city to its foundations. His funeral, at St. Paul's vast cathedral, was said to have been among the largest in the history of the city, and Holmes gave a eulogy so beautiful and heartfelt that all of the local newspapers printed it verbatim. George Washington Thomas, Rafferty's beloved partner, also delivered a stirring tribute. Three years later, he, too, was gone.

Holmes's exploits since the Eisendorf affair are by now well known. Once back in England, he gave up his small estate in Sussex and by 1921 had reestablished himself in London, where he began to take on new cases for the first time in years. His capture of Murchinson, the so-called laughing strangler who terrorized London for six months, was especially notable and earned him many plaudits. Of late, however, as old men are wont to do, he has slowed his pace, and during our weekly meetings at the Beefsteak Club our talk often turns to old cases like Eisendorf.

A few days ago, he showed me his latest missive from Katherine Krupp, who remains in Rochester with Willy Eisen. "We go sometimes back to Eisendorf," she wrote, "to explore Willy's old haunts, or what is left of them. The brewery still stands, but the lagering cave has been plugged up with mud. Willy is convinced the cave still holds fascinating secrets, and who am I to tell her otherwise? Indeed, I sometimes think the only happy people in this world are the ones who do not see it as it truly is."

"You could say the same about Eisendorf," Holmes remarked. "It was all a dream."

"More like a nightmare," I said.

Holmes folded up Mrs. Krupp's letter and put it his pocket. "Yes, Watson," he said softly, "I suppose it was."

LARRY MILLETT is the author of seven previous Sherlock Holmes adventures (all but one also featuring Shadwell Rafferty). He is an architectural historian whose books include *Lost Twin Cities, Once There Were Castles: Lost Mansions and Estates of the Twin Cities* (Minnesota, 2011), and *Minnesota Modern: Architecture and Life at Midcentury* (Minnesota, 2015). As a reporter for the *St. Paul Pioneer Press,* he covered many beats and wrote clues for the newspaper's legendary Winter Carnival Medallion Hunt, which annually attracts thousands of treasure seekers. He lives in St. Paul.